JED ROWEN

Encyclopocalypse Publications
www.encyclopocalypse.com

Copyright © 2024 by Jed Rowen
All Rights Reserved.

First Edition
ISBN: 978-1-960721-72-3

Cover Layout and Design by Kristopher Rufty and Sean Duregger
Edited by Sean Duregger
Interior design and formatting by Sean Duregger

The characters and events in this book are fictitious. Any similarity to real persons, living, dead or undead is coincidental and not intended by the author.

No part of this book may be reproduced in any form or by any electronic or mechanical means, including information storage and retrieval systems, without permission in writing from the publisher, except by a reviewer who may quote brief passages in a review.

PRAISE FOR DISC-OVERY

A weird and fascinating mystery tale that channels both Hunter S. Thompson and William S. Burroughs...yes, that weird! Cutting insights about modern life wrapped inside the street taco-craft beer pop culture of Southern California with a detour into *The Twilight Zone*.

— MARIO ACEVEDO, AUTHOR OF *THE NYMPHOS OF ROCKY FLATS*

Jed Rowen's debut novel is a mystery wrapped in layers of booze, pot, conspiracy theories, bromance, whacked-out mysticism, Southern California mythology, UFOs, more booze, and a whole lot of disc golf. This entertaining romp is a cult favorite waiting to happen!

— LISA MORTON, SIX-TIME BRAM STOKER AWARD®-WINNING AUTHOR

The *Sideways* of Disc Golf!

— SEAN PATRICK TRAVER, AUTHOR OF *GRAVES' END, RED WITCH* AND *WRAITH LADIES WHO LUNCH*

In *DISC-OVERY*, Jed Rowen has written an immersive, booze-fueled, mind-bendingly trippy sci-fi tale of UFOs, teleportation, and the hidden realms in our midst that only a few can truly see.

— JOSHUA GREEN, AUTHOR OF *DEVIL'S BARGAIN: STEVE BANNON, DONALD TRUMP AND THE STORMING OF THE PRESIDENCY*

A wild and quirky ride! This debut is full of surprises, UFOs, friendship, and delightfully, the sport of disc golf.

— JENNIFER BRODY / VERA STRANGE, AUTHOR OF THE *CONTINUUM TRILOGY*, *SPECTRE DEEP 6* AND *DISNEY CHILLS*

The inscription on the Statue of Liberty may call for 'Huddled Masses', but Jed Rowen gives them a voice. His wonderfully imaginative tale of personal redemption and the power of community serves as a love letter to the counterculture of the City of Angels. Too often fiction focuses on the celebrity and power associated with Los Angeles. Rowen deftly explores an eclectic mix of marginalized survivors of the Hollywood Dream. Their grace and guidance help to generate the courage to face an impossible task. Frisbee Golf, Sharin' Forties and Sci-Fi…Enjoy!

— BRICE WILLIAMS, ACTOR - *GREY'S ANATOMY*, *THE MINDY PROJECT*, *CRIMINAL MINDS*

With the story taking place in Los Angeles, Rowen pulled me into the City of Angels just like a Michael Connelly novel. With a plot that hurls itself into the dark corners of human nature, it gripped me like a Dean Koontz thriller! Within the first page, I felt like I had known the main character for a long time. For the entire novel, I felt like I was right by his side as the story took one shocking turn after another!

— ERIK HENGSTRUM, AUTHOR OF *THE CAMPAIGN OF PEERLESS KENT*

In *DISC-OVERY*, Jed Rowen takes you on a thrilling journey deep into Los Angeles, full of unexpected twists and turns.

— CARROT TOPP OF RADIOACTIVE CHICKEN HEADS

DISC-OVERY is a disc golfer's outlook into the deep-seated mysteries that are found underneath the City of Angels.

— SOPHIA JADE, MODEL/FASHION DESIGNER/ENTREPRENEUR

Engagingly plotted, irresistibly readable, and brimming with inside information conspiracy fans will enjoy.

— JEFF LEROY, FILMMAKER/DIRECTOR - *GIANTESS ATTACK VS. MECHA FEMBOT, RAT SCRATCH FEVER, CRACK*

DISC-OVERY is a gem of a novel, mixing humor with science fiction, as it reveals the mysterious underbelly of Los Angeles, through the wild adventure of its colorful and eccentric characters.

— B. LUCIANO BARSUGLIA, AUTHOR OF *THE GREAT BEYOND*, DIRECTOR OF *THE ELECTRIC MAN*

Absurd and crazy in all the best ways. Jed Rowen's *DISC-OVERY* is a wild ride that will have you hanging on for dear life...even after it's over.

— TIM MARQUITZ, AUTHOR OF THE *DEMON SQUAD* SERIES

A compulsively entertaining mix of inebriated humor, nostalgic sci-fi, and off the wall insanity!

— JOSHUA MILLICAN, AUTHOR OF *TELEPORTASM* AND THE *DEEPER THAN HELL* SERIES

To Jill

DISC GOLF, ALIENS, AND BOOZE
A B-MOVIE ACTOR'S ODE TO THE DRUNK NOVEL

I never thought anything could be worse than the acting biz. When I finally finished my first novel and ventured out into the big bad world of publishing, I realized the writing biz topped it. That was a pretty big surprise. Agents, publishing scams, pitch meetings, query letters…I realized quick how good I had it as an actor. Plus, say what you want about the movie biz, at least there are unions. There are WGA minimums, guaranteed actor day rates, residuals, per diems. Even the non-union stuff, you had labor laws on your side (well, in theory you do). In the writing world, there is a cartel of four or five publishing companies. They make all the rules with no unions of any power for them to contend with, only a bunch of agents who have some muscle. And they even felt like an extension of the publishing establishment. Gatekeepers.

I did my due diligence though, because I felt my debut novel deserved it after working so hard on it for so long. I researched how to write the best query letter, and sent out tons of them. I hit up every small publisher I could, messaged anyone I knew that had published anything, left no stone unturned. It wasn't about me, though. It was about the story. I wanted it out there.

Disc Golf, Aliens, and Booze

I had spent years acting, and anyone that's been an actor knows that you have to go all in. 100% commitment even to get the most marginal of results. It's that competitive and that rough. I was like a laser for years and years. I've been prolific and have managed to put together a modest body of work, through lots of blood, sweat and tears.

But there was this other artistic part of me that tormented me for all those years. The writer in me had been neglected and was pissed off. It never really let me have any peace even with every little victory I had as an actor. When I'd see my movies screen at film fests, or get a Blockbuster release (remember those), or win an acting award, the little imp of the perverse would unceasingly nag me…where is your novel, dude? You're letting yourself down, not living up to one of the purposes of you being on this planet, to tell stories not only as an actor but in arguably the most creative human endeavor, the novel.

It took me bottoming out after the economic meltdown of the early 2010's to finally get on the path that is the novel you hold in your hands now (or reading on your tablet or phone or computer screen).

I lived this novel. Well, maybe not the aliens. Or maybe the aliens. Hehe. But definitely the disc golf. And definitely everything that went along with playing this wonderful sport. The friendships and camaraderie. The competition. Being out in nature. The glory of hitting an ace. The booze.

Ah yes, the booze. As I wrote this novel, I realized how important drinking is to disc golf. Kind of like fishing. You can't fish without beer. Can't throw discs with the boyz without alcohol. I overdid it all those years ago playing disc golf after the economic meltdown. But when I sat down to finally write my novel, the drinking just fit seamlessly into the narrative.

It's a drunk novel.

DISC-OVERY is my debut novel. And my biggest influence as a writer…well, there are several. But one of them has always

Disc Golf, Aliens, and Booze

been Ernest Hemingway. His debut novel, *The Sun Also Rises* was also a drinking novel. The characters were mostly drunks. Some tormented by the war they were scarred from, but most by their marginalized lives where they struggled to cope. Much like the characters in my novel.

My book is a nod to this magnificent novel, and a salute to Ernest Hemingway.

I lucked out getting a publishing deal with Encyclopocalypse Publications. It sounds trite but I really think it was fate. It's so rare in life to get that perfect fit, to find the perfect home. Somehow my story found it.

But Encyclopocalypse is a genre publisher at its core. And I wrote *DISC-OVERY* as …get this…well…something…God forbid…*literary*. Yes. I wanted to write a novel that was in the spirit of *The Sun Also Rises*. Something that was a real freakin' novel. You know, literary shit.

So yes, you Encyclopocalypse readers who live, as I do, for genre stuff, my story has aliens. And government agents. And conspiracies galore. And intrigue. And action. And hot chicks.

But it's also Hemingway translated into genre.

So don't get mad if you gotta deal with a lot of literary pathos. And a lot of boozing like you've seen in those works your high school and college teachers made you read like Virginia Woolf, Faulkner, Hemingway, Bukowski, Eugene O'Neill, Tennessee Williams, oh the list goes on and on. Add my name to the list. Forgive the haughtiness, please. Those are are all literary giants. I am just a humble actor, a poor player.

But *DISC-OVERY* does belong on a list of drinking novels. I'm proud of that.

So before you turn the page and start reading this story, maybe fix yourself a martini or settle into a whiskey. Or crack open a bottle of wine or a six pack. But expect a little more than alien invasions, karate kicks or machine guns blazing.

Because *DISC-OVERY*, my friends, is literary. And it is one hell of a boozing novel, too. Cheers to that.

Jed Rowen
Los Angeles, 2024

1

I had to include almond butter in the picnic. It's ridiculously overpriced but it's Jane's favorite. As I toss it in my cloth grocery bag I wonder if there's anything left to get that could help win Jane over. I glumly look around as I doubt some organic salsa and seaweed snacks could fix a marriage on the rocks.

Finally, I decide on another bottle of merlot. More wine could help. As I walk to the check out, I grab some bottled water. I'm all set for the Last Meal.

I have half an hour. I jump in my car with the groceries and start the drive to Burbank. Cruising down Riverside Dr., I reflect on where it all went wrong with Jane. Neither of us was to blame. We just should have never happened. It was all contrived for fifteen long years. Maybe that's why the miscarriage happened. Something was telling us that a family was not in the cards. That this was never meant to be forever.

I pull one of the microbrews from the grocery bag. The label has a big zombie on it – yeah, I'm one of those guys who buys beer based on how cool the labels are. The taste is inconsequential. None of the different flavors of beer really bother me, from the murkiest IPA to a borderline cider. So I just grab whatever label is the most interesting. The zombie won out today. This was supposed to be for later on tonight. But, I think I need this microbrew now. Bourbon will be for later.

I glance around to see if there are any black and whites, and it looks like the coast is clear. I bring the beer down to the bottle opener on my key chain that's in the ignition, popping it open as I get a rush from the couple of seconds of terror of having my hands off the steering wheel. I quickly grab the wheel as my car has been veering to the right and chuckle to myself as I take a swig.

The tension I've been feeling starts to abate as the beer settles into my stomach and rises to my brain. I take another long pull. Then another. The zombie brew is doing the trick, I'm already starting to feel a lot better. But my angst pulls me back like some tug-of-war going on in my head, telling me that I shouldn't feel good. If I don't perform and bomb this picnic, it's over between me and Jane. It's showtime.

As soon as I start to psyche myself up, I realize I'm just not into the relationship anymore and want out of the marriage. It's been like this for a while. I know Jane wants out of it, too. I think that we both have been avoiding a final big confrontation, putting off the inevitable.

I take another swig and remember to keep the beer down low for a while. I'm entering the most fascist mini-city in the Los Angeles area – Burbank. When I arrive at the park, I'm twenty minutes early which is a perfect amount of time to sit and drink my beer before the picnic.

The buzz from my zombie beer is starting to battle the onslaught of emotions from the last fifteen years beginning to bubble to the surface as I sit in my car. The zombie almost kisses me every time the bottle moves close to my face for another chug. I close my eyes and feel the years just coarse through my veins, almost in a race with the alcohol that is traveling the same route.

All of the losses and failures in my personal life surge

DISC-OVERY

through me and finally seem to bottleneck at my eyeballs. I feel tears welling up.

I open my eyes, feeling like I'm going to scream but all I do is try to catch my breath before I guzzle the rest of my zombie beer. The alcohol immediately pushes back the morbid mental surge, and I toss the empty bottle underneath the car. I look in the rear view mirror, and see the redness in my eyes. I have *got* to get it together.

I make my way across the street into the park.

Immediately I notice how the leaves are jiggling in the wind, green and yellow dancing off of each other as the colors are cascading off the leaves and jumping up into the air. The wind starts to envelop me as I walk under the trees, as nature seems to take me in and embrace me. I've always loved nature. It wasn't really a part of my life in the concrete jungle of New York. I'm so thankful that it is in L.A.

The nice buzz I have from the zombie beer and this lovely little walk suddenly comes to a screeching halt as I remember what I came here for. Quite possibly the last day of my marriage. I sure don't feel up to this. I try to find my game face. I look around again and see the lush green of the park and the wind rustling through everything, making everything shake and flutter. I'm shaking, too.

I sit down at a concrete table and start to set out the food. My phone buzzes. It's a text from Jane. She's here. I look up, spot her, and wave. As she makes her way over, I uncork one of the wine bottles and take out the bread. I open up the jars of olives and artichoke spread, and set out the grapes, goat cheese, and all the other food. It's all looking pretty good.

I start walking over to Jane. She's slowly trudging her way up the path leading up to the picnic tables. Judging from her laborious walking, she's dreading this meeting as much as I am. She is wearing sunglasses with blue jeans and a white long sleeve collared shirt.

"Hey Jane, thanks for coming."

"Nice to see you, Jeff."

"I have a great little spread over here. C'mon, I hope you're hungry."

Jane doesn't say anything as I give her an awkward little hug that she half-heartedly embraces. We make our way over to the picnic table and sit down.

"Here let me pour you some wine."

I fill up both cups, and I raise my glass to toast.

"Cheers."

She mutters something.

We both take a sip of the red wine and I start putting artichoke spread on the bread.

"I brought your favorite. Almond butter."

"Oh that's so thoughtful of you, Jeff."

She takes off her sunglasses revealing pained eyes that seem to pierce right through me. As I look into them, I can see the deep bitterness they have towards me. I look down at my bread with the artichoke spread and take a bite. I'm almost afraid to look back up. She continues staring at me as I'm chewing until I finally see her reach over with a plastic knife for the almond butter and starts to scoop it onto the artisan bread. There is a long awkward silence as we both sit eating.

"How is it?" I ask.

"It's great. Unlike our current situation."

Well, shit. She's not wasting any time. She came ready to fight. The almond butter isn't working.

"It's bad enough that you dragged me all the way out here to L.A. But now I have to sit alone at our house every day wondering what I'm doing out here."

"Jane," I reply, "it was your idea that we should separate for a while. I didn't want to move out and leave you all alone. You made me."

Jane takes a bite of her almond butter bread and there is another awkward silence.

"Why did you really come out here, Jeff? It wasn't for that brokerage firm. You barely lasted a year there."

"I thought it was a good fit and a promising opportunity. We just weren't on the same page."

"Well it seemed to me that you never wanted to make it work there."

"Look Jane, I had to get away from New York. Everything that went down, how can you blame me? I needed a change. They had an opening here, and it all looked great on paper. It just didn't work out. But I love L.A. It feels like home."

"Well, I don't love it here. Not at all," Jane erupts. "I miss my family, and my old life in New York. I had a career there."

I start scooping out olives onto my plate and cut up some of the goat cheese. I'd need a much sharper knife to cut the silence that's descended upon us. After what seems like an eternity, I finally speak up.

"Maybe I want to be here where Sean was, Jane."

She looks up at me with the sullen expression I've seen her make so many times lately.

"All those years you never even talked to him," she said.

I put down the bread feeling the sting of that comment. A verbal uppercut right into my gut knocking the wind out of me. Resisting the urge to start screaming at her, I settle down and gulp half my glass of wine.

"Jane, you know I always loved my brother deeply. We got judgmental of each other's lives early on and it festered over the years. We got used to avoiding each other. What we let happen to us was so pointless and stupid."

I look down again at my plate of food. I remind myself to keep breathing as I think of all those wasted years between my brother and I.

"But I was always thinking of him. Even when we weren't talking."

Jane is looking down at her food now.

"I'm sorry, Jeff. That came out the wrong way. I know you loved him."

She looks up and our eyes lock for a bruising couple of moments before she turns away. I look down at the artichoke spread and realize suddenly how gross it looks.

"You know, Jane. I wasn't there for Sean when he needed me," I say in a hushed tone. "I'm realizing now that he couldn't just pick up the phone and call me. Maybe If he thought he could have done that, well, he might still be here today. I failed him."

Jane takes a long sip of her red wine. She puts down the cup and stares into it. I take another big drink out of mine. Good thing I grabbed that extra bottle of merlot. We're going to need it.

"I could see coming out here if he was still alive," she mutters. "For you to be here to help him. But to move out here after he's passed away and drag me along. I just don't understand it."

"Well, I don't really understand it that much either, Jane. It's just something I felt I had to do. It's like something was calling me out here."

I take a bite of my baguette.

"I like being where he used to hang out," I continue. "At his old stomping grounds. I go to some of the clubs he used to play at by myself but I don't feel like I'm alone. It sounds crazy but sometimes I swear it feels like he's hanging out with me."

I realize how ridiculously kooky this sounds but it's the truth. Another long period of silence follows broken up by maddening sounds of chewing and swallowing. I want to scream.

"Jeff, I feel like I'm in a void out here. I'm all alone stuck way out in Woodland Hills. I hate it. I have no life here; no career, no job, no family, no friends, nothing. Only an estranged husband who doesn't seem to be much interested in me anymore. Or in his old career. I just feel like you are not the man I married. I get through the days in a cloud, like I'm walking around like a zombie."

My mind wanders to that microbrew I pounded in the car.

"It's all day, every day, Jeff. I can't do this anymore."

She leaves that hanging in the air. This is it. The big whammy. I brace myself and pour more wine for the both of us. I tighten my grasp on the plastic cup in my hand waiting for the hammer to fall.

"Well, what do you think we should do?" I meekly ask, lobbing her a softball to whack.

"Jeff, I want a divorce."

The word hits me like a ton of bricks even though I knew damn well it was coming. I start to rub my head as I feel a headache immediately coming on. I remain quiet, having no idea what to say. My mouth starts drying out. I start to gasp for air as my heart starts racing. Jane just keeps looking at me with those piercing mad eyes of hers, keeping the pressure on. She's relentless.

I finish off my wine in one gulp. I look up at her and meet her stare.

"I guess that's the only real solution at this point, huh?"

Jane nods.

I gaze at her and wonder if there ever really was any spark between us. The blur of so many volatile years cloud over those early times of knowing her. I get a little reflective as I fill another cup of wine to the brim.

I guess at the very beginning there was *something*. An infatuation. Come to think of it, more like a *fling* that morphed somehow into a relationship that then mutated into a marriage.

"I want to go home, Jeff. Back to New York. I need to be with my parents right now. I need to start over."

"Okay, Jane."

I reach over and grab her hand. Both our heads sink and she starts to cry. I'm feeling tears welling up in my eyes, too. It's really over. The finality is hitting both of us hard right now. The marriage is finished.

I rub Jane's hand and move over to her and embrace her. It was the first real heartfelt hug we've had in quite a while.

"I'm so sorry, Jane. I'm so sorry for everything," I sob.

"Oh, Jeff. I'm so sorry, too."

We are both bawling and shaking as we hold each other tight. I'm realizing how badly we both needed to have a good cry. I can feel the warmth of her body and how delicate she is as she's shaking in my arms. It's funny how tough we both try to be with all the walls we've constructed around us, but how fragile we really are. We haven't had a moment like this in years. We slowly stop crying, I look into her eyes and there's a warmth in them I haven't seen in ages.

"I will always be there for you, Jane. Always. I'll be your friend forever."

"So will I, Jeff."

We smile at each other and hug once again.

"I don't think I've ever heard of anyone divorcing like this, crying and hugging each other over a picnic. We're acting like I just proposed to you."

We both laugh at this, and tears continue to stream from our eyes.

"Your famous sense of humor. I'll miss it," Jane muses.

She looks up at me wistfully.

"I have to go now, Jeff. I have a lot of planning to do. I'll call you in a few days, okay? We certainly have some details to go over."

"Yeah, we sure do."

Jane leans over and kisses me on the cheek and clenches my hand. She seems to have something else to say, but hesitates and turns around and walks off. All of that emotion in her face just abruptly vanishes as if someone just flicked off a light switch. I watch her go down to the parking lot as I grab my wine.

Wow, just like that. Fifteen years of experiences and commitment...*poof!* Gone. I guess I should finally feel relieved that the burden of a failed marriage has finally been resolved. But I sure feel lonely as I watch her drive off.

I close my eyes again and reach up and massage my temples. My head is throbbing with pain. I finally open my eyes and through my tears I see all the uneaten food that remains on the park table.

What the hell am I going to do now? I grab one of the napkins and start to dry my eyes. I take a few deep breaths as I start to settle down and decide the best possible thing for me to do right now...is to finish my lunch and drink the rest of the wine. A great idea. Finally, some clarity.

I begin to laugh at this glorious insight as I grab some bread and put the artichoke spread on it, as well as some olives and goat cheese. I splash some olive oil on and realize this little snack here is starting to become something special. I top off my cup of wine and I'm ready to dig in. I bring up the baguette to take a bite and out of the corner of my eye I see a small yellow flash and—

CRASH!

Jars and red wine splatter everywhere. My baguette goes flying out of my hands. Olives spill all over me and the artichoke spread projectiles across the park table. I start to fall back over on the bench, losing my balance and getting disoriented and then...*PLOP!* I land on the dirt.

I hear some vague yells in the distance, pushing my hands down on the ground and raising myself up.

"FORE FORE FORE!"

I shake my head a little bit and brush away some of the grass and dirt.

"FORE FORE FORE!"

"FORE FORE FORE!"

Turning around I see four figures racing towards me. They jump over the dry creek and start to sprint up the hill. Finally reaching me panting and out of breath.

"Hey dude! You okay?"

"Aw man, I can't believe this. Holy shit! Are you alright, man?" asks another.

The other two guys are simply looking at me wide eyed like they just ran over me in a car.

I start feeling around my body, checking in on all my parts. I move around and then get up onto my feet, dusting myself off. I stretch out my back and move my arms around, and everything seems intact.

"Uh, yeah, I think I'm okay," I respond.

"Oh my God I am *so* sorry, man, my disc slipped when I threw it. I didn't mean in a million years to hit you."

"Hey man," a bearded tatted up rough-looking guy in his late 30's points over to the picnic table. "There's your disc over here, Paul." He looks at me as he surveys the damage. "Shit, man, it totally wrecked your meal, bud."

They all glance over at the picnic table in sheer horror. They quickly move over to it and see the destruction their disc wrought on my lunch. The table is a disaster, food and red wine is splattered everywhere.

"Hey man I got some good news! One of your wine bottles survived! Hahaha...."

"Shut up Gary! Stop friggin' laughing," the burly guy exclaims.

Gary stops laughing and turns his attention back to me. I am looking at them warily but I am more disoriented and confused than mad. I'm still trying to figure out what just happened. I look up at Gary and he's holding my wine bottle in one hand and a small yellow frisbee in another. He comes over to me and hands me my wine. I motion to his frisbee.

"Is that what hit me? A frisbee?"

"It's not a *frisbee*. It's a *disc*," a voice from behind me says. I turn around and see a scruffy, emaciated man with no shirt on. He looks up at me with large bags under his eyes, and a face weathered from alcohol and drugs. I know faces like that. My brother Sean started to get one right before he died after years of partying.

"Hey man, we are so sorry for doing this to you," Paul says. "This is terrible. I don't know what to say." He looks like the leader of the group.

I am finally relaxed and have collected myself. There is a long silence as they are waiting for some sort of a response from me. I'm just looking at all of them, sizing them up. Besides the emaciated one, the other three are pretty big guys. No way I'm going to start anything with them. We stand around with only the noise of their panting from their sprint over to me. They wait for me to say something. All of their eyes are on me. I finally speak.

"I'll live, guys. No big deal." I chuckle.

Their faces break into smiles and they breathe a collective sigh of relief. One of them pats my shoulder. As we walk to the park bench, Paul takes out a cigarette and lights it.

"Hey I'm Paul. It's really nice to meet you."

He sticks out his hand and I shake it.

"I'm Jeff."

"Nice to meet you Jeff," the other stocky guy says as he juts his hand out. "I'm Gary."

"Hey there, Gary." I shake his hand and look at the other two guys.

Paul takes a pull of his cigarette and points over to the emaciated guy.

"And this is Andy," he says.

"Andy, it's a pleasure," I say sarcastically.

"The pleasure is all mine, sir," he quips.

"Hey, I'm Bill." I look over at Bill. He is also a compact, stocky guy with burly forearms who also looks gruff and weathered.

"Hi Bill."

"Look man," Paul says, "most people would totally just flip out if this happened to them. You are one cool dude." He looks over at the picnic table with all the food strewn everywhere. "I mean we completely ruined your lunch."

I look at the mess. I turn around to the guys.

"Paul," I say reflectively, "the lunch was already ruined."

He looks up at me a little puzzled but simply takes another drag off his cigarette.

"Can I see the disc?" I ask Bill.

"Yeah sure, man."

Bill hands me the yellow disc. I grip it and it's much smaller than a regular frisbee. I move it around in my hands. I like how it feels.

"I used to love playing frisbee," I say.

"Well, this isn't frisbee. It's disc golf," Andy says.

"Disc golf? I've never heard of that."

"Yeah, most people haven't. It's basically golf but you play with these discs instead of golf balls. You throw at a target, usually a basket, and try to get it in with the least possible throws. Most of the holes are 3-pars."

"Interesting," I say. "I was never much of a golfer. You know *regular* golf, ball golf."

Andy smirks at me as he takes the disc from my hands.

"When a golf ball dreams, it dreams it's a disc."

He takes the disc and moves to the edge of the small hill we're on. He winds up to throw it as his scrawny, emaciated body immediately takes on an athletic nimbleness to it, taking the disc all the way back and stepping forward with it. He releases it very fluidly, with a broad follow through and a loud snap of his wrist. The disc takes off launching out of his hand and takes a wide loop up into the sky.

I follow the yellow disc as it travels straight up into the clouds before it starts to careen left making a long arc back into the tree line on the far side of the park. It continues and spirals down, picking up speed as it fades off to the left. The disc crashes into the ground and immediately bounces up around fifteen feet, gliding until it hits the ground again. Then it then skips once, twice, and hits again on its side proceeding to roll slowly, around and around, giving one last little gasp of life and stands straight up on its side before it finally falls down. It is about seven feet from a lamp post.

"Good one, dude," Paul says.

"Thanks," Andy responds.

I'm kind of amazed at the flight of the disc and the dexterity of Andy's throw. Watching it had a therapeutic effect on me.

Paul places his hand on my shoulder.

"Hey Jeff. Thanks again for not going nuts on us. Here's a little token of my appreciation."

He starts going through what looks like a huge rectangular purse. He flips through it and finally finds what he's looking for.

"Here, man. One of my favorite discs. It's called a Valkyr. A great, easy disc to throw, and it can go forever. It's yours, man. Here."

He hands me the disc and it has a large picture of some winged creature on it. A much cooler emblem than any I've seen on my microbrews.

"Are you sure you want to give me this?" I ask.

"Absolutely, my friend."

"Well, thanks."

Paul takes another pull from his cigarette.

"It's yellow," he says. "The same color as the disc that just destroyed your picnic."

"It's also the color of friendship," Andy says.

I look over at Andy. Friendship. What a strange concept. It's been years since I heard that word in any serious context. I wonder how long it's been since I had a real friend. Or just experienced the joys of friendship. I guess since college. Maybe in my early 20s. A long time ago.

"Here," Paul says as he hands me a sharpie from his bag. "Write your name and number on it in case you lose it."

I dutifully scribble my name and cell number on the upper corner of the underside of the disc.

"We play disc golf two or three days a week here at the park," he continues. "The lamps are the holes. It's a whole secret course here. But on the weekends, we go to the real courses all around L.A. You should come with us some time."

"Yeah, maybe I will," I say.

"Let me give you my cell number."

He reaches over and turns the disc over looking at the digits I've inscribed on the plastic. He plugs them into his phone. A few seconds later a text comes up.

> Paul here. Sorry about ur lunch.

I smile and send him back a text.

> Lemme know when u go golfing.

His phone starts to ring an old Def Leppard song as it receives my text.

"Oh hey, you like Def Leppard?" I ask.

"Hell yeah, man. I saw them right before the pandemic. It was awesome."

"Yeah," I respond, "I was gonna go to that show but couldn't make it. Missed the tour they had with Motley Crüe, too. Another one of my favs."

I smile. I always like meeting people who are fans of old school '80's rock. It's one of the few things Sean and I had in common. Paul types in my name and saves me as a contact.

"Always cool to find someone who appreciates the classic stuff," he says.

"Yeah, man, definitely" I reply.

"I hope you take us up on the disc golf," Paul says as he takes a final big drag on his cigarette. "First time we go out, lunch is on us. It's the least we can do," he says as he motions to

DISC-OVERY

the food that is all over my clothes. We all laugh. Paul flicks the cigarette on the grass.

"We're outta here," he says. He walks off as the others start to follow him.

"Okay guys," I say. "I'll see you one of these weekends."

"Cool," Andy says. He has a very erudite voice, almost like a college professor. "I'll teach you everything I know about disc golf."

"Alright, Andy," I say.

I watch them walk off to the edge of the park where they've parked on the side of the road and make my way back to the picnic table and sit down. I pick up a plastic cup off the ground and pour myself some of the wine from the surviving bottle of wine as I study the cool emblem on the disc.

The Valkyr is so intricate. I grip the disc and move it around in my hands, studying this cool yellow aerodynamic piece of plastic. I'm finally relaxing a bit, enjoying the buzz of the wine as I take in the sounds of nature. What a wacky lunch.

Hearing some commotion from the other side of the park, I look up to see the guys noisily throwing their disc golf bags into the back of a pickup truck. They laugh boisterously as they step on their beer cans and kick them into the curb before piling into the truck and driving off.

I get up, still clenching that disc looking at my convertible in the distance. It's far from me, probably around two hundred and fifty feet. No way I'd make it that far. I aim at my car and try to remember how Andy threw the disc, taking it all the way back in a very wide throwing motion with a broad follow through.

I get into a stance and start to motion the disc forward. *Bring the disc all the way back*, I tell myself, *and then pull it forward. Don't forget to follow through. Just like tennis.*

I run up and take the disc back and fling it forward and I see a blur as I jerk my head around and my arm follows. I whip my arm around and there it goes!

It shoots up high and the wind catches it as it begins its ascent. It sails for a while and then starts to float down from its high arc. I immediately realize that it is going straight for the parked cars on the park's side of the street. I never thought I'd throw it that far.

THUMP!

Uh oh.

The disc hits a black Mercedes and ricochets off. The car alarm goes off and I panic. I frantically look around to see if anyone saw my disc hit the car. Amazingly, no one's around. I start sprinting and my heart starts racing as I'm rumbling towards the disc. I finally grab it, and notice a big dent it left on the Mercedes. Darting through the street to my car on the other side, I start up the engine and peel out.

I'm breathing heavily now, and sweat is pouring off me. Flying high with adrenaline, I speed down Riverside and turn the corner hard on Alameda St. hearing the screeching of my tires as I floor it up the street. I laugh out loud. I got away with it.

I'm cruising now and roll down the window letting the wind whip through my hair. I turn on the radio and Motley Crüe blares out as if on cue. I bang my hands against the steering wheel to the heavy guitar riffs and the drums. I'm pumped. I haven't felt this great in a long time. I'm ready to get on with my life.

2

It's been two weeks since Jane left town. I texted her a week ago, and still have not heard back from her. That last emotional picnic seems like it was all just a show, like she was performing in a scene study class. I have a feeling she's going to let her lawyer do the talking when we move forward with the divorce proceedings. She's acting very juvenile, and it's not only making me resentful, but even lonelier than I already feel.

I've always been a very social person, but I have no problem being by myself. However, the last two weeks without Jane have been tough. Even when we were separated, I always knew she was only a short drive or a phone call away in case I needed to talk to her. And even though we were apart, she was still in my life. I knew she was there if I really needed her. An emotional security blanket, I guess.

Now she has moved on and made it clear that we will not be socializing. I'm on my own now. I'm surprised at how deep the pit of loneliness is that I'm sinking into.

This big city isn't really helping things either. I go through my everyday life either staring at the walls or watching TV or venturing out to cafes, restaurants, bookstores and malls. No one seems very interested in getting to know me. People are busy, preoccupied with their lives and hustling with whatever they're doing. Everyone's in a rush, the way I used to be in New York.

Depression is subtly overtaking me every day. I feel it coming on like an astral python wrapping around my aura.

I take hikes, sometimes twice a day in the hills behind my place. The hot sun blazes away my sadness and seems to radiate a life force into me, sustaining me like it does to all the plants and trees around me. I soak it up every day like a lover's embrace, and let it zap away my despair and massage my hurt mind as it reddens my skin and nourishes my lost soul.

I love feeling the rocks under my feet and the boulders I walk over, losing myself in the sparkling brown canvas of earth that takes me into its vastness and calm serenity. I turn into the park's little walkways as shade envelopes me in its quiet hug as my feet get massaged on the mulch that's been poured all over these little trails.

But as the evenings descend upon me, so does my mood. It declines into the darker places. I wrestle with my demons throughout the night with the aid of too much booze, and then up and at 'em with a brand-new day filled with sunshine, blue skies, and those radiant hills.

Squirrels are my constant companions as they scurry about and peer over at me as I walk past. I've started to take nuts on my walks, and whenever I sit on benches in the dim shade away from the blinding rays of the sun, I feed all these new little friends that I've made. The same squirrels know me now aware that I come bearing snacks, and we can't wait to see each other. Their favorite is sunflower seeds. Sometimes they come right up to me and snatch them out of my hand. It took me a while not to flinch when they did that. I never imagined a squirrel could be a friend, but right now they are pretty much all I've got in that department.

I pass by beautiful young women with their boyfriends, girlfriends, or brave enough to just go it alone. They are completely oblivious to me as they rant to each other or into a cell phone about what seems to be the same series of conversations every day.

Some look straight ahead behind sunglasses, while others surprise me as they look up with alluring friendly greetings and flirtatious eyes. Sometimes there are conversations as we walk together. But when I get the nerve to give out my cell number, they never seem to follow up with me. Maybe I'm too old. Or maybe they just put it into a vast digital pile with all the other numbers they get from strange men they encounter all over L.A. The cute ones must get dozens of numbers every single week.

I think of the last ten years and how everything seemed to bottom out for me. Except of course for the fortune I'd made. My career was promising but nosedived into scandal and crisis. Luckily, I was able to parachute out with enough money to last me a long time, even after what I have to give to Jane.

I never want to go back to my former career and just want to get on with my new life, whatever the hell that is. A few weeks ago I was pumping my fist to Motley Crüe feeling like I was on top of the world and ready to climb up a new mountain. Now I'm sinking in a vast pit of despair with no bottom.

* * *

Back home I'm well into my second bottle of merlot, it's making me all warm and tingly inside. The music sounds great as I sing along while it blasts from my computer. It's not just classic rock. I like it all, you name it: rap, country, disco, pop, whatever. Thanks to the wine I'm feeling pretty good tonight and I'm looking around my place. I should probably tidy it up a bit, it's getting really messy. Dirty dishes are scattered all over the sink and clothes, magazines and books strewn all over the place. It's looking like a bachelor pad, that's for sure. Since it's much easier to clean when you are buzzing really good, I pound some more wine as I sing along to Judas Priest.

The dishes are the first chore to handle. Scrubbing away at all the dishes, I finally start to see the bottom of my sink for the first time in weeks. *So that's what it looks like!* I laugh to myself as I turn to fill up my wine glass. I take a little break as the soap suds drip over my hands and shirt.

I give the house a good look over and realize how much more cleaning I must do. The place has become a disaster area. My eyes follow all the things I need to tidy up, finally on the two brown storage boxes in the corner of the room with my brother's name on their sides in big bold print. Sean's boxes were a couple of my things that I picked up from Jane's rental a few days after our last meal together. Of course, she made a point not to be there when I came by to get my things.

I'd forgotten all about Sean's stuff. Or maybe I wanted to. It just hurts to think about the guy these days. Seems like eons ago when I was having fun retracing his steps in his old haunting grounds. But I've neglected Sean for a little too long and he is, after all, the reason I moved here. I came out here to discover him, as bizarre as that sounds. I need to start devoting myself to my little brother some more.

It's time to open those boxes. Hell, I'm so drunk that it might be the best time to do that. I dry off my hands, grab my Swiss army knife and walk over to the boxes. I start to cut through the tape.

As I rip the boxes open dust streams out resulting in a coughing fit. I hesitate and sit staring at the open box, feeling my eyes welling up. The emotion eventually bubbles over as I begin to cry.

That didn't take long.

Here I was feeling so good just a moment ago, confident I could handle this. It was inevitable, though. Alcohol can backfire on you when it comes to emotions. My little brother always had a way of getting under my skin. I break down and sob as I sit with my hands clasped around my head. Everything I've been holding back the last few weeks bursting out now.

DISC-OVERY

I let the tears pour out for a few more minutes and sit in a meditative zone, as the alcohol readjusts itself by starting to soothe everything going on in my head. Finally, I wipe my face with my damp shirt and slowly open my eyes.

I pull one of the boxes towards me and reach my hand into it grabbing what feels like something metallic. I take it out. A little gold bowl. I know what this is. A Tibetan singing bowl. *Cool!* I'd always seen these at shops over the years and always wanted to get one but just never did. Now I have my brother's.

I bring my other hand into the box and start to feel around, and I find the wooden mallet that is used with the bowl. I start to hit the mallet against the bowl like I've seen those monks do on the internet. I lightly hit the bowl; it rings out such a beautiful, piercing sound as it vibrates in my hand. This immediately has an intense calming effect on my frayed emotions. I let it flood over me with its healing powers.

When the sound dissipates, I lightly hit the mallet against the bowl again, and the high-pitched ringing continues its healing effect on me as it warms my soul with its ethereal tones melting away my tearful melancholy. I continue to sit letting the Tibetan bowl work its magic with its shimmering vibrations. This is so cool that Sean had one of these. It almost seems like a gift from him.

I put the bowl down and start grabbing other items from the boxes. They are mostly books and I stack them up next to the boxes. That's the one thing that Sean and I always had in common: we always collected a lot of books. As I'm taking them out of the boxes, I notice all the titles. Books on UFO's, the occult, conspiracies, mysticism. I knew that Sean had interests in these subjects, but it looks like he was really obsessed.

I take out a little box and open it up. Baoding balls. I move them around in my hands feeling the therapeutic effect immediately in my head. I used to have a pair years ago and lost them somewhere along the way. Now I have another set thanks to Sean. Tears start to well up again as I think about these wonderful gifts Sean's giving to me right now, instruments that are going to h elp me heal. I spin them around a few more times then put them away and place them next to the stack of books.

I rip open the other box pulling out a few cases of CD booklets. They're filled with movies. Lots of science fiction and horror films. I browse through the titles. Classics like *Bladerunner* and *Total Recall*, and a bunch of genre titles from the '80s. I put those aside and take out some more CD booklets. One is filled with Westerns, one of my other favorite genres.

I glance back into the box and pull out more CD booklets and look through them. All documentaries. Ten booklets in all. These must hold a hundred discs each, so that's about a thousand docs. As I flip through them, it looks like quite a collection. Tons of obscure crazy-sounding titles: *Nazi UFO's, Tesla, Hollow Earth, HAARP.* The list goes on and on. I can't wait to start watching these. I think I got everything out of the box but lean over and peer inside to see if there's anything I missed.

I don't believe it. Disc golf discs! Eight in all. I chuckle to myself as I remember the day those guys destroyed my picnic with that yellow disc after my last meal with Jane.

This is crazy. Sean played disc golf. The sport I was just so rudely introduced to.

I take them out and look over each of them. They sure have cool names and graphics. This one is an Ogre, with a fantastically hideous looking monster on it. This other one is a Troll. Here's a Blade. Another that is an Octopus, and it says it's a mid-range disc, whatever that is. And, finally, a Polar Bear. It's a bigger disc and says it's a putter. There are discs that are called putters? That's funny.

Well, now I must play this sport. Sean played it so I'm going to as well.

Immediately, I make a commitment to get really good at disc golf and take it very seriously. If disc golf gave Sean enjoyment and fun, it's yet another way for me to bond with him, along with watching all those documentaries he was into.

DISC-OVERY

I take out my cell phone and start going through my texts, looking for the ones from Paul. I find them and send a text.

> Hey man going disc golfing any time soon? Really want to join up with you guys. Psyched to finally start playing.

With both boxes now empty, I look at the stacks of all his movies, documentaries, the Tibetan singing bowl, Chinese baoding balls, and the discs. A very intriguing assortment of possessions. They certainly reflect Sean and fascinating guy he was.

Those deep and sad emotions I was feeling are starting to transform into a keen interest of absorbing all Sean's interests. I plan to comb through all these documentaries and books to get into my brother's head. I'll go play disc golf at all the courses around town he must have played at. Who knows, maybe I'll bump into some people who knew him.

After avoiding it for so long, I'll finally get to know my little brother.

My phone rings with a text.

> Hey stranger glad u responded we are going to the Ridge tomorrow want me to pick you up at the park we met at and I'll drive us

> Sure what time

I text back.

> How bout 8:30 am

> See you then and there

> Cool sounds like a plan

I pick up the Troll disc and grip it. I look at the graphic and the little devil monster looks up at me. I smile back at it.

Getting up, I head to my refrigerator and take out a microbrew, checking out the multi-colored salamander on its label. I put down the disc and flick off the cap with my bottle opener , taking a nice big swig. I tilt the beer up high and am eye to eye with the funny lizard on the bottle. I chuckle as I chug the beer.

I set it down and enjoy its effects. I'll have to bring a case of these microbrews for the guys tomorrow. What a brilliant idea! Man, it sure has been a while since I've just gone drinking with the guys. Since my early New York days. *Gosh, has it been that long?*

I gulp the rest of the beer down and slam the bottle on the counter.

I pick up my disc and walk back to Sean's pile of possessions. Everything Sean had is so cool. What a fun guy he must have been. At least I'm getting to know him now. Better late than never.

I can't wait for tomorrow. This is going to be a blast.

3

The alarm blares from my cell phone at 7:30 AM and I just let it ring and ring until I finally hit the snooze button. I'm exhausted. The whole idea of playing disc golf this early suddenly seems like a very bad idea. I just want to stay in bed. I nod off again and start floating around in a bad hypnagogic trip. I shift around in my bed in this uncomfortable zone until the alarm wakes me up again.

Blowing these guys off would be pretty awful of me so I throw off the bedsheets, get dressed and stumble towards Sean's stacks of possessions to find the discs. I pile them into my backpack along with the yellow Valkyr that Paul gave me.

On my way out, I grab the case of microbrews I bought late last night. The guys are gonna love these. It's the zombie label this time. I passed on the salamander.

Blinding light assaults me as I open the door but I manage to stumble into my convertible with all the brewskis and speed off as cool morning air rips around my head.

I drive on deserted streets looking forward to hanging out with my new friends. When I finally arrive at the park's back entrance, I see the guys congregated in the far corner of the large parking lot smoking cigarettes and drinking beers.

They tip their beers in my direction as I park. I grab my backpack and the case of beers and walk over to them.

"Hey," Bill yells over to me, "what's that you're carrying there, dude?"

"It's zombie beer," I yell back.

"Zombie beer? Never heard of it."

"Well, it's a microbrew. From Oregon."

"What?"

"Don't mind him, Jeff," Paul says. "He only knows malt liquor at the corner liquor store. He's drinking some green apple 12% liquid crack monstrosity for breakfast," Paul says.

"Bill probably thinks microbrew is a beer that comes in a very small can," Andy quips.

All the guys laugh.

"Shut up, dude. I know what microbrew is," Bill fires back.

He raises his malt liquor.

"I know this is ghetto shit. But I like it," Bill says. He guzzles the rest of it and throws the can aside.

Bill turns and looks wide-eyed at the case of beer I've carried over. He gleefully grabs the heavy case of zombie microbrew from me and takes it back to the white truck they're crowding around. As he sets the case in the flatbed and opens it up, he looks down at it as if he just discovered fifty bars of gold.

He slowly looks up at me with twinkling adoration in his eyes and lifts a bottle out of the case, holding it up to the morning sunlight. The psychedelic kaleidoscope zombie shimmers, and Bill is transfixed on it. He flashes me a big smile.

"This is the real deal, man." He laughs. "Thanks, new guy. What's your name again?"

"Jeff."

The three other guys start to walk towards me, smiling and drinking their beers.

"Well," Paul says, "looks like you made a friend for life."

We all laugh as Paul raises his brewski and we toast an odd chime of aluminum cans and glass bottles clinking together.

"Thanks for finally making it out here. I kinda gave up on you," he says.

"Oh, I've just been distracted with my divorce. If I didn't have that to deal with, I would have been out here with you guys a month ago."

"Well, glad you finally made it out," Andy says. He looks up at me grinning. His face seems puffier than the last time I saw him. He looks terrible. His clothes are ragged, and he reeks of cigarettes, booze and body odor.

Gary slaps me on the back.

"Thanks for the beer. C'mon man, let's get going," he says.

"We're going to the Ridge, man," Paul says. "The most fucked up course in town. You got guts starting off with this one, man."

"Hey, it's all about having fun," Andy says.

"We try to keep the drama out of it, but you know how people can be." Paul continues. "But golf still gets us away from the grind, all those pressures we gotta deal with. It's a good time, man."

"I can't wait," I say.

Paul flicks his cigarette away and we pile into his truck. He turns the radio to a hard rock station and turns it up loud as Gary breaks out a pipe and starts smoking pot. As we pull out of the parking lot and onto the city streets, Gary takes a big hit and as it boils his lungs, he starts to heave and grunt.

"Give me some," Paul says.

Gary passes the pipe up to Paul and he takes a hit as he manages to continue steering the car. He then passes it to me and I take a hit, then pass it to Andy in the back who goes to work on it. We're all feeling the effects of the pot as we move our heads to the pulse of the heavy metal riffs.

"This is the bomb man," Gary says.

"Pass it over here, dude," says Bill.

I haven't smoked in years, but my brain rejoices in being numb from the consistent anxiety it's been stewing in. I allow the grinding bass lines and awesome guitar riffs to take over and am feeling fantastic, turning around with a huge smile on my face.

I think to myself that these are probably the exact people that Sean used to hang out with. Working guys and dropouts. He'd fit right in with this crowd.

We zoom on the highway towards downtown until Paul finally takes an exit leaving behind the humanity encased in their vehicles, careening forward like frightened zombies. I'm glad not to be a part of that herd.

We reach the top of a hill with an incredible view of the sprawling city as nature starts to take us in from the paved over mayhem we just escaped from. Outside the swirl of trees go by in a flurry of green as Paul pulls off to the side of the road.

"We're here," Paul says.

We all stumble out of the car as Paul goes to the back and fiddles with his cooler opening it up. We cram as many zombie beers as possible into our bags. Paul tries to fit four of them into his bag, but gives up and opens the fourth beer, taking a satisfying gulp.

As we zip up our bags, Paul dumps the rest of the zombie microbrews into a cooler, nestling them into the ice. He puts the cooler in the front of the truck locking the door.

"C'mon let's go, you drunks," he says. He walks down towards the bottom of the hill, and we all fall in line.

We somehow manage to make it down the steep decline without falling on our faces or, more importantly, spilling our beers. Paul reaches a rubber mat and drops his bag right next to it on a dilapidated wooden bench. The rest of us catch up to what I assume to be the first tee pad.

Paul thoughtfully sips his beer as he gazes beyond the deep valley below us. He points to the top of the next hill over.

"You see it? The basket?"

I follow his pointed finger and squint to see what he's talking about. All I see is trees and bushes.

DISC-OVERY

"Uh. No."

"You see that oak tree on the edge of that hill?" he asks.

"Yes," I reply.

"To the immediate left of it. You can see it next to that first branch that's making a v-shape."

I squint harder and make out a big weird-looking metal basket with chains in the middle.

"I see it now."

"You want to put the disc in that basket," Andy jumps in. "It's a little bit different than hitting those lamp posts at the park. Those chains catch the disc if you hit them the right way."

"That's a tough throw from all the way over here," I pout.

"Yeah, and even if you make it over there, it can roll down the other side of that hill," Gary says. "Then you're hiking for a hundred feet or more. Not an easy hole. Not an easy course. You picked a real bitch to start out with, bro."

"Don't worry," Andy says, "just let it flow, watch your form and let the disc do the work."

Andy gets on the tee pad and does a quick two-step backwards as he looks behind as he brings the disc back. He's facing us as his back is to the basket in the distance. Then in a blur he whirls around and the disc flies spinning like crazy towards the other side of the valley. It looks like it's going to be too low, but it slowly climbs up out of the valley and just misses the trail on the other side. It glances off the top side of the hill and ricochets off wildly to the left, flying over the basket and smashing into another oak tree. The disc lands with a thud to the ground about twenty-five feet to the left of the basket.

"Wow," I exclaim. "How the hell did you do that?"

"He got lucky," Paul says. "That shot was going over the other side of the hill if that tree didn't save him."

"Wasn't luck," counters Andy. "You glance it off the side of that top of that hill at that angle, it's gonna hit the tree."

Gary laughs. "Yeah, whatever dude. You got lucky. Step aside."

Gary's turn. He starts to move as he winds up. He doesn't bring the disc back as far as Andy and he doesn't look as graceful. He grunts loudly as he whips his arm around and the disc juts way to the left in a big arc.

"Shit!" He yells.

We all watch the disc go way up high in the air and the wind catches it and takes it over the far-left side of the opposite hill. Gary looks at it with disgust.

"Early release program," Bill says.

Everybody laughs as Gary turns around walking off to look for his beer.

"Yeah, you would know about that, Bill," Gary says.

Bill looks down at his disc golf bag and flips through a bunch before he stops at a bright pink one. He takes it out and saunters up to the tee pad.

"Yes, I would know. They just let me out early."

Everybody laughs again as Bill takes a moment and scans the area before he lets out a wild yelp throwing the disc like a madman. Somehow the disc flies out in a straight line but is way too low. It hits well below the trail line on the opposite hill and then falls on its side and starts rolling down the hill. It's picking up speed as it just continues to roll, roll, roll.

"Oh no!" Bill yells, as everyone starts laughing again. The disc is not stopping. It rolls out of eyesight as he turns, and my eyes follow him as he goes to get his beer.

"Damn this course is fucked up!" he laments.

"Shit mother fucker!" yells Paul, I turn around to see his disc careen far to the right, sailing off into the vast wooded area past the far side of hill. Everyone murmurs their own commentary about Paul's shot as we all sip from our drinks.

Everyone's thrown except me. The guys slowly turn around, smirking.

"Time to walk the plank," Gary says.

Everyone snickers as Andy picks up my backpack.

"Let me see what you got in here," he says. He unzips the

DISC-OVERY

pack and starts flipping through the discs. "Oh, some old plastic here. Ancient.

Pretty beat up but these will work. Here's a good one. The Ogre."

He takes it out of the bag and walks up to the tee pad with me.

"Just throw it right at that oak tree to the right of the basket," he says. "This disc's overstable, so it will start moving to the left before you hit the tree and won't veer right over the other side of the hill, like Paul's just did. Just relax and throw it at the tree, and you'll be on your way to a par."

"Easier said than done," I say.

"Keep the disc level as you bring it back, like you're moving it along a table. Don't try to power it. Just shift your hips and follow through and keep moving. No heavy feet."

He hands me the Ogre and stands back and starts drinking the microbrew. He glances at the zombie on the beer bottle and looks back up at my Ogre disc.

"Lotta monsters out here today," he quips.

I take it and walk up to the tee pad. I'm so nervous my knees are shaking. Why am I so freaked out? Who cares how I throw in front of these clowns? But I can't help it, I'm petrified. I take some deep breaths and try to remember everything Andy just told me. I stand there thinking about it for a while.

"Thirty seconds on the tee pad, bud," Gary says.

"Shut up, dude, he can take all the time he wants," Paul snaps.

Bill and Andy just snicker to themselves as everyone waits to see how the newbie throws the disc.

I start to move forward and slowly take my arm back trying to keep the disc nice and level like Andy told me as my feet move forward. I keep my head straight and move slowly as I whip my arm around throwing it towards the oak tree and my body shifts fluidly to the right as I remember to follow through landing on my left foot coming around.

The Ogre comes out fast but a little high. It's on a nice line to the tree, and I start to think it might actually clear the valley area and hit the hill on the other side.

"There she goes!" yells Andy.

As the disc moves towards the oak tree, it dramatically sails to the left as it starts to glide. I'm ecstatic as the Ogre clears the valley and makes landfall about forty feet to the left of the oak tree. It bounces high and goes another twenty feet to the left. It finally comes to rest in a pile of leaves. I can't believe it.

"Nice shot, Jeff. You got an arm," Paul says.

"Good one, dude," Bill chimes in.

"I can't believe I got it over there," I say. "Shit, I'll open my eyes next time. Lucky shot."

"Nah, man, you listened to what I said," Andy counters. "You did everything I told you to do. You got nice natural form."

I'm flying high as we get on the trail that leads to the other hill.

"Hey Andy," I say, "what the heck does overstable mean anyway?"

"If you throw an overstable disc backhand, it goes to the left. It's understable if it goes to the right. And it's the exact opposite if you're throwing it sidearm."

"Sidearm?"

"Yeah, I'll show you how to throw sidearm today, Daniel-san."

Everyone laughs at his *Karate Kid* reference. Paul slows down until he's beside me, as Andy walks ahead to find his disc at the hill in front of us.

"Andy taught me everything he knows about disc golf," he says in a lowered voice. "He used to be one of the best players around until he started drinking. After that, he lost his house during the meltdown years ago and it's been downhill for him ever since."

DISC-OVERY

Gary darts off to the left to go look for his disc. He's cursing as he's going through brush and stepping over rocks.

"Where is my goddamn Troll?" he exclaims.

"Troll?" I say. "I think I have one of those. How many discs are named after monsters?"

"Come to think of it, quite a few," Paul answers. "I gave you a Valkyr. Ain't that some devil or something?"

"It's out of Norse mythology," answers Andy from far ahead on the trail. "They're female spirits that choose who lives and dies in battle."

"Oh, well, sorry scholar." Paul rolls his eyes.

We finally reach the other hill and set our bags down next to our discs.

"Hey, watch out," Andy says, "Gary's throwing now."

We look down the hill to the left and Gary is winding up. Then he throws a high, arcing shot far above us.

"Uh oh," Bill moans.

His disc flies over the edge of the hill where the basket is nestled next to the oak tree. It sails off into the distance down the other side of the hill.

"Shit!" we hear Gary yell.

Andy and Bill start chuckling as Gary yells from down below.

"What are you punks laughing at?"

They both try to stop their chuckling to no avail.

"Sorry, dude," Bill yells. "It's the pot, man."

"You're up next, Jeff," Paul says. "Gary's still the furthest out with that terrible throw down the side of the mountain but we don't got all day for him to go hike a mile to find it. Bill hasn't even started down the hill to shoot his. And I have no clue where mine went. We're playing 'ready golf,' so go throw yours."

I put my foot right behind my disc and pick up the weathered Ogre.

Andy starts walking over to me slowly.

"Not a bad throw for your first time. It took me months when I started playing here to clear that valley. You can throw."

"Thanks, Andy. I was an athlete back in the day. Played football and basketball. It's nice to be doing something athletic again with the guys."

"I played football, too."

"Oh yeah?" I ask.

"Yep, right here in Burbank. Strong safety. I was little but I packed a wallop on people."

"You're kidding, Andy. I played strong safety, too."

"No way!" he laughs.

"I loved it, man. I hit people like Ronnie Lott."

"Yep," Andy says. "He was my favorite. Him and Steve Atwater, remember that guy?"

"Of course. I loved Atwater. Great hitter."

"Hey you two, heads up. Gary's throwing," Paul warns us.

We stay quiet and wait for the disc to come back into view from down in the valley on the other side. We hear a big grunt, and a moment later Gary's bright red disc comes flying up over the ridge. It's not a bad shot and hits the other side of the tree, but it bounces off the ground and catches its side and starts to roll.

"Not again!" Bill says.

We all erupt into laughter as the disc starts rolling down the other side of the hill from where we came from. Paul laughs as well as he lights up a cigarette. After a few moments we hear Bill from way down below.

"Ow! Whose disc just rolled into me! How about a 'fore' guys?"

Gary comes panting up from the other side of the hill.

"Where did my disc land?" he yells at us.

"It rolled down the other side of the hill and hit Bill," Paul chuckles.

"What?" Gary yells.

"FORE!" Bill screams as his disc whizzes by us. It's driving straight for Gary. We watch it go straight for his head. Gary freezes as he realizes he's about to get clobbered in the face by a disc. As it races towards him, he clumsily drops to the ground like a sack of potatoes, the disc barely missing him. The disc juts up the hill landing twenty feet to the left of the basket.

We look at each other and again burst out laughing as we realize Gary was almost decapitated by Bill's disc.

"Great shot, Bill!" Paul yells.

"You almost took off my head, you asshole!" screams Gary.

"I yelled 'fore', dude!" replies Bill.

"You're right under the basket, Bill. Great shot!" says Andy.

Gary makes his way down to where Bill is to find his disc.

"I hate this fucking course," Gary mumbles. "Shit!"

"Is there a mercy rule in disc golf?" Paul asks Andy.

"I think it's like eight shots or something like that," he replies. "I'm not sure."

Gary walks by us cursing as he starts to descend the hill the other way towards the disc.

"Watch out, Gary," Bill yells. "I ran into some used condoms last time I lost a disc down there."

"Well, I'm gonna shoot now," I say.

"Please do," Paul says. "Take your time. If you throw it over the hill, you'll probably go through what Gary's going through right now. It's good exercise but bad golf. I strongly advise against it."

"Right," I reply.

"Speaking of exercise, I'm off to find my disc on the other side of the mountain. Good luck with the shot," Paul says as he disappears behind the trail.

"Hey let me see your backpack," Andy says.

I hand him the pack and he unzips it to look through the discs again. He stops at one.

"Ah, here's a good one. You got an Octopus, huh? Great disc."

He takes it out of the bag to look it over.

"Nice and heavy at 180 grams. This is the one you want. Put a little touch on it, Jeff."

"Okay," I say taking the disc.

I move behind my other disc I'd thrown on the first shot and put my right foot behind it.

"Nice and easy, but don't forget to follow through," Andy continues.

Taking a deep breath, I start moving my arms back and forth, trying to get a motion going before I actually throw it. I take it back a little and let it go with maybe a little too much on it, and a little to the right of the basket. The heavy disc goes high, though, hanging precariously over the deep valley behind the oak tree, and floats in the air until it comes back to the left over the branch of the oak tree falling about ten feet to the left of the basket.

"Shit, man," Andy says. "Great shot. You got a lot of balls to throw a hyzer shot like that over the edge of the cliff. Livin' dangerously!"

"Thanks Andy," I say. "Hey what does 'hyzer' mean?"

"It's when a disc fades hard," he replies.

"Fore!" we hear Gary from a distance. We look around as his disc rampages towards us. We're startled as it zooms over our heads past the basket and onto the other side of the hill where Gary had come from. We watch it go over the hill down the valley yet again. Andy and Bill look at me, and we smirk as we sip from our drinks. Bill gets ready to putt about twenty feet from the basket.

"Ow! You fucking asshole! Who threw that?" Paul yells from down below, where Gary's disc disappeared into.

We burst into laughter as Paul's disc comes screaming up from the mountain, hitting the oak tree to the right of the basket and falling to the ground nearby.

"Good shot, dude," Bill yells down at Paul. "You're right next to the basket."

DISC-OVERY

"Cool!" replies Paul from down yonder. "Tell Gary I'm picking up his disc that just hit me. That asshole."

"Yeah, pick it up," Andy chimes in. "Take the poor bastard out of his misery."

"Hey, you guys mind?" Bill says setting up to putt.

We hush up to let him concentrate as he's really focusing in on the basket. He flings a line drive right into the chains making a nice ringing sound.

"Awesome, man!" I yell.

"Killer putt!" Andy says.

"Good one, dude!" Paul exclaims, finally making his way up the hill.

Bill is beaming with pride as he grabs his zombie beer from a rock he'd set it on and toasts us. He proceeds to guzzle the entire beer down. Once the bottle is sufficiently drained, he burps loudly, tossing the beer aside and digging another from his bag. He snaps the bottle cap off with his teeth and spits it out.

"I used to know a guy who could do that back in college," I say.

"It's a handy skill," Bill quips.

Suddenly Gary comes into view on the trail, panting and moaning and covered in mud.

"I tripped down there and got all this crap on me. Where'd my disc go?"

"It rolled down the other side of the hill," Paul says.

Everyone stifles a laugh.

"That's it. I quit this hole. I'm done," he says.

"Yes you are. I picked up your disc," Paul replies.

He hands it to Gary, who snatches it away.

"Well, let the rest of us putt, will you?" Andy says.

Paul picks up his disc and gets in a putting stance.

Gary heads to his bag and breaks out a beer, opening it for a well-deserved swig.

"Fuckin' golf," he moans.

There's a crash against the chains again as Paul's putt falls directly in the middle of the basket.

"Good one, dude," Andy says.

"Nice one," I echo.

Andy is about fifteen feet away and focuses intently on his putt. He finally throws the disc and it glances off the side of the chains and falls to the ground.

"Dang it," he says.

Paul picks up the disc and hands it to him.

"Happens. Good drive, though, dude."

"I don't care about that," Andy replies. "I've told you a million times...you drive for show and putt for dough."

Andy puts the putter into his bag as I rummage through my backpack looking for a putter.

"You got a putter in there?" he asks me.

"I think so."

"Let me see."

He takes the backpack again and looks through it.

"You're in luck. A Polar Bear. Seems like you got all the discs you need. Where did you get these? I thought you said this was your first time playing. Did you go and buy a bunch of used plastic before you came out here with us?"

I take the putter from him and walk over to my other disc.

"Well, my brother used to play. When he died, I found these discs in his belongings."

There's an awkward silence until Paul speaks up.

"Damn. Sorry to hear that, Jeff."

I step up behind my disc and look at the chains in the basket. I take a deep breath and lightly throw the disc. It crashes against the chains and makes that cool ringing sound echoing through the forest.

The guys congratulate me—besides Gary who's still licking his wounds and pounding his zombie microbrew.

"The first time this guy plays on a disc golf course and he shoots a par. Amazing," Paul says.

DISC-OVERY

"I think we got a prodigy here, "Andy adds. "He listens. You're coachable, Jeff. I'm gonna make a player out of you."

I take my disc out of the basket and store it in my backpack.

"I can see why my brother played this sport. It's pretty cool. Glad I came out today, guys."

"Glad you came out too," Paul says.

We start walking over to the next tee pad.

"Well...we'll see if you still say that when you shoot a quadruple bogey out here and have to hike up and down these hills to get your disc," Gary says as he catches up with us, tossing his empty microbrew into the woods.

* * *

When we finish the ninth hole the auspicious debut of mine is a thing of the past. Not only have I failed to shoot another par, but I've lost two discs. I've shot two triple bogeys, three double bogeys and three bogeys. A terrible showing. I've also fallen down a couple of times. I'm covered with dirt and bleeding.

"Hey everybody. Look!" Bill announces. "See why they call this place Penis Park?"

We turn to where he's pointing and see a bush covered in used condoms. Bill laughs hysterically while the rest of us stare, wanting to throw up.

"Lots of people doin' the nasty up here!" he says.

"Yeah," Paul continues, "you don't want your disc falling in that."

"Gross!" Gary screams, laughing.

Once back at the truck we put down our bags inside the flatbed and Paul breaks out the cooler he'd stowed in the truck. We each grab a cold zombie beer.

"Cops," Bill says, barely moving his lips.

I feel a rush of panic as I hastily place my brew down on the ground next to my backpack, spilling some of it. Deftly, Paul slowly closes the cooler instead of freaking out and slamming it down— which would, of course, be a dead giveaway to hiding contraband. I look up slowly as the police squad car crawls by, both cops looking directly at us. They know we're drinking. They're making their point as they cruise by. We wait a few moments before resuming to drink from our microbrews.

"That was a close one," I say.

"Yeah, we all played it cool, though," Paul says. "You didn't flinch, Jeff. Nice."

"They come around here sometimes," he continues. "They're looking for gangbangers. If you keep a low profile, they don't mind the drinking too much, though sometimes they crack down on it."

"Sucks when they rifle through your bag," Bill chimes in.

"Yeah, most disc bags also carry a mini-bar and God knows what else." Paul snorts.

"They have a police academy right here on the other side of the park" Gary says. "C'mon, let's grab our stuff and give Jeff the grand tour before we start the back nine."

Paul puts the cooler away in the truck and we grab our bags and walk across the street to holes ten through eighteen. We pass a clearing around a slight hill that is covered with trees. As we go around the bend, the view of the city is striking, the full panorama of Los Angeles presents itself in its sprawling excess. We continue walking to the edge of the hill.

"There's Dodger Stadium," Paul points.

"Oh yeah, look at that. Man, you can watch a game from here," I say.

"Many people do," Paul replies.

"And if you look over there," Gary points to the right, "that's the twin towers jail."

"L.A. has twin towers?" I ask.

"Well, the jailhouse version," he answers.

I look at the ominous oddly shaped structure.

"I really hope I never have to go there," I say.

"It's not half bad, really," Andy says. "Lots of reading material, you eat three times a day. I really didn't mind it. I just hated it every morning when I realized I couldn't go play disc golf."

"I just got out three weeks ago," Bill says. "Early release program."

Everyone laughs.

"I've been so many times," Bill continues, "that every time I go back it's like a reunion in there."

Paul peers over his beer at the gloomy dungeon in the distance. "I was at the old county jail a few times years ago but I haven't been to this one yet." He takes another swig of his beer.

"Well, enough with the grand tour. Back to disc golf," Andy says pointedly.

We lumber over to the tenth tee and drop our bags.

Gary walks up to the tee pad with his distance driver. "I might surprise you guys this round," he says. He rips a massive backhand as the disc bristles through the air and sails through the trees directly at the basket. It sails just above it and skips several times until it's about fifty feet past it.

I raise up my zombie microbrew to my lips as I take a quick gulp.

"You're up, Jeff."

Setting the beer on a nearby rock, I open my backpack and flip through the discs until I find my Ogre. I grab it and take it to the tee pad and look straight ahead at the basket. Then I look around and smile at everyone. They smile back as they sip their drinks.

I've got a brand-new sport. And a whole new set of friends.

I turn around and face the basket bringing the disc back far behind me as I step into the shot and shift my hips around. Then I her rip.

The disc explodes out of my hand and races towards the basket.

"Good one, dude," Paul says.

Life is grand.

4

I spend most of the next day sleeping. All that drinking and chasing discs up and down hills in the hot sun has taken its toll. But as exhausted as I am, I feel terrific. I had so much fun with all my goofy new pals. I finally sit up and make my way over to the five-gallon jug of water on the kitchen counter. I reach for a few aspirin before guzzling a couple of glasses.

My wandering eyes rest on Sean's brown boxes in the corner. I drag them over to my bed and take out one of the CD booklets with the documentaries. I open it up and put a disc in the DVD player.

I sit back in bed as the documentary starts with a shaky camera filming a lady at a podium. Her nasally voice lulls on about occult phenomenon but in a very boring academic tone.

As the documentary drones on, I look down into Sean's box taking out some dusty folders. As I open one of the folders, I'm immediately drawn in by a series of beautiful sketches of nature. My eyes widen when I come upon a big drawing of a flying saucer, then another. Three more sketches of flying saucers follow, all with a backdrop of mountains, forests, and desert landscapes. All magnificent.

I remember what a great talent Sean was and feel tears

welling up. He was an awesome musician but an even better artist. I remember seeing some of his paintings at his college in Connecticut so many years ago. He had a special gift. Even held a few exhibitions at art galleries in New York City briefly before he moved to Los Angeles.

Funny how he was so into flying saucers, he appeared to have a real fascination with the subject. His boxes are filled with books on UFO's.

I put down his drawings and go back to the dusty folders, thumbing through them. One holds car insurance documents, another has his birth certificate and college diploma, another with lease agreements and the like. The final folder houses his tax returns. I stop at this one. I always wondered what Sean did to make ends meet. Whenever I'd pry, he would dismissively say he did odd jobs and leave it at that.

I take out the papers. The first is from a few years ago. I flip to the back page where the income figure is. One hundred and seventy-five thousand dollars. Wow. I had no idea Sean made that much. I was always under the illusion that he was a struggling musician and artist just barely making it. But now that I think about it, I can't remember him ever asking me for money. Not one cent, all those years. Usually struggling artists don't have a problem hitting up their family members for money, particularly those who they know are making oodles of money like I was. I always figured he was asking mom and dad for help. Evidently not.

I glance over the tax return and find the company name. ExecuSolutions. Thumbing through the previous year's returns, I find Sean's earnings. Two hundred and twenty-five thousand dollars. Another good year. Same company. I go back one more year. One hundred and ninety-five thousand dollars. ExecuSolutions again. When I get to the last tax return, I flip to the last page. One hundred eighty-three thousand. ExecuSolutions.

I sit back flabbergasted. I had no idea. Good for Sean. I'm

glad he was making decent money. Weird that he would choose to live in a modest apartment with roommates when he could afford something better than that. Well, maybe he liked living with his bandmates. I'm sure it must have been a lot of fun partying and rehearsing with them.

ExecuSolutions. I wonder what kind of company that is. I move over to my computer and type in the name.

Tons of stuff comes up.

Four indicted in botched security maneuver in Afghani war zone. Four private security contractors have been indicted by the Feds for murder for firing on Afghani citizens during a shoot-out during security maneuvers.

I look down at the next result.

The CEO of ExecuSolutions' shady past comes back to haunt him as four contractors are indicted....past involvement with South African mercenary firms comes to light as former guns for hire are rebranded as "Private Military Contractors" or PMC's.

Then the next one...

ExecuSolutions acquired by rival PMC Management Defense Services as Mike C. Milodread, CEO of ExecuSolutions, steps down amidst indictments of ExecuSolutions contractors who killed Afghani civilians last summer.

I scroll to a seemingly endless amount of articles about ExecuSolutions, none of them favorable. This is the last kind of company I'd expect Sean to be employed by. Even though he did ROTC in college, I'd never imagine he'd have any kind of career in the military, or an off-shoot of the military like the PMC's. Sean became very counterculture over the years and hated authority. He told me he only did ROTC for the loans and kept quiet about the experience. I barely remember he did it.

For years I thought he was a musician and artist living on the fringes of society, maybe finding work in restaurants or telemarketing or lowly sales... retail jobs. Now I discover he was pulling down six figures from a controversial mercenary company involved in shady operations worldwide.

I need a drink. I head to the fridge and grab a salamander microbrew. Before closing the fridge I make it a point to confirm there are plenty more. Looks like I'll need them. Lost in thought, I look up at the lady on my television still blabbering on about mystical nonsense. I try to focus on what she's saying as she's pointing to x-rays on an overhead projector.

I eject the DVD and read the title that is scrawled on the disc. *Alien Implants*. I put it back into the CD booklet and flip the pages of Sean's DVDs. Lots of weird titles. *Alien Abduction, Secret Government MJ-12 Files, Cattle Mutilations, Miracle Healing Shamans in Brazil, Suppressed Free Energy Devices*. I pause a moment and put down the booklet and pound my beer for a bit.

I pick up another CD booklet and look through it. *Tesla Technology, AREA 51 Alien Secrets, Secret Bases in Antarctica, Air America and the CIA, Edgar Cayce Prophecies, Aboriginal Healing in Australia, Cult Mind-Control Tactics of the Elite, Illuminati Sex Slaves*.

What in God's name was Sean into?

I take the DVD on Illuminati and put it in. A similar presentation comes up. A guy behind a podium with the same kind of amateur video production. He begins discussing the origins of the Illuminati—something I'm familiar with from the usual pop culture sources like magazines and TV shows. I've always had a mild interest in conspiracy theories. After all, the Pentagon released footage awhile back of UFO's with Navy pilots claiming could possibly be real. Multiple accounts of close encounters have been acknowledged and virtually paraded around for years by the government. What was a crazy conspiracy theory for decades was suddenly being acknowledged as credible. This "disclosure" is only the tip of the iceberg regarding our government and extraterrestrials.

I let the documentary play as I scroll through the myriad negative web pages on ExecuSolutions. I click on one.

> This former South African mercenary group financed by European black nobility, which was active in many parts of Africa since the '50's has found new life repackaged as a PMC or 'Private Military Contractor,' scoring multi-million dollar security contracts in the U.S. Government's adventures in Iraq and Afghanistan. This firm also got the job of providing security for Area 51, the U.S. Government's ultra-secret black site in Nevada. ExecuSolutions certainly has friends in high places as it has become both the darling of Uncle Sam's war privatization and black site security push and typifies the corporate outsourcing of formerly traditional governmental operations.

Unbelievable. What the hell was Sean doing working for a company like this?

I glance back at the television and the guy behind the podium is pointing at an overhead projection of different lineages of Illuminati families like the Rothschilds, Rockefellers, Carnegies, etc.

This is all a bit much. I take another pull from my beer. I grab the remote and turn off the television, then proceed to move all of Sean's folders off my bed. I lay down and look up at my blank, white ceiling.

I guess I knew my brother less than I thought. I wonder what he specifically did for ExecuSolutions. Was he one of the mercenaries? Why didn't he disclose this to me or mom and dad? I'm sure my parents would have told me about it. I conclude he never told them or anyone else in our family the truth.

I wonder if I should confront mom and dad with this.

Maybe not. It's possible they never knew about his secret life. Would probably shatter them to learn their son was not who they thought he was, opening a big can of worms and upsetting them. I'll keep this to myself for a while, or at least until I get to the bottom of this.

I roll off my bed to get another salamander beer and I take a big chug. I feel shaken. Getting antsy. I need to get out of here to clear my head.

After a moment's thought, I decide pay a visit to Sean's old roommates. His old band. Maybe they can clarify some of this.

I grab my keys and jump in the car, peeling out towards Ventura Blvd. Where the hell was Sean's old apartment again? I'm digging deep into the vestiges of my brain cells, and I get a vague street somewhere in Los Feliz. Hipsters galore. Next to a taco place down the street from an elementary school. I'll find it. Who knows if his old bandmates are still there, but it's worth a shot.

I speed over the hill into Hollywood. The sun is shining down on my head as gusts of wind ripple through the convertible. I pick up my cell phone to call my mother. She has to know *something* about her son's employment as a mercenary— I mean, private security contractor.

"Hey mom, it's Jeff."

"Hey sweetie. How are you?" she asks.

We go through the usual dance of mother to son small talk. I cut right to the chase.

"Hey, listen, mom, I wanted to ask you something about Sean."

"Okay."

"When he was living out here in L.A. all those years, what exactly did he do for work? I always assumed he did odd jobs."

"Your brother always told me he did catering work. He liked the flexibility of it."

"Catering, huh," I mumble.

"Yes. But you know how Sean was. Or maybe you don't

because you didn't talk to him for so many years long before he died, Jeff.

I roll my eyes as I take this little jab. I'm used to my mom's relentless passive aggressive behavior.

"He wouldn't return our calls for months at a time. The longest time we never heard from him was eight months. Not even a text. It was truly awful. Every time we finally got a hold of him, he told us he was on the road with that band of his. I always reminded him that he could have called us, but he always claimed he was too busy, that life on the road in a band was very demanding. I'd always argue that it would take just a few minutes to call and let us know he was okay. He would just brush this off. Your brother did this to us a lot, Jeff."

Eight months away in a war zone, I think.

"But what could we do," my mother continued, "he was a grown adult and if he didn't want to call us, he didn't have to. I just wish he had. He became so distant from the family all those years he lived out there in L.A."

"Yeah, that's pretty callous to act like he did," I said.

"Yes, well, I'm sure he had his reasons," my mom rationalizes.

She always enabled Sean and was an apologist for whatever he did. I always thought he was her favorite.

"Okay. Just curious. How's everything with dad?"

"He's okay. We might go up the coast later this month. Get some fresh air."

"That's a great idea," I say. "I'm in the car, and need to concentrate on my driving. I'll call you later. Love you."

"I love you, too, Jeff."

I hang up the phone and start biting my lower lip.

Sean lied to all of us. Old feelings of resentment and frustration I felt about him start to well up inside me. A reminder of why I cut ties with him for so long. Sean was always very selfish. He never thought of the family. I'm guilty of that, too, I guess.

DISC-OVERY

I'm no saint. I became a stereotypical greedy and ruthless self-absorbed Wall Street douchebag. Who the hell am I to be critical of Sean? But I never lied to mom dad as grossly as he had. Never lied about going to a freaking war zone. Never kept a secret life of this magnitude from them. The whole thing is bizarre.

Arriving in Hollywood, I make my way to Los Feliz. Sean's apartment was somewhere around here. I scan the abundance of boutique stores, chic restaurants, and hipsters. I may have to park and start walking to look for it.

As I'm attempting to locate somewhere to park, I spot the taco joint that I remember from the last time I visited Sean. I park my car and get out, immediately hit with the delicious smell of Mexican food. My stomach rumbles as I remember their awesome fish tacos..

Retracing my steps as best as I can, I feel out what I think looks familiar. Oh yes, here's that weird green house. I remember that. I continue walking and see the fence surrounding the elementary school. Getting warmer. I wander around different side streets and find myself at the little avenue he lived on. Ambrose Ave. Of course. Things continue to look familiar as I finally come upon Sean's apartment building. Satisfaction and relief wash over me. The Spanish tiles and the balconies. I can't believe I've actually found it.

A waft of marijuana smoke hits me as I ascend the staircase to the second floor and walk to the end of the hall where Sean lived with his bandmates. The last apartment on the left.

The door is wide open and television blaring. A guy is strumming his guitar watching some reality show. He puts the guitar down and grabs his bong taking a huge rip. I knock on the doorframe mid-exhale of pungent smoke. Startled, he coughs and turns around, acknowledging me with a nod.

"Hey there, sorry to disturb you," I say.

"Can I help you?"

"Yes, uh, I was wondering if my brother's old roommates

still lived here. They were two guys with long hair, one was short the other tall. They were here about a year or two ago."

"I remember those guys. They're long gone. Me and my buddies moved in here. Is your brother the one that died?"

"Yep."

"Sorry."

Kaleidescope tapestries adorn the apartment along with posters of all the classic bands: Pink Floyd, Led Zeppelin, Jimi Hendrix, The Doors. It never ceases to amaze me how some young people are so into the classics.

"It's okay," I say.

"You want a toke?" he asks me.

"Sure."

"Well, come on in then and close that door."

I enter the apartment shutting the door behind me and sit down on the sofa next to him. I didn't notice all the nose piercings he had. There must be half a dozen. How does he even breathe through all that metal?

"I'm Jeff."

"Hey man, I'm Chris."

He repacks the bong and hands it to me. I take a massive hit, he chuckles.

"Dude, you totally spanked that bowl."

I struggle with all the hot marijuana smoke in my lungs, coughing and sputtering it out. Chris shakes his head and continues to chuckle. He picks up his guitar and starts strumming again, the music sounding sublime as the pot sedates me.

"Yeah, man. Those guys were weird, dude," Chris remarks.

"What do you mean?" I ask him.

"Every time we'd come here to look at the place to check it out and finalize things, they'd be here arguing with each other and with these guys in suits that would show up. One time, the landlord was with us, and it just got really awkward."

"What were they arguing about?" I ask him.

"To be honest with you, dude, I think it was about your

brother. They were tripping out about him." Chris has set down the guitar again in favor of the bong.

"Do you remember what about, exactly?"

"No, not really. It was a while ago." Chris shrugs.

"Think about it. It's kind of important," I say.

He leans back and takes another bong hit. Setting down the bong, he ponders with red, glazed over eyes. Chris nods to himself, picking up the guitar again and strums a Led Zeppelin song. "Tangerine." God, I love that song.

He lets the music flow as he seems to be reaching towards a distant memory. Finally Chris says, "Interviews."

"What?" I ask.

"Something about interviews. Interviews that your brother did. That he wasn't supposed to do or something. They were freakin' out about that, wondering where they were."

"Interesting," I say.

"Every time I came in with my friends to look at the place or meet there with the landlord, they would try to stop arguing but it would always eventually just erupt as soon as we finished looking at the apartment. We'd walk out into the hall and they'd start going at it again. Finally, one day they were all gone."

After the final chord rings out, Chris hands me the bong and I take another hit.

"It just struck me as weird. They were really tense, those guys. I thought they were getting busted because the guys in suits looked like cops. Detectives."

"Were they?" I ask.

"No. I know cops, dude. But they looked pretty official. Like they worked for the government."

"Really?" I say.

"Yep. Oh yeah, another thing," he continues.

"What's that?"

"They rifled through the boxes that I think were your brother's. I remember because of this cool Tibetan bowl that was in there, and some Chinese balls. You know the ones you twirl around in your hand. I like those things, so it stuck in my mind. They were arguing about the contents of those boxes. I thought that was uncool because I knew your brother had died. I'm like, why are they going through the dead guy's shit?"

"Yeah, that is weird," I say.

He takes another bong hit, he offers it to me and I politely decline. I'm really floating now.

"Oh yeah. They were also looking at these CD booklets and talking about all these movies your brother had. Docs."

"Yes, my brother had a lot of those."

"They just kept going through them, looking for something. And making fun of the titles. They would go through all the booklets, being pretty rough with them, then just throw them down back in the boxes, as they'd keep cursing. And then they would kind of eyeball me and the landlord, getting really impatient with us that we had to be there. Then the landlord would get pissed at them. It was real awkward."

He strums his guitar again, this time singing some of the lyrics to "Tangerine." I look around the apartment, taking in the smattering of cool rock posters on the walls still amused that kids this young like music this old. I settle into in the relaxing marijuana mist and digest all of this. This is a gold mine of intriguing information.

"Can you remember anything else?" I ask him.

He continues to strum his guitar, lost in thought. Several long moments go by.

"Oh yeah. They confiscated all of the docs they found. Just took them after they rifled through them. That caused a big fucking argument. They all almost came to blows about that. Like who were they to just take your brother's shit. But the band guys once laughed about the fact that they were hiding most of your brother's DVD collection from these government assholes. I guess that's the stuff you were able to get."

I remember the day I told Sean's roommates they could keep all of his guitars and amps. They went back into one of

DISC-OVERY

their rooms and pulled out Sean's boxes that were tucked away. Curious they never brought up these government people who seized some of the collection. Maybe they didn't want to reveal Sean's secret life or that government people were after him.

"Anything else you can think of?" I take another big toke of the weed.

"No, that's about it. Just strange, man. Awkward situation."

I take a moment to watch the reality show that is playing. Some cooking show with the head chef yelling at everybody.

"Well, Chris. Thanks a lot for the info. It really helps. I'm trying to figure some things out about my brother."

"Hey man, I got a band and we're playing here in Los Feliz this weekend. You want to buy a ticket to the show? I got to sell like twelve more. Just ten bucks."

I figure that's a small price to pay for this invaluable information about Sean, not to mention all the bong hits, so I get out my wallet and pull out a twenty and give it to him.

"Gimme two," I say.

"Thanks dude!"

He quickly puts down his guitar and hurries over to his desk. He searches around until he finds the tickets, then turns around and hands them to me.

"This Saturday night. We go on at eleven sharp. It's going to rock."

I smile as I take the tickets.

"I can't wait," I say, though I have no intention of going. "Great talking to you, Chris. Thanks for the weed."

"You bet, man. See you Saturday."

I leave the apartment and as I make my way down the stairs the pot is making me feel even weirder about the situation. Maybe I shouldn't have had that last bong hit. I tell myself to breathe in and out as I make my way outside and towards my car. I make a mental note to get a couple of those tacos before I head back to the valley.

My phone beeps, interrupting my vision of delicious fish tacos, it's a text from Paul.

> Next sunday going to oak grove in pasadena its the first and oldest disc golf course ever hope you can make it

I stop walking to type a response.

> Of course im there wouldnt miss it for the world.

> Great ill send address and time later in the week looking forward to it.

> Me 2

Famous fish tacos again beckoning me, I walk down to the taco joint happy that I have fun plans for the weekend. Some delicious tacos and a couple of cold brews are just what I need right now. A temporary distraction from the frustration of another odd afternoon digging around in my brother's life, trying to figure out who the hell he really was.

5

The week flew by. I retreated into alcohol and marijuana. The secret life of my brother has caught up with me, and I don't want to deal with sobriety. Here I am, uprooting myself from the east coast to have some kind of spiritual bonding with my brother, and I discover that he's a soldier of fortune. Ridiculous.

I spent most of the week watching his documentaries, one after the other, while drinking zombie beer after zombie beer. My knowledge of the secret government and black budgets and UFO's has skyrocketed. Then as it got later each evening, I would hit the vodka. Five consecutive days of that. It's all been a blur.

I'm in no rush to find out more about Sean. I'll start digging around again when I feel up to it. I need to process all of this.

Sunday morning is here and I'm heading over to Buena Vista Park, where I'm meeting the boys. From there, we're going to that world famous disc golf course, Oak Grove. I'm ready to leave the darkness of these documentaries behind and have fun with my new friends throwing discs.

I got a coffee in one hand and another case of zombie beer in the other for the guys. That alone will keep me popular with the group. I cruise down Magnolia Blvd. into Burbank until I arrive and find the guys in the parking lot.

I pull up and they all stop drinking and talking and look over at me, smiling.

"What, am I late?" I ask.

"No, we're early. Getting our drink on before the day starts."

"I hear that," I say as I jump out of my car. I grab the case of zombie beers in the back and plop them into Paul's flatbed.

The guys applaud as I do this, and I take a bow. They come over and we all high five and do the man hugs.

"What up, dude?" Andy asks.

"Not much, man, just ready to go play," I say.

"Well, you're gonna love this course, Jeff. It's the very first disc golf course in the world," Andy says.

"Awesome!"

I look around and realize there are only three guys. Bill's not here.

"Hey, uh, where's Bill?" I ask.

"We heard he got picked up again," Gary said.

"Picked up?" I ask.

We get into the truck. The guys let me sit in the front.

"He had warrants. Cops caught up with him."

"Oh," I say.

"He might've caught a new case," Paul says.

"The good news is," Andy says, "we got four people, perfect for doubles so it's all good."

"And also," Gary adds, "there's more beer for the rest of us."

The guys laugh and I begrudgingly join in.

"He disappears every now and then," Paul explains. "He spends a lot of time locked up. Sometimes he just doesn't report to his probation officer. Just blows it off. Doesn't care. Then they issue a warrant. Then he plays a cat and mouse game with the cops. It's an endless cycle."

I don't say anything as the guys continue drinking.

DISC-OVERY

"We should blaze up," Andy suggests breaking out the pot. Everyone nods in agreement.

"This is a brand-new strain. It's called Death Star."

"No way, dude," Gary says. "That's a killer name."

"Call me Luke Skywalker so I can blow that shit up," I say.

Everybody laughs at this as we pass around the bong coasting up the 134 highway. Bill becomes a distant memory as we giggle like little girls for the remainder of the ride.

Paul takes an exit and turns onto Foothill Blvd., stopping and starting on residential streets, as we make our way into the mountains in the distance. We eventually get to a park, and I can barely make out the name on the sign at the entrance as we pass by it.

"What's the name of this park?" I ask.

"Hahamongna," Andy answers.

"What the hell kind of name is that?" I ask again.

"It's an American Indian name. This park is built on the remains of an ancient Indian burial ground," he continues.

"Bullshit," snaps Gary.

"It's true," counters Andy.

"I don't believe that mumbo jumbo." Gary laughs as he lights a cigarette.

I look back at Andy, and he's wistfully looking off into the distance, lost in thought. I guess this place strikes a chord with him. I turn back around, looking at the park as we enter. I see colorful discs fly about up on the course as we drive around the first hole to the parking lot. We finally park, and I look over at the first tee and a couple of groups are getting ready to play.

We get out with our disc golf bags and throw them in the flatbed. Paul breaks open the cooler. We start to fit as many beers as we can into our bags.

"Yo, you guys a drinkin' club or you playin' golf?"

Turning around, we see a skinny black guy in his late 40s. He's carrying a bucket with him and has a towel wrapped around his shoulder as he chuckles at the sight of us.

"I'd say more of the former," Paul responds.

"Hurlie!" Andy exclaims as he walks over to him.

"Hey, Hurlie," Gary says. Hurlie's eyes travel to the source of all the beers: the cooler. His eyes fixate on the multitude of beers remaining in the ice.

"You want a beer?" I ask.

"Hell yeah, I want a beer," he answers.

"You just made another friend for life," Paul says.

I reach into the cooler and grab him one of the zombie beers, and bring it over to him.

I go up to him with my hand extended.

"I'm Jeff."

"Hurlie. Nice to meet you."

He gives the zombie graphic a funny look and takes out his key chain which has a bottle opener. He winks at me as he motions to the crazy zombie on the beer bottle.

"This dude is trippin'." He laughs as he pops open the beer and takes a big swig of it. "Thanks, brah," he says as he tips the bottle to me.

"You're welcome," I say.

"You gonna join us out there, today?" Gary asks him.

"I got to finish a couple of cars here. If I get done, I'll join up for the back nine."

"Hey you might as well do mine, this thing is filthy. How much is it again for a cleaning?"

"Interior or exterior, and you want a wax?"

"Exterior with a wax."

"Twenty-five."

Paul takes thirty dollars out of his wallet.

"Here you go. The extra five is contingent on you finishing up so you can join us on the back nine. Been a while since we've played."

"Deal. I'll get her done by the time you guys get back here," Hurlie says.

We put our bags on and Paul puts the cooler with the

remaining zombie back in the truck. We all walk over to the first tee and watch the two parties ahead of us finish up their putts at the basket as we put our bags down on the benches.

"Let's flip for odor," Paul says as Andy and Gary start to chuckle.

"Flip for odor!" Andy says as he flips his disc up and everyone follows, throwing all our discs high as they all fall to the ground. Andy's disc and mine fall on the top where the graphics are, and Gary's and Paul's fall where the underside of the disc is facing up.

"All right, partna," Andy turns towards me. "Let's take it to 'em."

We bump fists, and I go back to get my beer.

Paul gets up on the tee, veers back and throws the disc wide to the right, missing the wide branch of the tree as it glides nicely back into the course.

"Good one, dude," Gary says.

Gary then gets on the tee and throws a line drive. We all watch it spin straight towards the extended branch of the big oak tree.

BOINK!

The disc hits the branch hard and falls straight to the ground as if someone shot it with a rifle.

"Shit!" Gary yells.

Andy then gets on the tee as I open my beer. His body is delicate with his skinny frame taking on his signature fluid rhythm as his feet dance around while he reaches his disc far behind him, looking back at it before he twirls around launching the disc out of his hand. We watch it fly high above the branch as it extends into the sky before it hyzers back deep near the basket.

"Nice shot, Andy," I say.

"Yeah, that was a great hyzer, dude," Paul echoes my compliment.

"Thanks," Andy murmurs.

He still has a lot of juice left in that emaciated body of his. I realize how proper technique and form can really overcome a lot of other physical limitations.

I grab my Ogre and take the tee.

The tree's massive branch extends far to the right, with its many tributaries of branches weaving around the main one making it look like a big massive claw waiting to snatch up my disc. I must go around it. I take a deep breath and start moving my legs, bringing the disc far back behind me. I realize there's a little incline with this tee pad that I hadn't noticed was there, and I'm wobbly as I turn my body back around. My right foot plants awkwardly as I start to lose my balance. I'm falling to the right but not before I throw the disc hard, and it whips back far to the right. The disc shoots directly at Paul who's drinking his beer. I can't believe what I just did. The disc just misses his head and flies into the street barely missing a SUV and sailing far beyond into the course on the other side of the street.

"Shit!"

"Haha, oh my God!" Andy says.

"I think I just shit my pants!" Paul exclaims.

"Dude! That was close!" Gary yells.

I have fallen down and quickly get to my feet and rush over to Paul.

"Hey man. I am so sorry, dude. I fell."

Paul looks over at me, calmly.

"Jeff, there are no 'sorrys' in disc golf."

I collect myself and dust myself off. I'm glad Paul's not pissed.

"Right. Of course. I'm glad you're okay. I guess I should go get my disc."

"Yes, you should," Paul says.

I run over to the other side of the street and look for my disc. I have no idea where it is, as I'm looking all over the place for it. Just then I hear, "FORE FORE!" I turn around and see a red disc coming right at me, it is mere feet from my head and my instincts take over as I drop to the ground. I can hear it whiz right over my face as I fall back onto my shoulders, luckily on a pile of leaves on the ground.

I still hit the ground hard and really feel the wind get knocked out of me as my forty-two-year-old body flails down on the ground.

"What the hell are you doin' man!" another disc golfer yells at me from about fifty feet away, walking down with his friends from another tee.

"You just ran into the middle of the range. What's your problem?"

"I'm sorry," I grunt as I get up, "it's my first time here, give me a break. I'm just looking for my disc."

I slowly get up as he's still looking at me with a scowl on his face. His friends all laugh as they're walking by to go to their discs down towards the basket. He's still looking at me as I finally get to my feet.

"Did you throw a silver disc?" he asks me.

"Yes! You saw it?"

He motions next to an oak tree thirty feet to his right.

"Over there, dude."

"Oh cool. Thanks, man. Sorry about getting in your way."

"No problem, man. Better watch yourself out here, though. Discs are flying everywhere. You can't just wander around unaware. You'll get beamed," the guy says as he walks by.

I trot over to the tree and find my disc. By the time I make it back to the guys, they are all sitting next to their bags with the beers out, waiting for me. I run up next to them covered with leaves and dirt.

"Oh, guys, I'm so sorry it took so long. I almost got nailed by a disc on that hole over there, and then I had to find my disc and—"

"Dude," Paul cuts me off, "what did I say about no 'sorrys' in disc golf? Relax, man. Drink your beer. We brought it up with us along with your backpack. Here."

He hands me my backpack and beer, and I chug it, laughing at myself. *Not a great start to the day*, I think. I don't expect to be great, but I don't want the guys waiting on me.

"We're gonna have to toke up at the next hole," Andy says.

"Awesome," I say.

"Well, let's finish up this hole then so we can get to that," Gary says.

We all put our bags on again, grab our beers and Gary and Paul walk over to Paul's disc which is about forty feet to the right of the basket. I follow Andy over to his great shot, which is about twelve feet from the basket. I head over to his disc and stand next to him as we watch Gary and Paul get ready to take their second shots.

Gary puts his foot right behind the disc and concentrates on the basket. Everything is quiet in the park as we wait for him to throw. He weaves the disc around the trunk of the tree, which is to the right of the basket. The disc glides until it hits a root, jumping up wildly as it passes the basket and falls eight feet beyond it.

"Good one, dude," Andy says.

"Nice shot," I add.

Paul then steps behind his first disc focusing on the basket for a few long moments before he backhands a wide arcing throw which glides back over to the right, heading straight for the basket. It's a terrific shot as it just misses the chains and falls softly on a bed of leaves.

"That's Paul's anhyzer shot," Andy tells me. "The disc is held with the left side tilted up as you throw it."

He takes his disc and shows me the grip.

"You throw it like this and the disc travels to the right. Opposite of hyzer.

"Anhyzer," I say aloud. "Left to right. Got it."

Andy picks up his disc and flips it into the chains. It makes a nice ringing noise as Paul throws his in the chains as well.

"Pars all around," Andy announces.

We all put our discs away in our bags and walk to the next tee.

*　*　*

The next few holes are uneventful except for a bunch of Armenian soccer players yelling at us when my drive went a little close to their goaltender. We managed to avoid a brawl as both sides uneasily try to claim their respective turfs hurling insults at each other.

I ride on Andy's coattails as he leads us to three consecutive pars. Now we are leaving behind the soccer field and baseball diamonds that adjoined the first part of the disc golf course, and we enter into a thicket of woods where disc golf really has hegemony.

I follow the guys into a wooded area that immediately has a calming effect on me as we all pass under a fallen tree that is lodged a few feet above the path. Walking into this little natural area reminds me of the sleepaway camp I used to go to as a kid in North Carolina, where I was immersed in nature with hiking and whitewater kayaking and rock climbing. One of disc golf's special gifts is getting people out in nature. As we come upon a small opening, Andy looks back at me smiling.

"I call this the Middle Earth hole. You'll see why."

We slowly come out into an opening from the little forest we've wandered into. There's a concrete tee pad on top of a mini cliff that overlooks a wide expanse of land below. Coming out of this enclosed natural corridor is almost a mystical experience. I take it all in, admiring the natural beauty around me. A big field of wild grass leads up to numerous cottonwood trees and oaks surrounding the basket way off in the distance. A myriad of colors reflect off the trees as the sunlight cascades against the leaves and grass. We take a seat on creaky little wooden benches behind the tee pad.

"Time to toke up and drink," Gary says.

Good call. We pass around a bowl and I open another zombie beer as we prepare for hole number five.

"The view is amazing here," I say.

"Yeah, this is one of my favorite holes on the course," Paul says. "Of course, it won't be too much fun if you fall of that tee pad."

I look ahead at the tee, and there certainly is a big drop off the end of it.

"I've done that before. Not a lot of fun," Andy says. "See this scar here on the side of my head?" He bends his head down and brushes his hair aside, and I see a massive scar going over his ear.

"That's a big one."

"I got a few other scars from this place, too," Andy boasts.

"Well, who's got the tee? Oh yeah, we still do!" Gary brags.

"Not for long," Andy says.

"All right, I'll throw in a second. Lemme just pound this beer," Gary says.

He gulps down the rest of his beer and lets a burp rip as he jumps up with his disc in hand, throwing his empty beer bottle into the woods. As he gets on the tee pad and stares far ahead at the disc golf basket, we all suddenly hear laughter coming from the path below the cliff.

"Oh wait, man," Paul warns, "hikers are coming."

"Okay," Gary says as he heads back to the bench and rummages for another beer in his disc golf bag.

We continue to hear the laughter as we see disc golfers—not hikers—come into view from down below. It's a gorgeous brunette with two guys, all carrying disc golf bags. I immediately perk up. The girl is strikingly sexy as she's carrying the conversation with the two other guys, following her like lackey dogs. The guys in the group suddenly become very quiet as all sets of eyes are glued on this stunning beauty. She turns to us, waves, and calls out to us.

"Thank you for not killing us with your discs!" she yells up at us in a thick Scandinavian accent. She flashes us a flirtatious smirk.

"No problem," Andy yells back.

She then turns around and wiggles her ass.

"Wheeheew!" Gary finally yells after the stunned silence.

Paul whistles loudly as she turns around to us and jiggles her ample breasts that playfully bounce around in her skimpy tank top.

I take a long pull from my beer, shocked at the show this girl just put on. Gary and Paul continue to inanely cheer her on as she walks by. I can't take my eyes off her.

"Pretty cute, huh?" Andy says, nudging me.

"Yeah, she is stunning," I say.

Paul and Gary settle down and start to pound their beers.

"She's one of maybe two or three girls that are regulars here at the park. Everyone else is a dude," Andy explains.

"Actually, she's the only lone female that plays down here," Gary interjects. "The other couple of girls who are regulars are always with their boyfriends."

"Don't let her looks deceive you," Andy says. "I wouldn't go near that girl with a ten-foot pole. She's very sketchy. Rolls with a bunch of Russian thugs. Probably mafia."

"Yeah, I've heard stories about her," Paul says. "Wasn't she the one who got those Mexican guys beat up real bad on the course awhile back?"

"Yep," Andy says. "That's the rumor, anyway."

"What happened?" I ask.

"A bunch of Mexicans guys were harassing her here a couple of years ago," Andy explains. "They all wound up in the hospital after getting a serious beating. Needless to say, no one's ever bothered her since then."

"I bet," I say.

"I hear she's a stripper," Gary adds.

"And some people say she's done porn," Paul chimes in.

"I've never seen her on any of the sites though. I don't know her porn name."

"It's Bella Biotch," Andy chuckles. "She's all over the porn sites."

Paul immediately takes out his phone and starts typing her name into one of his frequented porn sites.

"She's a wild one," Andy says, "but not a bad disc golf player. She can hold her own and will give you a run for your money. She's always hustling people."

"Yeah," Paul says as he's scrolling through the porn site. "I never play with her. She wants to bet on every shot."

"Sounds like a real classy lady, huh?" I quip.

"Yeah, someone you definitely want to bring home to mom," Paul laughs as he turns his phone to us showing Bella giving a blow job. We all stop and stare at his little screen as disc golf suddenly becomes very irrelevant. Paul turns his phone around as he starts scanning the porn site again. We chuckle to ourselves.

"I can't believe that shit," I say incredulously as I gulp down my beer.

"She has tons of videos on here," Paul grins mischievously.

We drink our beers until we hear other disc golfers behind us crash their discs into the chains of the previous hole's basket, awakening us from our stupor.

Gary puts his beer down and lets out another burp.

"All right. Back to disc golf. We got another group coming," he says.

He gets up to throw, and then we follow with varied results. The whole time I was up on the tee pad, I was freaking out about falling off the cliff so my follow through wasn't all there, but thankfully retained my balance enough to throw a pretty good drive. I realize that I have to develop a sidearm shot. Dancing around, throwing your head and arm back and twirling around is not such a good idea on tee pads that have ten foot drops.

DISC-OVERY

We make our way down the steep hill into the grassy field to find our discs and take our second shots. The setting of this hole continues to intrigue me with its otherworldly atmosphere as the wind ripples through the area, bringing a rhythmic dance to everything it touches. The trees, the leaves, the grass, the bushes all sway and move to a silent natural beat which flows throughout this enchanting part of the course.

Andy calls over to me.

"Look, over there. On that branch jutting out from that first cottonwood on the left."

I look where he's pointing and spot a hawk. It has a beautiful deep, dark brown color as it sits regally looking over at us. Paul and Gary have seen it, too, and everybody's quiet and standing still as we watch it take off. It glides over us, spreading its wings, and we watch it fly off majestically into the forest.

"Beautiful!" I exclaim.

"Way cool," echoes Gary.

"Yeah, dude," Andy says, "I love the hawks down here."

I turn back around and look at the cottontail trees swaying in the wind as I walk towards Andy's disc which is about thirty feet in front of mine. I pick up my Ogre along the way.

"You know, Andy," I say as we approach his disc, "this hole really does feel like Middle Earth. No joke. It's a little supernatural" I laugh.

"You don't know the half of it," he says.

I look over at him and notice through my beer buzz that he said that way too seriously. And a little unnervingly. Like he's seen Bigfoot out here or something.

A new gust of wind whips through everything and I force myself to focus on disc golf again. I go up to take my second shot. I throw without really taking into account the heavy gust of wind, and my disc gets picked up by it and careens way far to the left.

"Oops," I say as I turn to Andy.

"You got a tail wind. You gotta throw one of your mid-range

discs that's a little understable. I should've told you that. I was a little distracted."

I look at him and he still has that weird, serious look in his eyes. He looks through the discs in his bag until he finally finds the one he wants, and sets up for his shot. He kneels down and grabs some grass on the ground, throwing it up in the air and watching it float forward. He sets up his shot for a few long moments and flicks the disc far to the right, keeping it very low, and the wind takes it right up and into the basket. The chains ring so loudly as if they themselves are applauding the shot. All of us look at him in awe. Andy certainly has his moments.

"Dude," I say, "you're like a disc shaman. You read the wind perfectly."

"Thanks, Jeff."

Paul and Gary toss some halfway decent shots, and Andy and I leave hole number five with a birdie. We play the next four holes decently as I'm starting to slowly but surely hold my own with the guys, albeit with a lot of help from Andy. All I want to do is keep up. I'm happy with the way I'm playing.

After hole number nine, we head back to Paul's truck and throw our bags in. Paul unlocks his door and brings out the cooler setting it in truck bed. The cooler is attacked by many sets of hands as many zombie beers are extricated from its icy interior for the back nine. I manage to get three of the zombie beers into my bag and turn and see Hurlie walking over.

"What you think, Paul? You like my work?"

"Yeah, man, truck looks great. Grab yourself a couple of beers if you're gonna join us for the back nine."

"I am joinin' y'all, and I will take you up on that" he says as he cackles to himself. He lights up a cigarette as he leans over and grabs four beers from the cooler. He puts three inside his disc golf bag and opens the other one as he takes a big drag from his cigarette again, looking around.

"Last time I was out here, sippin' a brewski and smokin'...The Man pull up out o' nowhere and I got a ticket."

DISC-OVERY

"That sucks, man," Paul says.

"Sometimes I think I'm a target out here because of this—"

He slaps his forearm with his hand, and I'm trying to figure out what he's doing.

"Too black out here in Altadena," he says.

We plod along in silence. Hurlie senses the tension and loosens up a bit.

"But shit, man, every girl I meet tell me, once you go black you don't go back." He starts to cackle again as we start to walk across the parking lot to tee number ten.

"Well," Andy retorts, "my ladies tell me if you go white, you can go all night."

Everyone laughs at this as we pass by the middle of the parking lot. There's a little island in the center with some rocks and a tree and a few disc golfers are sitting on lawn chairs with a bunch of discs on display for sale. As we approach, I realize that gorgeous brunette from before is sitting behind the tree toking up on a joint and watching us as we pass.

"Oh, look," she says, "the guys I gave a little show to on hole five."

"If I had some singles, I'll strap them around your garter belt, honey," Gary says.

Everyone busts out laughing including the Scandinavian girl.

"I'll take your dollars later when I school you on the course," she adds as she starts to toke up again.

Everyone laughs again except Hurlie. He looks back at her grimacing.

"Uh huh," he says.

She goes back to talking with the guys in the lawn chairs. I'm staring right at her as I'm walking to the next hole, and she suddenly turns to me, catching me looking at her, and winks at me. That just made my day.

"That chick is really something," Paul says.

"What's her name again?"

"Her porn name or her real name?" Andy asks.

"Her real name," I reply. "I won't forget her porn name."

"Real name is Alisa. I think she's from Sweden."

"Is it true she got those Mexicans beat up, Hurlie?" Paul asks.

Hurlie takes a long drag from his cigarette.

"She trash, man. It's all true, and that's probably just the tip of the iceberg about what she do."

We step on to the disc golf course from the parking lot and go to the tenth tee and put our bags down on the bench.

"Okay. Let's flip for teams," Gary says.

We all flip and I get odd man with Hurlie and Gary are one team and Andy and Paul are another.

No one to lean on this round. No one to bail me out of my bad shots. I'm all alone.

"You cool with being odd man, Jeff?" Paul asks me. "We can re-flip if you want. The back nine is pretty challenging."

"Uh, no, it's cool. I gotta be on my own sooner or later, might as well be now."

"Okay," Paul says. "Well, you're up."

I grab my Ogre and walk up to the tee. The hole is a nice straightaway shot as the basket is not too far away and slightly to the left. Not a hard shot. I really concentrate as I want to make the most of these easier holes. I start to move forward as I bring my arm back and keep the disc level as I pivot around and hear a nice flick of my wrist as the Ogre flies smoothly out to the right, nice and low to the ground. It's a little short but it skips dramatically after it hits the ground and hyzers back towards the basket, and it picks up momentum as it—

"*BOINK!*"

The disc makes a loud noise as it hits the top of the basket and falls right underneath it!

The guys cheer. I can't believe I actually hit the basket. I was that close to hitting an ace, the disc golf term for a hole-in-one.

"Shot of the day so far!" exclaims Andy.

DISC-OVERY

"Almost an ace!" yells Paul.

"Fantastic shot," echoes Gary.

"You are da man," says Hurlie as he takes his disc out and saunters to the tee to throw. "It took me almost two years to finally hit a basket," he says as he nods to me.

He winds up to throw. Though not as emaciated as Andy, Hurlie's thin body similarly takes on an instant athletic dexterity as he throws the disc. He has great form as his legs and arms all work in tandem as the disc glides out of his hand for a very smooth shot. The disc goes out wide but hyzers back, skips high and lands about fifteen feet away from the basket.

"Nice shot, Hurlie. Smooth," I say.

"Well, thank you. You a tough act to follow, boy," he says.

He goes back to his disc golf bag and grabs his beer as Gary struts up to the tee.

"Hurlie's laying on the compliments with the hope that you'll keep supplying him with more zombie beer," Paul says.

Everyone laughs at this as I hold up my beer to Hurlie in a long-distance toast. He obliges me as we tip our bottles to the air and drink together.

Gary throws a decent shot, with Paul and Andy throwing good shots as well. I remind myself that this hole is not the hardest one I've ever seen. I better enjoy the high points now before the double and triple bogeys start happening.

We grab our bags as we walk down to the basket as I can't take my eyes off my Ogre as it rests directly underneath the basket. As we near it, I step back with my beer and wait to see the other guy's putt. Paul and Gary both go, and their discs land right next to the basket. Hurlie takes his time with his putt. He has an excellent stance as he concentrates on getting the disc into the chains. After a few long moments, he zings a line drive right into the middle of the basket and the chains echo throughout the park.

"Good one, dude," I say.

"Thanks, brah," he winks at me as he walks up to get his disc.

"I got all y'all discs, guys, go on to the next tee," he says, as he goes to pick up all of our discs.

"I think that is Jeff's first solo birdie ever. Am I right?" Andy asks the group, as we head over to the next tee pad.

"I think you're right, Andy," Paul says.

"He officially has the tee, too," Andy says.

"Yep, goes by the same odor, even though Hurlie hit a birdie, too," Paul confirms.

I say nothing, beaming inside that I technically am the leader of the pack. King for a hole. I savor the moment.

We take seats on the benches at hole eleven as we sip from our beers again and chill for a while. I look up and notice Hurlie lagging behind as he's inspecting my Ogre he's picked up from under the basket. I take a few sips of my beer as I check out the next basket still relishing my lead status.

The other guys are talking about how the Raiders are going to do next year and start arguing about the quarterback situation as Hurlie hands the guys their discs. Hurlie turns to me, intently staring straight at me as he raises my Ogre up in the air.

"Where'd you find this disc, Jeff? This was my boy Sean's disc. He ain't among the livin' no more, and here you is throwin' it. His name and number right on it. His old Ogre. I must've seen him throw it a thousand times out here."

You could cut the silence with a knife as the rest of the guys are so quiet you can hear the discs landing in the chains at the other holes.

"Sean was my brother. I got his discs out of his belongings that were left to me. You knew him, Hurlie?"

Hurlie's eyes widen and his mouth opens in surprise. I'm sure he thought I'd found this disc somewhere on a disc golf course and took it. Finders keepers.

"You are Sean's brother?" he asks in disbelief.

"Yes. I moved out here almost a year ago from the east coast, trying to discover more about him and what he was doing out here. These guys gave me a rude introduction to disc golf one day at a park, and then weeks later I found my brother's discs in his storage boxes. I realized then it was time I started playing the sport Sean loved."

"Damn," Hurlie says. "Small world. What a coincidence."

He looks at the disc again and hands it back to me.

"Did you know him well, Hurlie?" I ask.

"Yeah. We was buds. We played a lot of golf together. Sean was a good kid, man. I was real shook up when I heard he passed on. I'm sorry, Jeff."

"Thank you, Hurlie. I was pretty shook up, too. That's why I moved out here. As crazy as it sounds, I just wanted to retrace some of his steps."

"Right," Hurlie says a little uncomfortably. I look at the Ogre again with Sean's writing on it; his name in all caps and his phone number printed with a sharpie. I look back at Hurlie, and he's looking down now, smoking. He seems very pensive now, thinking of Sean.

We both sit down on the benches where the guys have been patiently waiting for this drama to end so we can get on with our disc golf game.

"You guys okay?" Paul asks.

"Yeah, man," Hurlie says.

I look up at Andy and the guys.

"Hey did you guys remember Sean at all?" I ask all of them. "He was a tall, skinny kid with dirty blond hair, played in a band."

The guys all think for a few moments.

"I don't know if I ever formally met him," Andy says, "but I do recollect someone looking like that playing with Hurlie and some other people. But then again, a lot of guys look like what you just described around here."

"Yeah," Gary adds, "you just described a surfer or a skater dude and there's a lot of that type who frequent this course."

"I think I remember playing once or twice in a group with you, Hurlie, when you were hanging around a guy who looked like that. I bet that was him," Paul says.

"Yep," Hurlie says, "probably was."

I'm looking down at the disc again and starting to get a little sad. I start drinking my beer. I notice the mood of the group is subdued and it's up to me to get it up again.

"Well, c'mon guys," I yell, "let's go, I want to keep my winning streak up."

"Atta boy," Paul says.

"Let's play," Andy says.

Hurlie quietly sips his beer and remains expressionless. I go up to the tee to take my shot and the next basket is at a diagonal through a thicket of trees to the right.

"If you had a sidearm," Paul says, "this is where you'd use it."

"Yeah, tough to get a backhand through there to the right," Andy adds.

"Well," I say, "no better time than the present."

I grip the sidearm the way Andy had taught me a couple of weeks ago at the Ridge, and it feels as awkward now as it did then. I tell myself to keep it low as there are branches jutting out everywhere. I take a couple of steps, holding my breath and flicking a sidearm shot. The disc flies out very slow and flaccid. It maintains a decent line but hits a tree about halfway down the short range of this hole. Well, at least it went somewhere.

"Not a bad shot," Andy says. "You're still on track for a par. You want to shoot again? You're odd-man so you can have two drives if you want."

"No, that's okay, I think I'll take two shots from there," I say.

The rest of the guys throw their discs and we walk towards our shots as the mood of the group begins to pick up again. The guys start to joke around and resume their argument about the Raiders quarterback, but Hurlie is still silent. I'm hoping he can

DISC-OVERY

shake off the subject of my brother. I don't want to be a downer here on the course.

We all putt out, I walk away with a par and both other teams birdie. I lost the tee. Oh well, at least I had it for a hole. We get through the next few holes decently. I hold my own with a few bogeys to go along with a couple of pars and that's pretty good in my book. We arrive at the last hole on this part of the course before the holes extend out to a whole other area of the park. The basket is hidden from view as it is way far out to the left.

I take out my Ogre again—which I know will hyzer well and get out on the pad to shoot. I take the disc back and really fling it. It's a solid drive that catapults out and takes its signature hyzer run to the left.

"Dude," Paul says, "that was an awesome shot. You really got an arm, Jeff."

"I appreciate it," I say.

"Yeah," Andy adds, "you got a lot of potential at this, Jeff. You have a real natural stroke."

I'm feeling terrific with all these compliments. The rest of the guys throw their drives and everyone reads the course nicely. We grab our bags and head through the small tunnel that opens to the notorious next few holes of the back nine. As we pass the overlay of the trees, the sun hits us as we step into the wide open space.

I look to the left and am stunned to see a massive complex come into view. There must be a couple of dozen buildings that take up an enormous swath of land in an area far beyond the fringes of the park. As I stop and look at it, a bizarre yellow helicopter takes off from one of the structures and heads our way. I gaze at the chopper. I've never seen one like it before. It has odd black stripes and a weird design to it. Andy walks by me on the way to the next hole so I tag along with him.

"Hey man," I say, "what the hell is that place over there?" I ask.

Andy glances over at the massive structure.

"That's EAD."

"What's EAD?" I ask.

"Experimental Aerolab Dynamics," he explains.

"I didn't know it was right here next to a disc golf course. What a crazy looking helicopter," I say as it continues to fly towards us.

"I saw them out on the field here with that Moon Rover, remember dat thing?" Hurlie says. "We was laughing at them driving it around, and some dumb ass threw a disc at it, and it actually hit the fuckin' thing. They tripped out and sent some police over, and they started harassin' us. We was like, shit, man, this is a disc golf course. They got that whole complex over there, and that ain't enough for them? They tryin' to take over our course? No way we lettin' that happen. The cops got even more pissed when we said this and told us to shut the hell up, and if we mess with the Rover again they gonna bring out the paddy wagon. We left the Rover alone after that."

We chuckle at this as we continue to walk to the next hole.

Andy looks over at me and speaks in a hushed tone.

"I've met old-timers here that have told me stories about what goes on over there that would make your head spin."

I slightly grin at what Andy said, thinking he was joking. But he isn't laughing or horsing around.

We approach the next tee whose basket is far off into the distance, and I look back around to the left again at EAD, with its sprawling complex of buildings behind imposing gates and fences.

The wind picks up around us as the enormous compound suddenly takes on a spooky tinge to it. I pick up on a strong sense of foreboding about the facility. Maybe it's just the pot or the booze but a feeling creeps over me that the more I find out about this place's secrets, the more I'm going to find out about my brother. That's exactly what I intend to do.

6

I spend the next few days not sleeping well as I delve into Sean's documentary collection. At this point, I could probably write a book on CIA black ops in Central America, the Golden Triangle, NASA cover-ups, suppressed healing therapies, you name it. I can articulate the physics of how a UFO flies; how HAARP orchestrates earthquakes, hurricanes, and tornadoes. I'm learning all about the secret government, MJ-12 and the Illuminati and Bilderberger groups, and how they rule the world. I'm watching so many of these docs that I can feel my old self start to break down, like an old coil of me that I'm attempting to shake off.

It's another way of bonding with Sean. I knew he watched every single one of these docs and was affected by every one of them. I want to do the same thing. I want to know how he felt as he let all his old viewpoints and belief systems shatter away from the sheer truth of these videos. I want to grow just like he grew.

I don't understand how watching these docs could vibe with him becoming a merc. Did he break down into some existential dark phase? Some nihilistic cycle of despair about the true state of the world that made him want to go kill others for money on high risk, suicidal missions? Had his existence become so excruciating in such a cynical world that he developed some kind of death wish? I don't know. But I'm getting a clearer picture of what was going on in his head, that's for sure.

After watching what felt like eighty of these docs with probably over 900 to go, I can already feel the bogus layers of propaganda and disinformation I've absorbed from the mainstream over the years just melt off me in globs. I'm glad to see it go.

I drink the whole time I'm watching these. Sometimes I fall into deep despairing moments. Subjecting yourself to a massive flood of the ugly truth of the world can be a little overwhelming. And when a little more of the dam of my previous psyche breaks every day, I also think of how alone I am in my life and everything I've lost the last few years; my wife, my brother, my career, old acquaintances.

I don't have a job or a career to focus on. What am I going to do now? Thank God I have plenty of money in the bank but there's a dark side to that, as I spend days feeling lost with no goals. I don't have to go somewhere every day and, as crazy as it sounds, that can develop into a problem. An idle mind is the devil's playground. I can't go back to what I did before. Old contacts are long gone and bridges have been burnt on both coasts. I hate that business anyway. It's over for me.

I'm out here in a new city, starting over again with no direction. It's tough and lonely.

I have to get out and interact with people again. I turn off the TV. I'll get back to my binge watching soon enough as well as this self-imposed pity party. It's time to get out into the world.

I look around and my house is becoming a mess. Empty alcohol containers and pizza boxes strewn all over the place, piles of dirty clothes. Stereotypical bachelor. I have to get out of here. Throwing some clothes on and grabbing my disc golf bag, I grab my car keys and bolt out the door.

As I drive toward Oak Grove, I decide I'll do some exploring and playing golf all on my own. Hopefully I'll bump into Hurlie again and we can talk more about Sean.

The last time I was here with the guys, I'd sobered up by the time we left to memorize how we got to the park. I'm a little fuzzy on this last section, however, as I realize I may have made a left instead of a right. I pass by the outskirts of that Park Hamaga-whatever it is, going the wrong way. Now I'm going to have to make a u-turn to get back to the park. I see the Experimental Aerolab Dynamics entrance and figure I'll just do a u-turn there. I pull up to the front and see two security guards. Maybe they can help me out.

"Hey there, I just took the wrong turn going to that disc golf park, I was wondering—"

"Get out of here, now!" one of the chiseled security guards yells at me.

"Excuse me?" I ask.

"You heard him," the other security guard snaps at me. "Exit now!"

I glare at them as I turn around and drive away. Dickheads.

Back on the road, I'm still smarting from the ill manners of those security guards, then I see the basket of the first hole and a disc flying towards it. I enter the parking lot and pull into a space. There's Hurlie, washing a car on the other side of the lot.

He sees me pull up, and I wave to him. He nods at me as he goes back to cleaning the car. I'm wondering if he's too busy to talk. I grab my disc golf bag and walk over.

"Hey Hurlie."

"Yo, man."

"Just figured I'd get out of the house and play some disc golf."

"Cool. Have fun. I got to finish up this car."

"Yeah, no problem. Hey, uh, do you want to wash mine?"

"Nah, man. This is the last one for the day. I'm takin' a break after this one."

"Oh," I say.

He's still not really making eye contact with me and being surprisingly dismissive.

"Well, if you want to join up and play some holes, I'll be—"

"Meeting up already with some guys, Jeff," he says a little curtly. "Maybe I'll see you out there."

"Yeah, man. Cool."

"Right," he says as he scrubs the hood of the car.

I turn around and walk away.

That was weird. I wonder what that was all about.

I arrive at the first tee and put my bag down on the bench. I remember what a disaster this hole was last time. I take out my Ogre and walk over to the tee. That branch extending so far to the right is just as intimidating as I remember it. I put the disc down and inspect the branch.

It is a pretty gnarly looking thing. It looks like some kind of grotesque, massively deformed claw. I closely observe all the intersecting wooden tributaries that wrap around one another in some hideous embrace like a bunch of snakes trying to choke the life out of each other as they writhe in a collective death grip.

I bring my Ogre up and focus on getting to the right of that branch. I bring the disc back as I reach far behind me and then move around fast and snap my wrist as the disc flies out. It doesn't go very far to the right, and instead hits the branch with a loud thud and falls to the ground. I turn around frustrated and grab my bag to go shoot my second shot.

I get up to the disc and put a marker at the edge of the Ogre while I pick the disc up and put it in my bag. I take out my Octopus mid-range disc and line up behind the marker and try to concentrate on the basket that is pretty far away. It would suck to bogey on the first hole.

As I struggle to concentrate, I suddenly hear a very loud, sharp *caaaw* from above on the large branch extending from the tree. It is so shrill that I have to regroup and step back for a moment. I look up at the branch and wonder what could make such an unpleasant sound. I scan the branch and again study all its unsettling contours. The horrible wailing suddenly erupts again and I jump. I keep looking for the source of the sound and finally spot the perpetrator: a big black crow. I take a few moments and study it. It's a carrion crow with its signature all-black bill and feathers. What an imposing looking bird. It looks so formidable, like it's ready for battle. It flies off and croaks out that shrill *caaaw* again.

"Are you bird watching or playing disc golf?"

I turn around and that dark-haired beauty from the other day on the course is standing on the tee with hands on her hips, looking right at me.

"Excuse me?" I say.

"You heard me," she says. "Are you going to throw or look at the birds?"

I smirk to myself as I remember the show this young lady put on the last time I was out here.

"Well, I think a little of both," I answer.

"You know, disc golfers and bird watchers don't get along on this course. You're going to have to pick a side."

I think for a moment as she waits impatiently for me.

"I'll go with the disc golfers. They seem like they could win in a fight with the bird watchers."

She smiles, warming up to me a little.

"You mind if I join you?"

"Not at all," I respond.

She winds up and throws with excellent form. The disc sails out of her hand and I hear the loud snap of her wrist as she follows through exceptionally. The disc flies beneath the branch about ten feet to my right and goes past me another forty feet. She's not a big power thrower, but I can tell already how accurate she is. She grabs her disc golf bag and starts walking towards me.

I turn around to focus on my shot. I'm not feeling a big hyzer shot here. I think I want to just throw the disc straight at the basket. I put some zip on it, and the disc holds a nice line as it flies right past the basket and falls against a little mound of leaves that stops the disc in its tracks, about eight feet past the basket.

"Nice recovery," she says as she walks up to me. She smiles and extends her hand.

"I'm Alisa, nice to meet you."

"I'm Jeff, pleasure is all mine," I say as I shake her hand. I look up at her beautiful dark eyes and, up close, I notice her party-weathered face. She's not wearing any make-up. Her skin is not great but she's still beautiful. I'd say she's about twenty-nine or thirty, though someone could mistake her for a few years older. She's barely hanging on to her youth.

"Let's go putt," she says, as she starts to walk to the basket.

I grab my marker and sling my bag over my shoulder as I catch up to her.

"So, you want to play this nine for a finsky? I'll give you a couple of strokes," she asks.

"What?"

"A finsky for the front nine. I'll give you two strokes."

This girl is not wasting any time trying to hustle me.

"No thanks, Alisa. I'm out here for fun."

"Oh relax," she responds. "It makes the game interesting, makes you focus on every shot and play harder."

"If you want to bet, go find someone else."

"Okay, mister. I got the message," she says rolling her eyes.

She reaches for her putter as she puts her bag down on the ground. She kneels down into a stance and rocks back and forth, cradling the disc in her hands, concentrating on the basket. She suddenly whips it forward and the disc crashes against the chains. She just sank a thirty foot putt. Very impressive.

"Good shot," I say.

"Thanks, mister" she says.

DISC-OVERY

I would've been out five bucks if I took her up on her bet. This chick can play.

We walk forward to the basket as I move on back to where my putter landed, up on the pile of leaves. I drop my bag, pick up the putter and throw it against the chains for a par. Alisa takes it out of the basket and hands the disc to me.

"Nice putt," she says.

"Nothing compared to yours," I say. "No wonder you asked me to bet on the game before you threw."

"I'm one of the best putters out here," she boasts. "I don't have the arm like most of the swinging dicks out here, but I eat them alive with my short game."

I smirk to myself as we walk over to the bench of the next hole. Alisa is a shark.

"I just started playing disc golf with a bunch of new friends," I tell her. "We've been going to some of the courses in the area like the Ridge."

"Yeah, I play there, too. This place is my favorite, though. It's my home course."

She takes out one of her drivers and walks over to the next tee pad. She seems to be putting on a little show with how she's stretching and moving that body of hers all around before she throws. Probably a strategy of hers to distract the guys she's playing with. Well, she won't take me out of my game.

Suddenly she turns around reaching far back with the disc and then lunges forward and flicks the disc out of her hand. It stays low to the ground and starts to curve around the big tree in front of us and follows a corridor that goes to the upper part of the small hill that leads to the basket at the far end of the hole. It skips a few times before it lands about twenty-five feet to the right of the basket, behind a bunch of tall bushes. Still a very good shot.

"Did you see that thing spin?" she asks me. "I love the Troll, such a wonderful understable disc. It moves like a flying saucer."

She walks back and sits down at the bench as I grab a disc from my bag. I look up at her and she's taking a pipe out of her bag and loading it up with some weed. I turn around and go up to the tee and squint into the distance, trying to find the basket.

"It's way ahead to the right of that tree in the middle, up that corridor behind that thicket of oak trees way ahead. You see?"

I continue to squint until I find the patch of oak trees she's talking about and I finally find the basket with the yellow top right in the middle of them.

"Ah yes, I see it. Different location from the last time I was here. Those oaks are hiding it."

"Yes, they moved them from the long positions for the tournament they had here last week," she says as I hear her take a long toke from her pipe.

I concentrate on the basket far ahead as I slowly move my arm back, doing everything I can to keep the disc level as I move my legs and reach back far with the disc before I spin forward, launching the disc as it goes far to the right, avoiding the trees in the middle. It follows the same path as Alisa's disc but it's a little high. It sails a little to the right and floats down into the trees at the far corner of the hole. Pretty decent throw.

I turn around and walk over to the bench to grab my bag. She blows out another batch of pot smoke towards me and gestures the pipe at me.

"Do you want some?" she asks.

"Sure," I say, taking the pipe and her lighter and toking up.

"Not a bad shot," she says.

I fill up my lungs with smoke as I grimace to hold it in for a few moments before finally coughing it all out. I hand the pipe back to her.

"Thanks," I say. "I adore that Ogre."

"Ah, the Ogre. I threw that disc for years. It looks like yours has broken in a little bit too much. It might be time to get a new one."

DISC-OVERY

She picks up her bag and we start walking together towards our second shots. It feels good to talk to such a pretty girl.

"So, I'm trying to place your accent. What is it?"

"I'm Swedish."

"Oh. Yeah, I thought it was Scandinavian but sometimes it sounds a little Russian."

"I hang around a lot of Russians, so maybe it's rubbed off on me a little bit."

Oh yes, her Russian thug friends.

"Disc golf is big over in the Scandinavian countries. That's where I started to play. But playing back home really sucks. Try finding your disc in a mound of snow. Not fun."

"I can imagine," I say.

"You can play disc golf twelve months out of the year here in L.A.

We walk along a little bit in silence as the nature sounds become more noticeable with the effects of the marijuana. I glance over at this beauty. Her eyes have suddenly become deeper and sadder, I notice the pain this girl carries with her.

"When I first came to L.A., I knew once I found a disc golf course I'd feel more at home here. As soon as I discovered Oak Grove, I knew I'd be okay. No matter what this city threw at me, I knew I could always come here and everything would be all right."

This tough girl with an attitude suddenly has given me permission to see a more fragile side of her. I wonder why. I have a feeling she doesn't let anyone see it. Though, knowing her, maybe she's just softening me up to try to hustle me again.

My mind is swimming in these thoughts until I look up, realizing my disc is off to the side.

"Okay, I need to go get my disc and shoot," I say as I walk off to the left.

Alisa continues to walk up the little hill to the right to get to her disc, which is behind several big bushes that completely block the view of the basket.

I get to my Ogre and realize what a tough shot it is. The basket is right above a slope that a disc could just roll down, all the way to the next tee pad. I take out my Octopus as I crouch down a little bit, putting my foot against the Ogre. I figure I'll throw a big hyzer off to the right and let it crash down at the foot of the branch of oaks where the basket is and hopefully it will skip into the middle of all of them. I don't look at the basket but pick a target to the upper right of it to aim at. I settle into my stance and flick the disc high and wide, and the disc finishes its ascent before it begins its dramatic hyzer down towards the basket and then-

CRASH!

I don't believe it. Right into the chains.

"Wow!" Alisa yells. She claps her hands. I'm a little stunned at how the disc seemed to be guided into the center of the chains, almost drawn into them by remote control or by some powerful magnet. I stand there in a moment of clarity that everything that I planned out for the disc— its flight path, where I was aiming, how I thought it would end up— came to fruition exactly as I had mentally mapped it all out.

"You have quite the *hyzer* shot," Alisa says in an exaggerated German accent, laughing as she winks at me.

"Thanks," I say as I get my disc out of the basket.

Alisa walks behind the tall bushes where her disc is. I'm wondering how she's going to get out of this little predicament as she can't even see the basket from behind them.

"Right between all those oak trees. Very impressive, mister," she says from behind the little green wall of nature.

I smile very self-contentedly, loving the fact that not only did I do something impressive in front of her, but I'm going to beat her on this hole. No way she birdies from behind those bushes. I walk up to the basket to get my disc.

"Wait, dude. I have to putt," she says curtly from behind the green wall, about forty feet away.

DISC-OVERY

I stop in my tracks as I look back at the tall bushes. There are a few long moments of silence. I wait patiently.

Suddenly the disc bolts from over the bushes, cutting through the air vertically as it spectacularly twirls around and around making its descent, finally falling into a horizontal position before crashing into the chains.

I cannot believe what I just witnessed.

"Music to my ears," Alisa says, still behind the tall bushes. I can hear her toking up behind them. She finally emerges with a stoned smile on her face, doing the tomahawk motion with her right arm.

"That was the tomahawk shot, mister," she giggles.

"You had to rain on my parade, didn't you," I lament. "Had to upstage me, huh."

I go retrieve the discs out of the basket as she smiles with the pipe in the middle of her lips.

"That was one of the most incredible shots I've ever seen, Alisa."

She tokes up and holds in the hot smoke in her lungs as long as she can before she blows it out towards the basket.

"Lots of weapons in my arsenal of shots," she says in quite the raspy voice.

We head over to the next hole through the wooded area. I look around at all the trees and brush and realize we are going up to that hole up on that little cliff.

"I love this hole," I say. "I call it the Middle Earth hole."

We both crouch beneath the fallen tree that is a few feet above the trail that winds up to the tee pad overlooking the field below where the basket is.

"Yes, I love this next hole, too. It is probably my favorite on the course. Let's go sit down on the benches here and take a break."

"Sounds good to me," I say.

We continue on the trail stepping over rocks as we make our way to the opening with the view of the wide expanse of the next hole. The tee pad is up on the cliff, and we set our bags down on the benches behind it.

Alisa takes out her pipe again and starts to load up her marijuana into it. She takes a few tokes and passes it to me as she gets up and scans the area, looking in all directions intently.

"What's up?" I ask.

"Cops. They have binoculars. I'm always on the lookout for them. Otherwise they will snag you."

She sits back down again and reaches for the pipe.

"Coast is clear," she says with a smile. She takes the pipe from me and starts to toke up again.

"Go ahead. Throw," she tells me.

I stumble upright and feel very stoned from the pot. I tell myself to concentrate on not falling off the damn tee pad cliff into all the rocks below. I focus on the mechanics of the shot and do a short wind up, bringing it back and then skip my feet across and let it go.

It flies out nicely, staying very low and manages to come back towards the right before it finally hits the ground and skips another thirty feet.

"Very nice shot, mister. That was an excellent anhyzer," Alisa says.

"Thanks. I'm trying to get better at that shot. My Troll is perfect for it."

"Yes, I love my Troll, too. Great understable disc."

She puts the pipe away and grabs a pink disc from her bag as she walks up to the tee pad with an instant sobriety. She's moving in for the kill as she steps into her shot, showcasing a sidearm that I need to include in my repertoire. Her form is resplendent as she follows through with her front foot firmly planted against the edge of the teepad right at the edge of the cliff. She knows how to work that limited space with such deft savviness, as opposed to my bumbling backhand where I'm simply hoping my flailing body doesn't fall over the cliff.

I'm marveling at this beauty as a pink blur rockets from her right arm as it spins off into the distance, far outperforming my previous showing. It shimmers in the blue expanse of sky, as the pink dot flirts with a seeming immortality as I wonder if it will just fly off forever like a flying saucer going up into space. After its otherworldly performance out of the gates, though, the disc remembers its limited human energy origin as it fades gracefully to the immediate right of the basket as it dives into the dirt abruptly, stopping obediently, almost under orders of its sultry Swedish master who threw it.

I start clapping my hands as she looks back over to me with that million dollar smile of hers.

"Take a bow," I tell her.

She moves around with her back facing me as she bows, mooning me with her ample backside as we both break out laughing. She does a few more bows, each time showing me a nice angle of her impressive posterior as I continue to applaud. Finally, we both grab our bags and start to walk down the rocky little slope from the tee pad to the field below. It's a small miracle that I manage not to fall as buzzed as I am from the weed.

"Check it out," she points ahead. "It's snowing."

I look up and see a cascade of white flakes blowing into the field from the trees near the basket.

"What the hell?" I say.

As we continue to approach, it looks like a snow machine is behind the trees carpeting the area with flakes, as a white flurry starts to envelop us as we walk towards it. The pot makes the flakes take on a hazy shine in the fading sunlight. I look over at Alisa and she looks as dazzling as the tree shavings moving all around us. We've both stopped walking and are letting this shimmering whirlwind of glistening white flakes just smother and encircle us. Alisa turns to me with her piercing dark eyes and smiles.

"It's beautiful, isn't it?" she asks.

I stare into her eyes and they seem to pull me into her soul, as the sadness I noticed in them from before has turned to a radiant tranquility. I realize then what she told me before, that she feels at home here on this course, that all of the problems of life melt away when she comes here. I'm sure the pot helps, too.

"It's the cottonwood tree over there," she says as she points over to the big tree which hangs over the disc golf basket about fifty feet away. "It sheds, and it creates this wonderful aura of flakes around it that shake and sparkle in all the sunlight that hits this big open area."

She heads towards her disc as we both move forward, leaving behind this magical little scene.

I walk over to my disc and put my bag down still trying to process the quasi-mystical experience I just had with this beautiful girl in the cottonwood flakes. I take out my putter and line up behind my Troll and look over at Alisa who flings the disc right into the chains as the sound reverberates throughout the trees. She skips towards the basket like a little girl, clapping her hands, giddy from making the putt.

"Great shot," I say.

"Sorry, Jeff. You should've putt first, you're further out."

"No 'sorrys' in disc golf, Alisa."

She acknowledges my adept little application of disc golf parlance with a wink of approval as she waits for me to putt.

I concentrate on the basket which is partially hidden from the branches of the cottonwood, and I fling a bad shot that hits right into the tree. The disc stumbles around in the branches before clumsily falling to the ground. Ah, if only my putting was as good as my witticisms.

"Uh oh," Alisa moans. "You don't want to three putt."

I wind up doing just that. I don't really mind double-bogeying, though, after that mystical moment with this beauty. I put the putter into my bag and we start walking to the next hole.

"That was quite the religious experience with you in the cottonwood snow," I say.

She turns to me and smiles, and dimples form around her mouth as I continue to be entranced by her.

"I've had many experiences here like that," she says. "This place always reminds me that there is still so much beauty in such an ugly world. Every time I have to leave here, I know I'm leaving paradise and going back to that city of devils."

She becomes serious as she stares down at the ground as she walks along. She is so beautiful as the sadness I saw before in her eyes reappears briefly before it slides away again into her stoned stupor. She skips along and twirls around almost to purge that sadness that descends upon her from time to time.

"I really love it here, too," I respond. "I'm going to be spending a lot more time here at Oak Grove."

She stops when we turn past the woods as we enter a clearing. She motions to the Experimental Aerolab Dynamics base far off in the distance.

"That place. That big fortress they built here for their rockets and space shit. They put it here for a reason. They know the power of this place."

She looks off wistfully at the imposing government lab for a few moments.

"They know a ley line is here. A vortex to a higher dimension. The Indians knew about it before them."

She starts walking again and looks over at me with that enchanted look still in her eyes.

"And I know the power of this place, too."

I walk along with her, as much in a daze from this girl as I am from all the booze and pot.

She puts her bag down on the bench of the next tee pad and takes out her pipe again. We both look up at the Experimental Aerolab Dynamics base again as we suddenly hear the loud roar of rotor blades disturb the tranquility of the park. A multicolored helicopter lifts off out of the compound and darts off into the mountain range. We both stand in silence as she takes a few more tokes and hands the pipe to me. I place it to my lips and light up the bowl.

"I have seen every aircraft imaginable go in and out of there over the years. Late at night once, several years ago, I saw a flying saucer fly into the base."

I chuckle as I cough up the pot. I wasn't expecting that.

"Bullshit," I say, through the chuckle-coughs. "I think you might have had a few too many 'shrooms that night."

"No. It was real. They have them there and work on them. They always have. Deep underground. Very few people who work there know about it. It's top secret."

I roll my eyes as I bring the pipe up again to my lips, still giggling.

"Well, if it's so top secret," I ask, "how come you know about it?"

She turns to look at me with a little smirk as I light up the pot.

"You'd be surprised who I've gotten to know here at this park over the years. There are no secrets, Jeff. People talk. Especially to pretty girls."

She takes out a disc and walks up to the tee pad, looking far past the disc basket she's going to throw to, instead studying the maze of buildings and nondescript structures that make up EAD behind the barbed wire fencing that encircles it.

"That's why they invented this game here so many years ago with these little discs. Right down the street from where they work on the big saucers. So, on their lunch breaks, they could study how discs fly when they throw them. Like little models. Like little toy flying saucers. It helped them understand them in a more intimate way, touching them in their own hands. They saw the physics of them in action, their aerodynamics, their amazing spin and how they glide in the wind, in the air, around trees and over hills. It's all so much more intimate when you're holding and throwing them."

I'm flabbergasted at what she's telling me. She fondles the

DISC-OVERY

disc in her hand as she waxes poetic about secret government flying saucers.

"Then," she continues, "they'd go back to work and take their secret security clearance elevators far underground to go tinker with their big recovered UFO discs."

She steps forward while she brings the disc far behind. Her face turns all the way back so I can see her clearly before she twirls around and snaps the disc forward. It's a little high but has more power than any drive she's had yet today. It lands about ten feet to the right of the basket. Another great shot.

A bunch of guys that are standing on the tee pad at the next hole turn around when they hear the disc crash to the ground.

"Jessie!" Alisa yells, startling me out of my buzz. She waves at the three guys at the next hole.

"What up girl!" Jessie yells back.

"You want to play for a finsky?" she yells.

"Sure!" Jessie responds.

She turns to me and takes her pipe back from my hand.

"It was nice playing with you, Jeff. Time to make some dollars, though."

She starts walking off to Jessie and his friends at the next hole, dropping me like a bad habit. I muster up some courage and call after her.

"I'd really like to play with you again. Can I get your phone number?"

She turns around with a little twinkle in her eye.

"I'll see you around, Jeff. Work on that putting. You know what us disc golfers say, right? You drive for show-"

"...And putt for dough," I quip with a beaming smile.

She winks at me and walks off to the next hole.

7

I finish three over for the day, which is a pretty good score for me. Oak Grove is a tough course with a lot of pitfalls, and I have yet to score an even or an under par on it. I'm feeling upbeat about my game as I make my way to the parking lot to go home.

I notice Hurlie sitting all alone in that little island of rocks and grass where a disc golf basket amusingly serves as a putting green. He's smoking a cigarette looking blankly off into the distance. He doesn't see me approaching as he sips on a straw protruding from a beverage wrapped in a brown paper bag.

"What's up, Hurlie?"

He looks up a little startled.

"Hey," he responds.

"Mind if I sit down?" I ask him.

"Go ahead."

I have a seat and Hurlie says nothing looking down at his beer.

We both sit in silence as I'm trying to figure out this new dismissiveness he has towards me.

"You know, Hurlie, you were a lot friendlier before I told you I was Sean's brother."

He reacts as if I just hit him with one of my discs.

"You trippin', man," he says.

"No, just making an observation."

He takes another long pull from the straw. He looks very subdued as he stares off again for several long moments. Finally, he speaks.

"I knew Sean really well," he says. "Went through a lot with him. It took me a long time to get over him dying. Now you here bringing all that stuff up again."

I settle down now as his passive aggressive behavior from today is understandable.

"You knew him well, huh?" I ask.

"Yeah, man. We was close. Into the same shit."

"Like what?"

He takes another drag from his cigarette looking off at the soccer game which is taking place right next to the first hole. Players are yelling in Armenian at some disc golfer who throws his bag on to the ground.

"As soon as I met that dude," he says, "we just clicked. We both had similar ways of looking at things, of lookin' at society; how things are, who really run things."

The disc golfer proceeds to kick their soccer ball into the street. Several other disc golfers get into the shouting match as we both casually watch this scene escalate from afar.

"I remember when I first met him, we was playin' on this course. I started goin' off on judges, and how they all Freemasons with they bullshit gold-tinged maritime flags in they courtrooms."

Hurlie flicks his cigarette into the parking lot. The shouting match between the soccer players and the disc golfers is getting worse.

"Your bro knew exactly what I was talkin' about that first day we met. We broke off from the rest of this group of golfers we was with, and spent the rest of the day throwin' discs together, talkin' about everything from alien underground bases to pyramid power. We was inseparable from that day forward."

I can't believe my luck in finding this guy, someone who got to know my brother so intimately.

"I got his belongings from his old apartment," I tell him. "I've been watching all those docs from his massive movie collection. He certainly was into some far-out stuff," I say.

Hurlie looks up at me a little surprised.

"You got all those?" he asks.

"Yep."

"I know that collection well. I borrowed many, seen most of them," he tells me. "Some of mine are in there, actually. I gave him a bunch. You watchin' them, huh?"

"Yep. They're amazing. And I'm getting to know more about Sean with every single one I see," I say.

Hurlie's looking down again, lost in thought. There's another long, heavy silence in the air.

"Man, what you doin' now?" he finally asks.

"Nothin'. I was just gonna go home."

"You wanna come back to my place? I got some ribs at home. We can eat and hang out. Talk."

"Sure," I say, a little surprised by the invitation.

"Let's go. I'll drive. I'll bring you back here later."

We get into his old Buick, and we both cruise out of the park and hit the highway as he lights up another cigarette. He turns on the radio as he sips from his brown bag-cloaked beverage. He takes out his straw and starts chewing on it as he passes me the beverage. I take it and look down at it through the paper bag, and it's that same weird green apple high-alcohol forty-ouncer that I saw Bill drink a few months ago.

I raise it up to my lips and take a big drink of it. The artificially engineered fake fruit booze concoction—probably made of toilet water from a lab underneath a highway in some god-awful part of St. Louis— certainly does its job sedating me. I notice a slightly metallic tinge of the green apple as I lick my lips. It tastes more like a bad scientific experiment than a beer, but oh boy, does it give you a buzz. I hand it back to Hurlie and he puts the straw he's been chewing right back into the can and takes another big pull from it as we start to head downtown.

He looks around at me smirking and raises his voice above the loud jazz music that's emanating from the Buick's ancient radio.

"This shit is drug in a can. You'll see it around the disc golf crowd the more you play."

"I've already seen it," I reply.

We both laugh as he turns the radio louder. I feel the car swerve to the right as my body pulls to the left as we exit the highway. He deftly maneuvers through a bunch of streets and finally we pull in front of a nondescript white house. We get out of the car and he opens the front gate.

"Follow me. We goin' around the back."

I dutifully follow to the left side of the house on a little cobbled sidewalk as Hurlie leads me past a bunch of potted plants and bags of soil to a garage in the back. He crouches and grabs the bottom of the garage door and pulls it up, revealing his very comfortable-looking dwelling area replete with all the amenities you need: a sofa, kitchen table and chairs, refrigerator, sink, TV, and plenty of bookcases filled with DVD's, books, VHS tapes and magazines. It's nice and cool inside as I hear the swamp cooler that Hurlie thankfully left on all morning spill cold air into the garage.

"I like it, man," I say.

"Thanks, Jeff. My mom owns the property here, and she lives in the house. I converted this a while ago, and it's my home. It's all I need, and all I want. And it's rent-free."

He takes out a big plastic container from the refrigerator and throws it down on the kitchen table. He grabs a couple of the green apple monstrosities from the collection I notice he has in the fridge, too.

"Here's them ribs. Dig in," he says. "And, of course, another from the green apple vineyard," he cackles as he goes to pull down the garage door.

I smile to myself as he doesn't offer any plates, napkins or utensils. I'm starving so I just rip off the top of the container and grab one and start devouring it. It's delicious. I realize I should slow down and savor it because it really is just that good. I finish it, and almost start gnawing at the bone, I love it so much.

"Try to come up for air," Hurlie says as I reach for another rib.

I start devouring it as Hurlie goes over and browses his bookcases. I practically forget about him as I enjoy my little feast.

He finally comes over to the table as I'm grabbing for another rib, and puts down a few books. I glance up at some of the titles. *Tibetan Tunnels to Agartha*; *Nazi Paperclip Astronauts on Mars*; *Arcturians and Pleiadians*; and *Vortexes of California*.

"These are Sean's books. I borrowed them a long time ago. Take them."

"They're his, huh?" I ask. "You can keep them if you want, Hurlie. Something to remember him by."

"I already read them. I think he'd want you to read them. These were some of his favorites, and he always was passing them around to people. He wouldn't want me just sittin' on them. He thought knowledge and truth was supposed to be disseminated. So take them and read them. That's what Sean would've wanted."

We sit in silence for a while as I finish another rib. We both continue to pound the green apples as Hurlie starts to have that same distressed look on his face he started out with at the park.

"I took you here to give you yo' brother's books but also to talk to you about something, Jeff," he says.

He's looking straight ahead as he takes out a cigarette and lights it up.

"Sean got into some really weird shit when he was out here,

man," he slowly explains. "Kinda went overboard with it. Started playin' with fire, Jeff. Got way in over his head."

I look up at him as my buzz starts to melt away. I can feel my breathing start to speed up.

"What are you trying to say, Hurlie?"

He gets up and goes over to his TV, then puts in a disc from one of his DVD collections. It's a shaky video of bright lights darting around in the sky.

"This doc was one of yo' bro's fav'rites. *Peruvian Flying Saucers.* He would come over to pick me up to play disc golf, and we'd pound beers and watch this doc before we'd go to the course. Watching the real thing would put us in the mood, you know. Get us seein' the physics of them, how they flew, how they'd spin and dart in the air. He always thought the Peruvian flying saucers reminded him the most of how these plastic discs flew."

"Do you believe those are real?" I ask.

"Yeah, they real. Absolutely they real. I love this doc. When I start to miss Sean, I throw it in. Sometimes I feel he's watching it with me, right here in my crib, like we used to before he passed on."

"Funny you say that, Hurlie. Sometimes I feel he's with me when I go to some of the old clubs he used to play at on the Sunset Strip."

"I used to go watch him play all the time at those clubs," Hurlie reminisces. "He sho was a kick ass guitar player. That last band he was in for awhile, they rocked. I used to be the only brothah in the crowd," he laughs.

I take another long drink from my beer as I patiently wait for him to continue with the revelations about Sean.

"We'd hang out. Talk about flying saucers. Talk about all the books we'd read, and all those other docs in his collection. He was real interested in UFO's, you know, how they flew, how they made with they own gravitational force field inside, and all sorts of other theories about how they could pull off flying the way they did. We'd do this almost every weekend for months on end, and then he'd just stop returning my calls because he'd go off on one of his overseas contract jobs. And then, months later, when he'd get back in town, I'd get a call from him wanting to get together again and throw discs and drink and watch docs together. This would happen on and off like that for almost eight years.

"The last time when he stopped returning calls, there was a lot of bad shit goin' on with him. I just thought maybe he bolted. Left town. Or, you know, got another merc job. Then I get the call out of the blue he's dead."

Hurlie looks down at the stupid green apple emblem on top of the can.

"He was my best friend, dude."

I look over at him, the tears welling up in my eyes.

"What happened to my brother, Hurlie?"

He continues to look down at the can and then starts to pound the beer. He takes a few long moments before he speaks.

"Your brother found out about some secrets at Oak Grove. Met a guy, someone who worked there a while back, who was dying of cancer. He gave your bro a deathbed confession about what really has been going on around that park over the years. I don't know how he met this dude. He was one of the OG's of OG. Sean got this guy to spill the secrets of Oak Grove on video."

"What kind of secrets are you talking about?" I ask.

"Oak Grove is haunted, bro," Hurlie responds as he looks down at his bottle. "It's a vortex. Was an ancient Indian burial ground. Those Indians knew the place is powerful man, and so did those guys that started Experimental Aerolab Dynamics back in the day right down the street. You think it was a coincidence that this flying saucer game, disc golf, was invented a distance driver's throw from EAD?"

"You know I was just talking to that girl, that hot chick,

what's her name? Uh, Alisa. She was talking about the same thing," I say.

"You hangin' around that crazy Russian?"

"She's Swedish," I correct him

"She ain't no Swede. She a Russian porn girl. Stripper, too. Escort. She bad news. Got a couple of Mexicans beat up by her Russian mob friends when they was harassin' her on the course. Steer clear of that ho, Jeff."

I start to smile as I drink my beer. I can't believe this crazy train wreck of a chick.

"Anyways," Hurlie continues, "Sean took it one step further with getting this old guy to confess. The guy tells him in the video how to access the underground government base where they tinker with them flying saucers they got; where all the secret government groups hang out."

"Are you telling me there are government bases underground at Oak Grove?" I ask incredulously.

"Government bases and all sorts of other shit, dude. Extraterrestrials down there. And they don't all necessarily get along, neither. They go at it sometimes. Skirmishes. Shit blows up down there. Reminds me kinda of the gangs up here in the city. They try to co-exist in they turf but go to war from time to time. OG is a trip, man."

"Do the other guys know about this? Gary, Bill, Paul? Andy said something a little weird the other day when we were talking about EAD. Does he know? You ever bring the guys here and watch UFO docs together?"

Hurlie takes another sip of his beer and then looks at the green apple emblem a little reflectively.

"Nah, man. Some guys you just play golf with."

I get up and put my beer on his kitchen table. I wobble a little bit and put my hands down on the table to steady myself. I close my eyes trying to digest all this information into my alcohol-soaked brain.

"So what are you telling me, Hurlie? My brother got into

this, snooped around and people wound up killing him? Is that what you're saying?"

Hurlie takes a long drag from his cigarette.

"I don't know, man. Maybe he just OD'd. But he was on a lot of peoples' shit lists for doing that video. And supposedly he went down into that underground base, too, and they found out about that. They got *real* pissed at that."

"*They* meaning the government?" I ask.

"The government, the aliens, that merc company he worked for. Everybody. He would antagonize people, brag that he had this video of that scientist guy. Dude was brash. Sean had a big mouth. He'd threaten to put it online or take it to the media. He was nuts. Had no idea who he was messin' with.

"I warned him constantly," Hurlie continues, "that he was playin' a dangerous game. But like his mercenary jobs, I think he got a rush from it. He was an adrenaline addict.

Hurlie puts out his cigarette and takes a long drink from his beer.

"So I have my suspicions about his supposed overdose. But I can't prove nothin'. And neither can nobody. And if you start pokin' around down there, Jeff, you might wind up like him."

I sit in stunned silence. I try to remind myself to breathe as I feel like all the oxygen was just sucked out of his little dwelling place. I'm feeling a little faint. I need some water.

I go over to the sink and fill up a glass of water. I gulp it down and splash some water on my face as my legs feel wobbly. I grab the edge of the sink and try to maintain my balance.

"Yo, man. Take a seat before you fall down," Hurlie says.

I manage to get back to the couch and Hurlie goes over to this little mini-pyramid and opens up one of its sides and takes out a bag of weed. He starts loading up his pipe and takes a big hit off it and passes it to me.

I take it and smoke out of it as we both look at the UFO's on the TV darting back and forth. They have a hypnotic effect as we keep passing the pot pipe back and forth. Every toke from this potent strain pushes back an advancing army of mental demons unleashed by these revelations. But I start to whimper as I feel the tears dripping down my alcohol-numbed cheeks. Hurlie peers over at me as he hears my light sobs. Then looks back at the UFO's on the television.

"I didn't want to tell you this shit, man," he says softly. "I could've just let it go, kept blowing you off when I'd see you out on the courses. But I decided to bring you here and tell you all this stuff. You know why?"

I shake my head.

"I'm doin' this for Sean, man. I owe him."

"You owe him?" I ask through teary eyes.

Hurlie continues to look straight ahead, following the UFO's on the screen.

"They caught up with yo' bro right before he died. Took him out into the desert to some warehouse and beat him up."

Hurlie takes a long pull from his beer. He looks over at me, with a deep haunting pain in his eyes.

"They wanted him to give someone else up. They wanted a name."

"Of who?" I ask.

"The guy they saw on surveillance tapes down there in the underground base with him. Sean wouldn't give that guy up, no matter how bad they beat him or what they threatened him with. They harassed him for months about this after we went down in the base."

"We?"

There's a long silence as he struggles with his emotions.

"That other guy was me."

Hurlie gets up and walks over to his bookcase.

"I was the other guy that went down with him to that base. Your bro never gave me up. He could've, and who knows? Maybe they would've spared his life. I feel a lot of guilt about what he did for me. I don't know, though, sometimes I feel he had a death wish anyway, and not giving me up was a way of fulfilling his suicide pact."

"He took a lot of high-risk contracting jobs in some real dangerous places around the world. I think I agree with you, Hurlie. As I've been learning more and more about him, my brother seemed to have an undeniable death wish."

"Yeah, I know all about those merc jobs he took," Hurlie echoes as he starts to sip on his drink again. "He went to some of the worst war zones in the world. Some of these places, shit, man, I didn't even know we had troops in."

"Well, technically those guys really aren't troops, they're contractors so they don't really count in any official anything," I say. "For the last several months I've been researching all about these contractor companies that the government outsources to do their dirty work. Uncle Sam is privatizing wars, and mercs don't officially exist. They are like a ghost army. And my brother was a part of all that."

"Well, he never snitched me out," Hurlie proudly says. "You know, he always talked about you, Jeff. How he wished he could talk to you about all of this. But he just didn't feel he could. He was all alone, tormented with it. So he confided in me, told me everything. I became kind of like his surrogate brother. That's why you here, Jeff. All of this stuff he told me, did for me, turned me on to, I always thought the whole time he really wanted to talk to you about it all."

Hurlie turns to me, deeply serious.

"So you need to hear all of this, about all his dark secrets, and what really went on down there at Oak Grove. Because he always wanted to tell you about it the whole time. So I'm fulfilling a dead man's wish, doing this with you because I owe him.

Hurlie turns back to the flying saucers on the screen and gulps his drink again.

"He never gave me up."

The army of demons have totally taken over my brain as I

just want to scream. I go over to his pot pipe and light it up again and take a big long toke.

"Hurlie, why couldn't he go to anyone about this?"

"About what?" he asks.

"About getting beat up and tortured by these people?"

"Man, he did go to the cops. They didn't do shit. Most of them didn't even believe his fairy tale stories about government agents doin' this to him. But once the higher-ups found out about it, well, shit, who you think was doing this to him? The feds, brah! Who you think the local cops answer to? When the FBI, CIA, NSA, DOD, and a bunch of big merc companies based out of D.C. are involved? What you think Pasadena PD or LAPD can do about that? What they gonna do? Nothin' brah, they take they marching orders from Uncle Sam. They helped cover up his death, I'm convinced of it. They part of it."

Hurlie is ranting away as he's becoming emotional. He retreats to the refrigerator and opens the freezer and takes out a bottle of vodka. He gets two shot glasses from a cupboard and sets them on the kitchen table. He pours two shots, picks them up, and brings one over to me.

I take it and we both shoot them. It helps along with the pot to calm the storm that continues to swirl in my mind as the revelations come down like a hailstorm.

"I have to do something about this."

Hurlie winces.

"Jeff, they will kill you, dude. Just like Sean. You'll both be dead. What is the point of that? You can't beat them. Think about what you up against."

"I want to expose them. Get a video out about what they're doing underground at Oak Grove and put it out in the world, get it out on the internet. Finish what Sean was trying to do."

"They gonna come after you, dude."

"That's my problem. I can't let this slide. They have to pay a price for what they did."

Hurlie returns to the kitchen table and pours himself another shot of vodka and downs it.

"You a dead man walkin', Jeff."

I join Hurlie and pour myself another shot of vodka. I hold it up and look directly into Hurlie's eyes.

"How do I get down into the base? Can you show me?" I ask as I shoot the vodka.

Hurlie grabs the bottle of vodka and drinks right out of it.

"No, but that scientist in that interview can. That's who showed us."

"What do you mean?" I ask.

"That deathbed interview. That scientist guy spilt all the beans on how to get down there. It's a secret Tibetan mystical way of doing it, something you'd never think would be possible."

"But you did it. Why can't you just tell me?"

"I don't know exactly how Sean got us down there. He did some meditation with one of those Tibetan singing bowls, recited some mumbo-jumbo, and then we was transported down there."

"What?" I ask, confused.

"You'll see what I'm saying when you watch the video," he says.

"Well, where is the video of this?"

"You got it."

"What do you mean, I got it?" I ask, incredulous.

"It's in one of those docs in that big collection of his you got."

"Are you kidding me?"

"Nope."

I think to myself how those old roommates of Sean's were telling me about those agents who ransacked his belongings, confiscating his DVD documentary collection. I guess I got the golden egg in the docs of Sean's they hid.

"Which one?" I ask.

DISC-OVERY

He hesitates, realizing he's about to give me the kiss of death.

"It's about halfway through the one about Agartha."

"Agartha?"

"Yep. It's called *Secrets of Agartha*, if I remember correctly."

I take the bottle of vodka and pour myself another shot. I gulp it down. Hurlie is eyeing me very intensely.

"Don't say I didn't warn you. And no matter what happens, you got to keep my name out of it. No matter what. I only doin' this, sayin' all of this out of respect for Sean. I ain't doin' this to sign my own death warrant."

I make eye contact with him for a long moment.

"I promise you, Hurlie, on my brother's soul, that I will never involve you in this. No matter what happens."

We sit in silence and sip our vodka shots.

"I wore a ski mask that night when I went down there with him. That's how they don't know who I am. I'd suggest doing the same. You got to be real careful, dude, real furtive, real undercover. If you don't prepare, and be real slick, they will find you and kill you, man. And when you put it out there on the internet, you better be long gone from here, Jeff. Like out of the country."

"I hear you loud and clear, Hurlie. I'm going to do my homework and go in there and get out before they knew what hit them. And when my videos go viral on the internet all over the world, it's gonna be sweet payback for what they did to Sean."

Hurlie looks at me again with those pained, haunted eyes and pours us both some more vodka. He raises his shot glass in a toast.

"Here's to Sean, dude."

I raise my shot glass to his and clink it. We down the vodka shots and watch as the lights in the kitchen flutter a couple of times. My heart beats wildly as Hurlie and I look at each other aghast, wondering if Sean just clinked his own vodka shot with us from some invisible realm.

8

Hurlie drops me off as the sun is setting at Oak Grove. We clasp hands as we say goodbye for the night. Our friendship is established now and forever. Sean was a brother to both of us, someone who endeared himself forever on our souls and whose absence will always be a void in both of our lives. But we both somehow feel Sean around us from time to time, and he still guides each of our lives in his own way. I know he is leading me right now to finish what he started, and I finally feel like I have a real purpose in life instead of just floundering around. I wave goodbye to Hurlie as he speeds off out of the park up to the highways above. What an afternoon.

I slowly walk to the car, exhausted from all of the drinking, the pot, and the intense emotional few hours I've had with Hurlie. I wonder how I'm going to make it home. The brisk early evening air whips by my face, nurturing me in its cool caress, helping to heal my alcohol drenched teary-eyed cathartic afternoon. When I get to my car, I lean against it, drifting off, feeling my legs wobble beneath me as I slump against my front hood.

I finally open my eyes as the sun continues its descent on the horizon. The leaves are rustling in the light wind, having one last dance in the fading sunlight before darkness descends with only sparse moonlight feebly illuminating the park. The thought of getting on to that highway seems a lot worse than hanging out in the park a little bit longer. Especially if I could play a couple of holes of disc golf. *What a great idea!*

I grab my disc golf bag and head to the first hole as my life has never felt as clear and focused as it does now. I finally have found a real purpose. A quest. Maybe this is Sean's posthumous gift to me. However, I know I'm about to embark on something there's no coming back from.

I began to understand Sean more by watching his movie collection, getting into his head one documentary at a time. But this is different. With this new adventure I'm getting a taste of the rush of adrenaline that took him to overseas war zones year after year.

I put the disc golf bag on the bench at the first hole as I look up at that evil-looking branch that extends over the first part of the fairway, its baneful contours as hideous as ever. I zip open my bag and take out my Diamondback disc. It's time to let a sidearm rip, to go right underneath that devil of a branch instead of trying to hyzer a shot way around the right of it. My sidearm has improved as of late, and my confidence is growing with every forehand shot.

I grasp the disc and look ahead at the small gap of about eight feet that's between the ground and the branch to the far left side of the fairway, about one hundred feet away. It's a tough shot, but I'm going for it. I concentrate as I start to move my feet slowly forward as I take my right arm back with the disc, all the while focusing on that little eight-foot window I have to get this little blue disc through.

I move forward faster and shift my body more to the right as my body moves almost perpendicular to the fairway ahead of me as I continue to step forward until I finally whip the disc forward, my body turning toward the fairway.

I can hear my wrist snap as the blue disc shoots out of my

hand, erupting like a missile as it speeds off just above the ground, zooming along just like those flying saucers Hurlie had on his television screen at his little guest house.

The disc looks fluid as it glides along just a couple of feet above the grass. This has to be the best sidearm shot I've ever thrown as it jets along with a momentum I haven't seen before in any of my shots.

It passes through that small eight-foot corridor with room to spare as it sails towards the green soccer field. I'm entranced as it powers forward until it finally hits the grass, turning dramatically at an angle from the impact of hitting the ground, catapulting towards the basket that sits between the trunks of several trees before it...*smashes into the chains!* The disc halts in the middle of the chains, almost posing for the mental picture before it finally falls down into the bottom of the disc golf basket.

I stand frozen in a state of complete shock and euphoria. I can't move. There is an overwhelming silence in the park. Like the entire world has stopped. My mouth is wide open as I try to process what has just happened. I have just hit an ace. A hole in one. The pinnacle of disc golf. The closest thing I've ever had to a religious experience. I look around to see if anyone is present to have witnessed this. No one's in this part of the park at dusk. I'm all alone.

I grab my disc bag and start walking towards the basket as I am still numb from what has just occurred. I slowly start to breathe again as I make my way up onto the fairway still transfixed on my light blue Diamondback disc sitting on the bottom of the basket. Smiling to myself, I think of those flying saucers that Hurlie and Sean used to watch together as they pounded beer, psyching themselves up for the round of disc golf. I think about everything that has happened in the last few hours. It truly has been a magical afternoon.

I finally reach the basket and take my Diamondback out and look at it longingly. I might have to retire this disc now and put it up on my wall. I look at it and marvel at its cool light blue color. I've never really paid much attention to the dazzling blue hue of this disc. I move it around with my hands, seeing how the light of the early evening bounces off it. I smile broadly as I'm holding it like a baby in my hands in front of me. And what a cool name, too! The Diamondback. Reminds me of some of those old paperbacks I used to read about the old west when I was a kid when a snake would—

"Are you going to kiss it?"

I look up to follow where that familiar voice came from.

"Alisa?"

"I'm over here, behind the tree next to the bench at the second hole."

I look over at the big oak tree up the hill to the right of the second tee. Alisa is sitting almost hidden in a big hollow in the tree with a joint in her hand, smoking it as she smiles at me. I can barely see her from this angle until she emerges from the deep cavity of the tree.

"That was quite a shot, mister," she says, smiling.

"You saw that, huh? So, I have an official witness."

"You sure do," she says walking over to her disc golf bag that's sitting on the bench next to the second tee.

"After I hit it, I scanned the area for people and thought it was deserted. I had no idea you were here."

"That oak tree is one of my secret hiding places for smoking weed on this part of the course. Remember what I told you. The cops are always lurking at Oak Grove."

She unzips one of the side pockets of her disc golf bag and takes out a Sharpie.

"Here let me sign your disc. That's what people do who've witnessed an ace."

I hand over my disc as she scribbles her name on it. Her lively smile accentuates her stunning beauty as I'm glad she's here to share this moment.

"Oh yes, one other thing, though," she says. "We have

another tradition when a person hits an ace. You have to give all the witnesses who are present a dollar. Looks like I'm the only one, so you got pretty lucky today. When I hit my first one out here, I was with like ten people. Hitting that ace cleaned me out that day."

"Are you kidding me," I protest. "Is this another one of your hustles?"

"It is no hustle," she replies curtly, her lively smile vanishing from her face. "Ask anyone who plays disc golf. It is one of the traditions out here. Either respect that or take up bird watching."

I concede and grab my wallet, pulling out a dollar bill as she continues to scribble something on the underside of the Diamondback. I give her the dollar as she hands me back my disc. I turn it over and read what she scribbled.

A FEROCIOUS FOREHAND! – Alisa

I start to smile again as I look up at her.

"Yeah, my sidearm has really been getting better for me. This shot though, as soon as I threw it, I knew it was something special. My best ever."

"I saw you throw it," Alisa recounts. "As soon as it left your hand, I knew it had a chance. I think that you've found your shot. The sidearm suits you. You have great natural form with it, unlike your backhand which is a little awkward. No offense."

"None taken," I say. "My backhand has always felt a little stiff, you're right. Amazing how you pick up on these things."

"They call me the disc witch out here. Along with other names," she smirks at me. "Some of which are not too flattering."

"The disc witch, huh?"

"Yes, when people think they've lost their discs, I usually find them. Just by feeling the wind around me and understanding all of the angles and the lay of the land, I can figure out where they're hidden. It's like a sixth sense. People are always amazed."

DISC-OVERY

"You love this sport, don't you?" I remark, smiling at her beautiful dark eyes.

"Yes, I love it. I will always play it. And Oak Grove will always be my home course. If they ever deport me, I'll just come up through Mexico to be here again." she says.

Our eyes meet for a couple of moments until she glances down at her sharpie and puts it in her bag. She lights up her joint again, darting her eyes around, scanning for cops. She strolls over to the second tee pad and I follow her.

"Do you want a hit?" she asks me.

"No thanks. I'm finally sobered up after a long afternoon and it's getting dark, and I got to drive home now," I say.

"Suit yourself. I'm staying and playing."

"But it's getting dark. How do you play at night when you can't see anything out here?" I ask.

She tokes up a few more times as the conversation pauses. She finally catches her breath as she finishes wheezing from the pot.

"Why do you think they call me the disc witch, honey?"

She turns to go through her discs as she finally settles on her pink Relic.

"You get better when you play at night, when you can't see where the basket is, but you know its placement. You have to pay attention to precisely how you throw it, to gauge exactly where it lands. It brings your concentration to a whole other level and develops that sixth sense I just told you about. It refines the intuitive aspect of my game giving me that special edge. So, when I come here during the day, I tear up these guys with the big arms. The silly meatheads just know power. There is so much more to this game than that."

I stand smiling at her and our eyes meet once again. I think about what Hurlie told me about her but I don't care. I'm totally intrigued with this Swede, or Russian, or whatever the hell she is.

"What are you smiling at?" she asks me.

"Oh, you are fascinating to me, that's all," I reply.

"Oh yeah?" she says.

"Yeah," I reply, continuing to smile.

She turns away, breaking up our eye contact as she steps on the tee pad and brings up her disc.

"Come by sometime at night," she tells me while looking away at the disc golf basket a couple hundred feet away. "I'll teach you the ways of the disc witch. It will up your game."

I smile even more broadly.

"Which night?" I ask.

"Any night. I'm usually out here."

She steps up and flicks the disc and it glides nicely, close to the ground as it doesn't flip over and starts winding back to the right side of the fairway, disappearing into the darkness of the woods.

She grabs her bag and looks back over at me.

"Come find me," she says with a wink.

She turns back around and walks off towards her first shot.

I watch her vanish into the night.

I wonder to myself, what's more dangerous out here? The secret government in their underground base or this chick?

* * *

I walk back to the parking lot still giddy from my ace. I can't wait to gloat about it to all my disc golf buddies! I haven't talked to them in a minute. I text Paul and moments later my phone beeps.

> u da man

The text says.

> lets play soon k?

I type.

> ok

hey I want to text andy and tell him about my ace whats his #

> he doesnt have cell phone

well ill go to him where does he live ill surprise him

> hes homeless lives under bridge next to railroad tracks near san fernando rd

Shit. I didn't realize Andy was homeless. I respond.

u think hes there now

> maybe

ok ill try to find him

> good luck

thanx lets play next weekend

> ok

I get in the car and head out to find Andy. I take the 210 West until I hit the 2 South and take that to the 134 West until I find the exits for Burbank, and then just head north towards the mountains in the distance.

I finally reach the edge of town where auto mechanic shops start to appear, as well as welding and sheet metal companies. Then there are all those nondescript office buildings, storage units and warehouses. And, of course, a strip club or two thrown into the no-holds-barred zoning here. It all seems like a smuggler's paradise with everybody up to no good. Who the hell knows what goes on in all these warehouses behind all the barbed wire fences and walls.

I finally see the part of the bridge from the street I'm on, and several people are sleeping in an encampment outside. I venture over there as Andy could very well be in one of those sleeping bags underneath the tarps. I park on the curb down the street and make my way over to their makeshift community.

I'm scanning everybody there, seeing if Andy is somewhere in the hamlet of tents or buried in unmatching multi-colored layers of heavy clothing that adorn the homeless in the cold evenings. They sit around on discarded couches, as mangy as some of the dogs that they keep as pets, drinking and smoking, as lamps and radios are powered by outlets on electric utility poles adorned by rotting bookcases and moldy tables. The whole place showcases the unfortunate widespread and popular contemporary American shanty town aesthetic of exterior decorating.

I walk away from the group thinking he might have splintered off from these people. He is a bit of a loner, though he can be quite the socialite with a drink in his hand playing disc golf.

But Andy is nowhere to be found. Trying to find him out here actually seems futile, particularly at night. I begin to walk back to my car continuing to scan the area looking for him. It's certainly a rough section of town, as gang graffiti is sprawled over the sides of vacant buildings. Dour fast food parking lots beckon for the next drug deal to take place with those at the fringes of society mingling in a kind of no man's land at the periphery of the city.

I study the construction workers scurrying about in the early evening as the light wanes, finishing up another exhausting day of work, along with painters whose jeans and shirts are splashed with a potpourri of paint, walking around like moving modern art paintings.

I sit on my car and scan the working class neighborhood again. A Mexican lady pushes a stroller on the sidewalk with a

DISC-OVERY

kid holding on to her hand as she passes by a liquor store. I look at the place and its steel-rod exterior, keeping all the alcohol inside nice and chilled. It's basically a massive cooler in a big metal cage. My eyes rest on someone drinking outside of the doors on the street curb with a red hooded sweatshirt. I watch the figure bring the forty-ouncer up to his lips and take a big drink from it. It's Andy. I should've known all along how to find him. Just follow the booze.

I make my way over to him, crossing the street and careful not to bring attention to myself. I want to surprise him. He is transfixed on his can of alcohol, staring down at it, almost mesmerized by the manufactured elixir encased in aluminum that helps him cope with life out here on the streets. I'm nearing him as I start to notice how terrible he looks; his face is worn and puffy, and his clothes are filthy and torn. He barely notices me as I approach him. He looks up and squints at me.

"I hit an ace, Andy."

A little smile forms on his face as he brings up the forty and guzzles some of the booze down. It's not the green apple varietal, just straight up malt liquor. He's dazed as he looks up at me, completely inebriated and on who knows what else judging from the look of his eyes.

"What course?" he manages to ask.

"Oak Grove."

"What hole?"

"The first hole."

"No shit," he says as he looks down at the street right below him. He starts chuckling as he takes out a pack of cigarettes. He takes one out and lights it up.

"Not an easy hole to ace," he continues. "I never have. No one's aced that hole in a long time. Congrats, Jeff. A toast to your first ace!"

He raises his can of malt liquor and toasts the air in my direction as he pounds the rest of it. He finishes it and grimaces from the booze, then proceeds to throw the beer can in the gutter to his right.

"How about celebrating by buying me another beer?" he asks.

I look down at him. He is totally pathetic sitting on the curb next to the gutter.

"C'mon, I'm the friggin' granddaddy of the game! You know how many courses I've designed? I was playing this sport when they threw frisbees, not discs. You should be honored to buy me a drink on the night of your first ace, goddammit!"

He looks back down after he finishes his moronic tirade.

The absurd aspect of what he just said is actually true. He's one of the granddaddys of the sport. I've learned from many people in the disc golf community over these last months that he was one of the pioneers of the sport over the last several decades in Southern California, instrumental in designing courses, setting up tournaments, and even getting sponsors back in the day.

"What do you want?" I ask.

He looks up at me glowingly as I've said the magic words.

"Any forty will do just fine," he says with a big smile on his face.

He goes back to dragging on his cigarette and I wander into the liquor store moving towards the back, searching the refrigerators for the green apple toxic toilet water from St. Louis. I finally find it. The green apple varietal and its kindred malt liquors are basically the bastard stepchildren of regular beer. Kind of like the way disc golf is to traditional ball golf.

I grab two and bring them to the register. The clerk rings me up and I pay him and he puts the beers in individual paper bags.

"Hey do you have any straws for those?" I ask.

"Sure," the clerk answers and reaches down and grabs a couple for me. I bet people ask him for straws for their brown bag boozing all day.

DISC-OVERY

Back outside, I walk over to Andy and sit down next to him on the curb, handing him his malt liquor. He grabs it and takes it out of the bag, immediately guzzling then letting out a big belch. He laughs and wipes his mouth with his sleeve.

"Charming," I say as I open my green apple brew, still in the brown bag, and put the straw in it and take a long sip.

Andy pounds the malt liquor a couple of more times and closes his eyes, relishing the buzz.

"Why don't you keep it in the brown bag and sip on it with a straw so not everybody in the whole world can see you drinking in public?" I ask him.

"Rules, rules, rules!" he mocks. "I'm gonna do what I want. They can take all their rules and shove 'em!"

He pounds the beer once again and starts laughing. I take another long pull from my drink and savor the metallic taste of the GMO synthetic green apple bad booze concoction.

"So how many aces have you hit in your career?" I ask him.

"Seventy-three," he replies.

"Wow! That is incredible!" I exclaim.

"Well, you're on your way," he tells me, slurring his words. "You keep playin' like your playin', and you're gonna be real good, man."

"Really? You think so?"

"Yep. If you keep listening to my goddam advice!"

He takes a long drag from his cigarette as his body sways a little bit.

"You play with a lot of restraint and discipline. Don't try to just kill it every time. You're thinkin' about each and every shot. It's a cerebral game," he slurs. "A thinking man's game. You understand this. You're gonna give those guys out there on the course a run for their money, Jeff. Goddamnit, you're gonna give 'em hell!"

"Gee, Andy. Thanks. That means a lot to me, you saying something like that. I mean, you know this sport as well as anyone. You really think I can be a decent player some day, huh?"

"Absolutely, Jeff. But you gotta stick with it, and work on that putting," he slurs, rocking back and forth. "Because you know what they say, you drive for show-"

"And putt for dough," I say smiling at him.

"Oh. I've told you that before, huh?"

"You and just about everybody else on the course," I reply.

We both laugh and go back to drinking our respective domestic toilet waters.

We sit in silence for a while, both focusing on getting more of a buzz going, though I think Andy certainly has been working on his for a while. I look ahead at the encampment of homeless people underneath the bridge. There's a blue tarp towards the back and several of them are setting up their shopping carts near their sleeping areas. One of them is listening to the Dodgers game on a radio he plugged in to one of the light poles.

I look back over at Andy, who's gazing down at the street again. He really does look terrible as his face tells the tales of many years of drug abuse and alcohol blackouts. He looks despondent.

"Hey, Andy, I wanted to ask you something."

"Ask away," he responds.

"I've been playing a lot at Oak Grove the last few months. Met a lot of people down there, you know, regulars. I talk with them. I've heard a lot of weird stories about that place. You've mentioned to me the other day you've heard similar urban myths over the years. That it was built on an Indian burial ground. Shit like that."

"That's no myth. That's real."

"Do you think the place is haunted?" I ask.

He takes a swig from his forty and rubs his face, and pulls out his cigarettes again.

"A lot of bizarro shit happens there."

He looks down at the street again. There's a long period of heavy silence.

Andy takes another drag from his cigarette as he looks up at the encampment under the bridge.

"The Devil's Gate Dam's at the edge of the park," he continues ominously. "It's shaped like a Devil's Head."

He takes a drink from the forty and another long drag on his cigarette.

"I went there once many years ago."

He looks over at me with his dark eyes suddenly filled with fear.

"And I'm never going back."

Andy's pupils tear into me as he lets me glimpse into a very dark part of himself. A place far inside of him filled with terror and madness. For that split second, he lets me see what he's been carrying around inside him for so long that has reduced him to sleeping under a bridge. All because of what he saw that night, so many years ago at the Devil's Gate Dam.

He stares ahead, out at the encampment.

"I've seen a lot of creepy stuff at that place over the years. All sorts of apparitions. Weird ships coming out of EAD. Even creatures that I've never seen before. Several times, I swear I saw a chupacabra. I've heard strange voices there in the howling wind at night. I can go on and on, Jeff."

"Hey, man," I finally break the silence. "Do you want to split a fifth of vodka with me?"

"Yeah," he says as he's still working on his forty. "Go get it, and let's go for a little walk. I got to get up off this curb and move around."

"So do I," I say as I get up and stumble into the store.

I purchase a fifth of vodka and catch up to Andy who's walking along the side of the street. I take out the bottle and take a swig and pass it to Andy who does the same. He hands it back to me and I put it in my pocket. Dust mingles up in the air from the street and we turn away, struggling not to cough. We continue to walk along. It feels good just to get the blood flowing and clear my head after that unsettling alcohol-drenched conversation we just had. I can tell Andy's feeling good walking around, too.

He starts meandering off the sidewalk after the row of buildings to the right of us ends and a barren field starts which extends to the highways in the distance. I watch him wander out into the field and I follow as I take out the vodka again. He extends his hand for the booze and I hand it to him. He takes a few sips from it and hands it back. We keep drifting off into the field, and I wonder where the hell he is taking me. He finally takes off his backpack, unzips it, and reaches in and grabs a couple of discs.

"You got discs, huh?"

"Yeah, we're gonna loosen up a little bit. I throw out here a lot, on this abandoned rocky field next to the highway. I play safari. It's a great place to practice your stroke on, especially at night because the streetlights out here illuminate the whole tract of land, all the way up to the highway. So we're gonna make our way out towards the highway up there. We'll climb up that hill to the 101, and I'm gonna show you something."

"Sounds like a plan," I say.

"Here's an Ogre for you. I know you like that disc. And I have some mid-range discs, too, and putters in here," he motions to his backpack.

He looks ahead and points to a tire about two hundred and fifty feet away.

"You see that tire?" he asks.

"Yep," I reply. I'm surprised how well lit the area is.

"Three par to the tire."

"Okay," I say.

We both throw pretty good drives as mine goes about twenty feet farther than Andy's. He grabs his backpack, and we start walking towards our discs. We don't talk as we still hear the wisps of cars far behind us, scurrying about through the concrete tributaries of the city. We stop at Andy's disc and he takes out a mid-range disc before he plops his backpack down. He steps up and plants his foot right behind the distance driver he threw and proceeds to throw a laser towards the tire. It starts low but sails high as it passes over the target, falling finally about thirty feet past it.

"Dammit," he says.

He grabs his backpack and distance driver and we walk up to my disc.

"What do you want? I got a Seal or a Turtle for mid-ranges," Andy asks.

"I'll take the Seal."

He reaches into his backpack and takes out the disc and hands it to me. I walk up to the distance driver I threw, which is halfway submerged underneath the sand. I kick it over and nestle my foot against it and concentrate on the beat up old tire, which is about ninety feet away. I throw a fluid backhand shot that sails a little wide to the right before it settles into a nice hyzer that comes back dramatically towards the tire. It hits the dirt and skips over the tire and lands about ten feet to the left of the big discarded piece of rubber.

"Good one, dude," Andy says.

"Thanks," I reply.

We walk towards the old tire and as we get closer he reaches into his backpack and takes out a putter for me. I take it and we both go our separate ways to our respective mid-ranges. I get to mine first but wait for Andy to go, as he's further out.

He gets in his stance and gets in some quasi-meditative state as he's seriously concentrating on the target. He stays there for a few comical moments as he suddenly looks up wide-eyed and flings the disc at the tire. It hits it with a thud and bounces away.

"Nice shot, man," I say.

"Thanks."

I smirk to myself as I realize that after all he's been through, Andy's still got game.

I settle into my stance as I concentrate on throwing the putter a little to the right of the target, hoping it will fade into the tire.

I finally throw it and I can feel it kind of slip out of my hand as it misses badly to the left and very short.

"Wow, that sucked," I say in disgust.

"If you wanna get it in, you gotta get it up," Andy says.

"Yeah, that was weak, man."

I putt out and we walk along the field towards the highway.

"Your turn," he says to me. "Pick hole number two."

I look around at the barren field in front of us that's lit up by the streetlamps as well as the moonlight from far above. I finally find an empty forty-ouncer about three hundred feet ahead.

"Okay, three par to that forty-ouncer. You see it?

"Do I see it?" Andy responds. "Shit, I drank it last night."

I smile as Andy goes first since he shot a par on the last one and I bogeyed.

He returns to that weird half-assed meditative state as he gears up to throw and suddenly whips his body around in that surprising nimbleness he's capable of. I hear his wrist snap as the disc launches out of his hand as it goes in a gorgeous line drive straight ahead towards the bottle lying on the ground several hundred feet ahead. It's a fantastic shot, coming from a combination of muscle memory and sheer talent to that old competitive streak he's had all these years. The disc maintains its line as it starts to approach the bottle, and then it starts to dip and *clink!* It hits the glass bottle.

I turn around to a beaming Andy, admiring his latest disc golf masterpiece.

"You had to rain on my parade, huh?" I tell him.

"You couldn't be the only one with an ace today, rookie," he replies, grinning from ear to ear.

"Great shot, Andy. Unbelievable. Sure as hell gonna be one tough act to follow."

I walk up to the spot he threw from to tee off.

I stop and turn around and look at him.

"Aren't you forgetting something?" I ask him.

"What?" he stammers.

"My dollar. You owe me a buck. You know the rules."

His smile disappears as he didn't expect this from a newbie like me.

"How the hell do you know about that?"

"That chick Alisa told me all about that warped disc golf etiquette when I hit my ace today," I tell him. "I had to cough up a buck."

"You're hangin' around with her?"

"Yeah," I reply.

"You better watch out for that one. She's trouble."

"So I've heard," I say.

"I think I have a hundred pennies back at the encampment. I'll count them out for you when we go back there," he glumly replies.

I turn around smirking to myself. I have no intention of collecting a hundred pennies from him. I'll let him sweat it for a while, though. I stare at the forty bottle in the distance and step forward and let it rip. It's a terrible shot, slipping out early, going high and far to the left, typical of what happens when I try to kill it instead of throwing it fluidly and following through.

"Early release program," I mutter out loud.

I look over at Andy as we walk towards my shot and his shit-eating grin has returned. Hitting an ace far outweighs the loss of a hundred pennies.

"How about I buy us another round of drinks when we get back to the liquor store, and we'll forget the dollar you owe me, okay?

He's beaming now.

"Deal, buddy!"

We continue walking towards my disc, and he moves in front of me and proceeds to pick it up and put it in his backpack.

"Hey!" I say.

"I want to get back to that liquor store and start drinking. So let's just hike up to the highway and I'll show you what I took you out here for, and then we'll go drink."

"Okay."

He then picks up his disc and meanders back to me.

"C'mon, follow me," he says as he trots forward.

We walk another hundred yards towards the expressway where he leads me up a little path to the overpass. I'm huffing and puffing a little bit as we move up the steep incline towards the cars up above. I wonder what in the world Andy could possibly want me to see up here.

When we arrive at the top, the noise from the cars zooming by is stifling as Andy stands behind a concrete barrier. He motions me over to him. I step over the barrier to a small enclave where he is, and we both lean against the fence.

"Look over there," he tells me.

I follow where he is pointing. It's a billboard with a big vodka advertisement on it. I've seen the same ad all over the city. It's illuminated by the big lights on top of the billboard for all to see on the expressways.

"Couldn't you have just pointed out this vodka to me back at the liquor store instead of walking all the way over here to see it on a billboard? I told you I'll get you whatever you want!" I practically yell over the noisy traffic.

"Listen, Jeff," he says. "Look at the bubbles in the far right corner, next to the girl drinking it. You see them?"

I peer over at them and find the bubbles next to this anorexic redhead on the right of the billboard.

"Yeah I see them. So what?"

"Look at it closely. Concentrate on it, tell me what you see."

I look at the bubbles closely but they just look like bubbles.

"They look like bubbles," I yell at him again over the awful traffic of the 101.

"Look *closer*, Jeff," he yells back.

I lean back on the fence and really focus on the bubbles.

"Look at the face staring back at us," he says pointedly.

And then I see it. Out of the random images of ice, the eyes appear to me. They come to life as they meet my gaze. I then follow the eyes to the horns above it. Chills run up my spine as I find myself looking into the eyes of a demon. My eyes move to the right and find yet another demon face forming out of more bubbles.

This leads to the cocktail the redhead is holding out in her extended arm, and I see dark black spots in the center of the ice cubes in her drink forming demon eyes. They peer back at me and I follow yet another set of spiked horns that form out of the jagged edges of the ice right over them, which form the hideous face of another demon. The malevolent figure leads me to yet another and another until I see a multitude of demons looking back at me masquerading as ice cubes in the drinks of the other partygoers all over the billboard. It is the canvas of the devil, evil eyes of hideous demons look down at me and over every oblivious lost soul of Los Angeles. I am short of breath. I lean back as I feel lightheaded from this ghoulish sight.

"Did you see it?" Andy yells at me over the traffic mayhem.

"Yeah!" I yell back. "I got to get out of here, man!"

I stumble back towards the path and step over the concrete barrier to make my way down the steep little path, trying to catch my breath as I feel like I'm hyperventilating. I need to get away from there. I move my legs faster down the hill outside of the expresswayWhen I'm halfway down I feel like I can't catch my breath and my right ankle suddenly gives way with a sharp pain. I feel myself losing my balance and fall to the right. Then I slam down on the hill and start to roll. The earth moves all around me as I tumble until it finally slows down I stop, face planted in the dirt.

Tasting the dirt in my mouth, I lie still panting heavily. My ankle is killing me and my rib cage also hurts. I lay there hearing myself breathing until I feel Andy's hands on me.

"Dude! Are you okay? Jeff? Talk to me!"

I lay there awhile longer, trying to catch my breath.

"Yeah, man. I'm okay," I mumble. "Just let me catch my breath."

I finally turn over onto my back and look up at Andy's weathered face.

"Dude, are you hurt?" he screams at me.

"Just twisted my ankle, man. I'm fine," I say struggling to sit up.

He's looking down at me very concerned.

"Are you sure?" he says.

I stand up and move around and feel my right ankle and my right rib cage protesting from the movement, but nothing is broken. Just bruised.

"Yeah, man. I'm all right. Just took a nasty spill. Had to get away from there."

"I'm sorry, Jeff. I didn't want you to freak out. I was just trying to make a point."

Andy allows me a few moments to get myself together.

"C'mon, man. Let's go get that drink," I say, turning towards the direction of the liquor store.

We say nothing for the next few minutes as the awful noise pollution from the expressway gets quieter with every step. My ribs hurt but I know what broken ribs feel like, and there's no way I'd be able to walk like this with busted ribs. After another hundred yards or so, the noise from the highway begin to die down. I take a moment and sit down as I am exhausted. Andy sits down next to me, a look of concern on his face. My breathing is getting under control as I close my eyes and try to catch up with myself.

DISC-OVERY

I try to digest what I just saw on that billboard as well as recover from that spill I just took. Finally feeling under control, I open my eyes. Andy is sitting there, holding one of his discs and drinking from that forty he'd stashed in his backpack.

"That was really freaky, Andy."

He continues to look at his disc, bending its rim back and forth and eyeing its contours.

"I think this disc is getting a little warped. It doesn't throw as straight as it used to. I might have to put it to bed soon and get another one," he says somberly as buying a disc is a major expense for him. He keeps scanning it until he finally puts it in his backpack. He looks down on the ground reflectively.

"You know, I heard they just opened up this brand new disc golf course in Switzerland. It's in the Alps. They put a basket there in such a way that when you hit the chains with a disc, the sound bounces off all over the mountains so that even people back at the tee a thousand feet away on the other side of the mountain can hear it ringing."

He takes out a cigarette and lights it up. "I want to go there before I die and hear that ringing through the mountains," he says as he looks up back at the encampment. We both look over at the homeless people trying to set up a tarp, a couple of them are bickering over a shopping cart. Another one kicks over a garbage can and starts yelling at the others as he storms off. That idyllic scene that Andy just described in the Alps seems like light years away from this dreary urban setting. His home.

"I took you over there, Jeff, to that unholy billboard, to make a point."

"A point about what, Andy?"

"There's a lot of evil in the world, Jeff," he says, his eyes meet mine. "You don't have to go out and search for it, like you're going to do at Devil's Head. It's all right in front of you. Around you. In the most unlikely of places. In advertisements on billboards, in the symbols of corporate logos, the architecture of malls. All around us, everywhere."

I look into that profound pain in his eyes, the ones that have not only seen the traumas of street life, but tell of the horrors of the supernatural and the hidden evils lurking in the mundane of everyday life. When you can identify the reality of the darkness that secretly pervades so much of our society, that knowledge can destroy you, drive you mad. Waking up to it is not easy. I know because I'm dealing with it, just like Sean did, watching all those documentaries and digging around for the truth at Oak Grove, following in his footsteps. It's shocking and terrifying. It's easier to stay asleep as you go through life, one of the many millions who live a lie every day.

It is then that I understand I am playing with fire, exactly what Hurlie spoke to me about. And what Andy is warning me about by taking me to see the billboard. I am flirting with the dark side and it can ruin me, much like it has killed my brother, put Andy out on the street, and has terrified and endangered Hurlie as well. It would be much easier to walk away from all of this.

But I owe it to Sean. Since I wasn't there for him while he was alive, I'm going to follow through with his unfinished business. Even if it destroys me.

"Thank you for showing me that, Andy. You gotta wake up sometime."

Andy looks back down on the ground again.

"Nobody said it would be easy," he says. "I'm just trying to help open your eyes a little bit. To things I see every day."

He looks up at me with deep concern as a chilly gust of wind adds to our anxieties, we shiver for a moment.

"Let's go get that drink then, Andy. Anything but that brand of vodka on the billboard, though."

He smiles at me as we both get up and head over to the liquor store.

9

I spend the next couple of days trying to process everything that I'd been through the last week or so. I keep drinking my whiskey and wine. After that billboard, I'm laying off the vodka for a while.

I can't bring myself to sit down and watch the doc with the interview with the secrets of Oak Grove in it. Some warrior I am. I don't feel intrepid or adventurous, only weak and frightened. I cower in my house, pulling the sheets over my head as I lay in bed wondering why I'm considering risking everything to complete my deceased brother's crazy failed mission.

A couple of weeks pass. I finally limp over to Sean's doc collection and flip through the pages of DVD's looking for the title *Secrets of Agartha*. I spend a half an hour maddeningly scanning the titles before I finally find it.

It's on one of the discs that has four other docs on it with all the titles barely legible scribbled on the corner of the disc. I take it out of the plastic sleeve and look at it closely. Just another ordinary looking disc out of a thousand. But there are secrets buried somewhere in this one. Secrets that probably got Sean killed.

I slide it in the DVD player and get ready for whatever is on this disc that will seriously rock my world.

I settle into watching this very interesting documentary about the inner earth. Evidently, the earth is hollow and there is an inner world that Admiral Byrd accidentally discovered during his trip to the North Pole. His ship went through a secret opening at the top of the Arctic Circle, and he went down and visited a beautiful world inside the earth where he encountered benevolent beings who told him how the earth was in dire straits because of its incessant wars and conflicts.

It is known as Agartha, the documentary goes on to talk about Shambala, which is sometimes confused by the concept of the inner Earth, which is believed by the Tibetans to be a vast network of underground tunnels which—

Suddenly, the documentary goes to a white fade out. I sit wondering if the documentary is simply over. Sometimes these docs end abruptly as they were recorded or dubbed over erroneously or are just plain defective. I wait patiently and I stare into the white void on my screen until it transitions into what looks to be a hospital bed with an old, sickly man lying on it. He has long gray hair and looks haggard as he reaches for the glass of water on a small table to his right. He takes it and crouches up as he struggles to drink from it. He finally manages to take a sip without spilling it all over himself and places it back on the table to his right. I hear the voice from behind the camera and shudder. It's Sean.

"Wilhelm, thank you for taking the time to talk about this with me," Sean says to the old man.

Sean's voice immediately brings up a flood of emotion because I haven't heard his voice in years. We stopped talking seven or eight years ago, it's eerie hearing him. It's like he's being artificially brought to life again. The old man struggles to speak.

"It is something that I can't live with anymore. And since I don't have long to live, it's time to tell someone about it."

DISC-OVERY

Wilhelm gasps for air as Sean patiently waits for him to continue.

"Living with a secret can tear you apart inside. You can feel it just eat you alive, devouring your soul. The torment literally gobbles up your heart, your blood and guts, everything deep within you. They say what I suffer from is cancer. They are only partly right. It's really my dark secrets that are consuming me and sending me to my grave."

Sean adjusts the camera, shaking it until he fixes the tripod and slowly zooms in on Wilhelm's face on the bed. As the camera moves in, it is striking how haunted the old man's eyes are. Decades of anguish show in his pained pupils as he struggles to continue.

"I could never speak out publicly about this, for obvious reasons. I have seen several colleagues slip, making statements casually in public about what goes on down deep in the crypt here. And then, we'd all hear about some unfortunate car accident this person had, or how one of them suddenly dropped dead of a heart attack. It would send a message to the rest of us about what happens to people who have loose lips."

Wilhelm slowly looks to the right as he trails off, gazing at the glass of water again. He reaches for it and tries to grasp it and he knocks it over and it crashes to the ground, shattering. A moment later, Sean walks into frame to clean up the broken glass. I gasp seeing my brother for the first time in years. He had aged since the last time I saw him. Long hair, but slightly balding on top and a little more hunched over than I remember. Also, it looks like he was walking with a slight limp.

Sean finishes cleaning up the broken glass and hands Wilhelm a bottle of water. He turns to go back and as he does, looks directly into the camera, and it's like our eyes meet gazing at each other for a moment.

He steps out of the frame to go behind the camera and it jarringly moves as he adjusts it once again. He zooms back a little bit as we see Wilhelm drink out of the water bottle. He finally puts it aside and speaks again.

"But what do I have to lose, now?" Wilhelm continues. "What are they going to do? Come and kill a dying man? I don't know even know if I'm going to last the rest of the week."

He pauses and tries to collect his thoughts.

"Almost my whole career was spent being afraid of what I knew was going on underneath that base. Thirty-five years of being a coward and not telling the American public, or really the world, what I had seen far below this quaint park in Pasadena, where families have picnics and kids play soccer."

"And people play disc golf," my brother adds.

Sean slowly zooms in on Wilhelm's weathered and pained face, suddenly breaking into a smile.

"Yes, of course," Wilhelm replies. "How could I forget the sport my esteemed colleagues invented right at Oak Grove? We couldn't figure out how those discs we recovered actually flew so we thought making little plastic ones and chucking them around the park down the street could clarify all the secrets of UFO's."

Wilhelm starts chuckling to himself.

"How silly to think that."

He grabs the water bottle again and takes a sip.

"We never figured out anything about those saucers. But we'd boast to the Russians how we figured out how to reverse-engineer them. All lies.

"MJ-12 and all their CIA lackeys and black-ops people that made up the secret government, they were all shaking in their boots with what was going on down there. They had made a deal with these little alien bastards that gave them their spacecraft where they'd teach these power-crazed military and government elite how they could rule the world. What a bunch of crock.

"You wouldn't believe what I would see down there over the

years. Military brass screaming at the aliens about all their lies and reneging on their promises; shootouts that would happen in the underground corridors with all the infighting among the secret government. Presidents visiting the area to make some meaningless speech in L.A. to a labor union or at some Hollywood big-wig's fundraiser; all the while the real reason they came out here was to be ferried down underground to meet with MJ-12 and the alien group down there. People wouldn't believe what was happening right underneath their neighborhood park.

"The magical rituals that EAD was founded on were just the tip of the iceberg. The real secrets were the elaborate network of tunnels that go deep underground to the base that house these recovered spaceships. And the aliens who took up residence there. These are the things very few people really know about. You have to get down there by being transported in a magical shuttle that the alien group provides. They're able to send us down to that secret base through miles of all that packed earth dirt by special teleportation.

"That's why most people working at EAD or even in the elaborate tunnel system underneath it wouldn't really believe the rumors of another, even more secret base where the aliens were. They'd see the MJ-12 people around, see the President, see all the secret government people. But almost all of the workers had no idea all these elites were being secreted from there to another base deep down below where the real heavy shit was going down."

Wilhelm pauses here to take another drink. He slowly breathes in and out trying to relax as he's getting a little worked up with his confession. He closes his eyes almost in meditation before he continues.

"They took me to their super-secret base because I was one of the top physicists at the time, and they wanted me to figure these spaceships out. I could only get so far with them. There was stuff they could do that me and all the other big brains they brought down there just couldn't figure out.

"Every time I was down there I thought that it might be my last. But they kept me alive. They were always watching me real close. I believe they even planted agents in my social circles up in my regular life in Pasadena to see if I ever talked about what I witnessed or what I was working on. I think my nosy neighbor was actually a government agent. Some of the guys at my tennis club would ask intrusive questions. They had all sorts of eyes on me. I had to be careful.

"But I don't care anymore. I'm dying. I want the world to know what's going on down there and what these jokers have been up to."

The old man slowly breaks into a smile and looks directly at my brother.

"And also to let everybody know the true origins of disc golf."

They both break into laughter as Sean moves into frame again with his disc golf bag. He pulls out of his discs and hands it to Wilhelm. The old man cradles the disc, bending it, eyeing its contours as he studies it.

"Ah, the Owl. Famous bird of Freemasonry. The first disc I ever threw. I remember when they designed this one. All of those scientists back in the day started with these oversized frisbees and they finally got it right with this one. All based on trying to figure out the flying saucers we had at the EAD garage. If we couldn't figure them out, well, at least we could transform those big unwieldy frisbees into these smaller, sleeker discs that have amazing aerodynamics. We made this sport!"

He gets reflective and emotional as he hands the disc back to Sean.

"I'd agonize over how the real flying saucers would pull off their amazing acrobatic maneuvers that defied logic and science and everything else our limited human intellect could understand, while the disc models we threw would all just come

DISC-OVERY

crashing down to the dirty ground after their short flights. But I would still love watching these plastic discs fly through the air, how they would glide with the wind currents, grandiosely flying too close to the sun, mimicking for a moment the alien craft they were a pale reflection of, before gyrating down unceremoniously to the dust of the earth again.

Wilhelm drifts off again, lost in all the memories of being out on disc golf courses.

"How I loved to watch them fly, spinning in that beautiful symphony of physics, where a disc is the most perfect aerial flying invention. I would have visions of us conquering the world with our guys up in flying discs putting on a show for the rest of the world who would cower at what we accomplished with this alien technology.

"There was a time here at EAD where we thought we were on the cusp of conquering the entire planet. If we could figure out these spaceships and engineer them ourselves, America would rule the world. There were a lot of high hopes. We felt like those astronauts going to the moon or the guys who figured out the bomb at the Manhattan Project. We were going to change the world and make our country the best."

He starts laughing again as he sips from the water bottle.

"And we all eventually failed. Couldn't figure them out. The only ones that could fly them weren't people. They were the aliens who were always lying to us about everything. All of our hopes and dreams were squashed. After a while, the government wanted nothing to do with us scientists who worked so hard trying to reverse-engineer these ships. The program folded, and the secret government made other plans at world conquest."

The old man closes his eyes again and the only noise in the room is the sound of his rhythmic breathing.

"How silly I was to get caught up in trying to rule the world. Ah, the follies of youth."

Wilhelm drifts off into silence, closing his eyes and taking a break from the heavy dose of reality he's immersed in. The rhythmic, almost melodic sounds of his breathing fill the room. He finally opens his eyes struggling to speak. He looks more somber and serious as he starts to continue with the next part of the interview.

"The government then started throwing us all under the bus. Firing us, marginalizing us, eventually killing us. You wouldn't believe it, Sean. How they ruined lives, destroyed careers. How they murdered. They ran roughshod over everyone involved in that program. When they realized we couldn't help them rule the world, they wanted to rinse their hands of us. And they did.

"But I managed to stick around, along with some of the others. One of them was a German. I got to know him. We bonded as we were in fear of our lives, wondering what Uncle Sam was going to do to us. He helped me through that crazy time. He had been through it before as he was part of Operation Paperclip and was brought over here after WW2 because of his involvement in the Third Reich's own flying saucer program. So he was used to being at the mercy of the government. Being expendable. He got me through it. I thought it was quite absurd, me bonding with a former scientist from the Third Reich."

Wilhelm reaches for the water again and grabs it and drinks. His eyes are wide open, their deep well of pain telling as much as his words about all the dark intrigue he'd been through.

"And as we got to know each other better, bonding under the imminent threat of being executed by secret government assassins, this man told me even more of the secrets of Oak Grove. How the tunnels were connected to a vast network of bunkers the elite had built for decades that extended to all sorts of locations underneath strategic locations throughout California and beyond. How there were other networks in different parts of the country. And how it was all tied into Tibetans who had built their own underground network of tunnels for the Nazis, and later the U.S. And how it was all tied into our moon landings and secret missions to Mars.

"This old Nazi," Wilhelm continued, "befriended many Tibetans early on in his career who told him all about how they were able to construct such magnificent underground systems. There were secrets even beyond the physical construction of them that were never divulged to their American masters. He spoke of how the Tibetans could teleport themselves to them at whim. Even from up on the surface. And how the Nazis never understood how they did it. The American government was astounded by this phenomenon."

Wilhelm stops and takes another break as he reaches for the water. He takes another sip as he mellows for a bit, looking up at the ceiling.

"This man bestowed on me these ancient Tibetan mystical secrets. Taught me these things in case I ever truly feared for my life. How I could get out of this underground base by teleportation. And how I could teleport back here, too.

Wilhelm looks straight at Sean now.

"It's about the prayers, Sean. The Tibetan prayers, when enunciated a certain way with their singing Tibetan bowls, the sound of it all had a magical power. It transports you. He would always talk to me about sound. How our government, the Tibetans and even the Reich had always known the power of sound, and how it can manipulate the space-time continuum around us.

"And so he taught me these things. How to teleport with these mantras and sacred prayers. I learned how to do these magical rituals, with Tibetan singing bowls while chanting their secret mystical words. And I'm going to tell you about them now, Sean. You will know these secrets. And you will be empowered by them. You will be able to teleport down into those tunnels far below, and even into the secret base below them. I was able to do this, and so shall you. And your assignment, Sean, will be to document these places, and put them on the internet so people can see the truth of what is really happening down here. That, Sean is what you are called upon to do. This is your mission. I have chosen you to impart this wisdom to because you are worthy, my friend. I'm entrusting this to you."

Wilhelm is looking directly at Sean now, who is standing to the left of the video camera.

"I will go down there, Wilhelm," Sean says, off-camera. "I want to help inform the world of what is really happening with UFO's and MJ-12. And the truth about the secret government, and all of the disinfo and lies, and expose it all.

"Wilhelm, I have seen all of the deception overseas in my contracting work. I've been used as a pawn in all their games, all their lies. Talk about being expendable. I've murdered for them. Tortured for them. I've sold my soul for what amounts to petty cash doing their bidding. And I can't live with myself anymore with what I've done. I need to do something righteous. Something to absolve me. To help me get my soul back. I need to help humanity instead of being in the pay of those who keep us all down. And I'm ready to die now. Ready to sacrifice what is left of my life to atone for all of the horrors that I've wrought upon the innocents of the world. I'm finally ready to do good. Even if I have to pay the ultimate price."

Sean steps forward into frame as he walks over to Wilhelm and sits down next to him on his bed. They both lock eyes.

"Many are called, Sean," Wilhelm says. "But few answer."

"I'm ready, Wilhelm. Ready to complete this mission."

Wilhelm reaches for a book that is next to the bed.

"Please get the Tibetan bowls over there," Wilhelm says as he points to the other side of the room.

"Bring them. Listen to my chants, Sean. Learn them now with me. Learn how to synchronize them with the bowls, and you will become godlike. And with this special power you will be able to expose these elitist power mongers and enlighten the world."

DISC-OVERY

Sean looks over at the bowls on the other side of the room where Wilhelm has pointed to. He gets up and walks out of frame to go get them.

And then for the next few minutes, I sit in utter amazement as I watch Wilhelm and Sean perform their magical ceremonies.

10

> Sylmar this morning?

I squint into the screen of my phone and peer up at the top of the message. It's Paul. And it's 6 AM. He woke me up. I'm glad he did. I miss those guys.

> Sure man what time

I text back.

> 8 am

> See you then bud

A smiley face comes back from Paul.

I get up and out of my pajamas I've worn for the last few days and step into the shower letting the hot water engulf me. I've been in a daze since seeing that doc with my brother and Wilhelm. I'm armed with the wisdom of the Tibetans on how to descend into the caverns, tunnels and the underground base itself underneath Oak Grove. I've even memorized the magical prayers and mantras, and know when to ring the Tibetan bowl to make it all happen.

I'm rehearsed but not ready. I was a high stakes risk-taker on Wall Street but I've never dreamed of doing anything like teleporting down into an underground joint alien/government base to take video footage. That's nuts. Yet this is what I'm taking on.

After I step out of the shower and get dressed, I look around for my disc golf bag. I find it underneath my coffee table and head out the door. Before I know it I'm on the way to Sylmar with Megadeth blasting away.

Before I reach the course, I stop off at the nearby liquor store. After all, what is disc golf without some brews? I purchase a case and notice all the discs for sale behind the counter as the clerk rings me up. How entrepreneurial.

Pulling into the parking lot, I see the guys near the 'putting green' practicing their putts as they sip on drinks. I park and get my disc golf bag and beer and walk over to them.

Paul, Gary and a new guy are there.

"Jeff, this is Tom. Bill's still locked up."

"He'll show up one of these days, hopefully soon," Gary says.

"All right, well, that's four. We have enough for teams," I say.

"Actually we have an odd man," Paul tells me. "Andy's passed out in my truck."

I look up and over into the truck and sure enough there's Andy passed out in the flatbed snoring loudly.

"He's passed out at almost all of the other courses," Paul says. "I refuse to carry his ass off a course again. Not gonna happen."

"I don't blame you," Gary chimes in. "Next time he pulls that shit, we leave him."

I put the beer down on the flatbed next to Andy.

"Help yourself, guys," I say.

We hang out and catch up as we imbibe more of the beers until we decide to start playing. We stuff as many of the brewskies as we can into our disc golf bags and make our way to the first tee. Andy—finally awake from his impromptu slumber, groggily follows us. We had woken him up by pouring beer on him. He cursed us at first, and then scolded us for wasting beer. I think the only reason he got up to play with us was to start drinking again.

We flip for teams and I get odd man out. Damnit. I'm all alone now, nobody to bail me out of bad throws.

"Hey, man," Gary says, "Andy and Paul told me you got an ace."

"Yeah, they told you about that, huh?" I reply.

"Where was it?"

"The first hole at Oak Grove."

"Are you serious?" Gary adds. "That's a tough hole. Nobody aces it."

"I got real lucky."

"C'mon, odd guy, you're up," Paul says.

I grab my beloved Diamondback and step on to the tee and peer through the trees barely finding the basket way off in the thick of the forest. So many damn trees.

I slowly move forward and turn my body as I reach back with the disc before I whip back around, turning on my right pivot foot as the disc bolts out of my hand and sails to the right of the cluster of trees. It glides fluidly along finding the little corridor of open space until it wraps around the last tree, hitting the ground and bouncing forward about thirty-five feet to the lower left of the basket.

"Terrific shot," Paul says.

"Yeah, man," Andy, "nice one. You're getting better and better."

Gary and Tom both nod their approval at me.

"Thanks, guys. We'll see how I hold up. We still got eighteen holes to go."

"Ain't that the truth," Tom says.

The rest of the guys take their shots as I kick back with my beer. We then grab our bags as we walk down to our second shots under the shade of the trees, drinking our brewskies. The light of the morning sun ripples through the trees as we walk, and I look up and see how it splashes off the desert mountains in the distance. It creates an orange-yellow hue that reflects down into the valley with a swirl of light and color.

I hear the birds of the trees start to chirp. They seem to be serenading us atop the branches as we walk below them. We walk along laughing and joking, the booze making its way through my system, giving me a perfect little buzz as I feel the soft earth below me, cradling my feet.

I wait for the other two teams to throw their shots, realizing that my shot was far and away the best of the bunch. Gary's shot goes off into the sidewalk which is OB, but Tom picks up the slack and shoots his disc right near the basket. Paul and Andy then proceed to hit pretty good second shots. I walk up to my first shot, take off my bag and grab my putter. I put my little marker disc at the top of my Diamondback and put my new favorite disc back in the bag, catching a glimpse of Alisa's scribble before it's lost in my collection.

I step up right to the tip of the marker and focus on the basket. There are three trees directly in front of it, so I decide to throw a high hyzer shot and hopefully wrap it around these trees and into the basket. I concentrate for a few more moments, visualizing the path of my putter before I throw it, and then send the disc off. It glides nicely until it starts its descent to the left. I'm watching it spin, almost mesmerized by the beauty of the red disc swirling in the air as the physics of its flight take it on its rhythmic mathematical journey. There's probably some equation that can perfectly figure out exactly where it's going to land. It sails right over the basket and hits a tree right beyond it. Thank God it didn't land on the sidewalk, which is OB and a big penalty stroke.

"You want to take another from there? You got two shots, you know," Paul asks.

"Nah," I reply. "I'll take two putts."

"Good idea," he says.

We all hit our putts and walk over to the next tee pad.

I'm still first on the tee pad throw a nice sidearm that stays low and hits near the second basket. The other two teams go, and we put our bags on and walk towards our second shots. I catch up to Andy as we walk along together.

"Still thinking about that billboard, man. Keep pointing out that demonic shit whenever we're around town. I want to see wherever it's hiding in plain sight."

"You got it. Plenty out there."

We splinter off as we go to our respective discs, and everyone shoots pretty good second shots but nobody birdies. We all putt out, and walk over to hole number three. We put our bags down on the bench and pound the rest of our beers.

We all dig into our disc golf bags and find another brew and pop it open as we all take turns driving off the tee pad for hole number three.

This time I hit a tree that's about fifty feet down the fairway. My good fortune has run out.

"Shit!" I exclaim.

"Hey you've had the tee for two holes now," Andy tells me. "You're gonna have to work for this one."

The other guys throw pretty good drives as we again get our disc golf bags and start to mosey on down the fairway to our second shots. My shot's by far the worst as I approach it quickly. I take out my Bomber disc which is a great fairway driver, which is something between a distance driver and a mid-range and get ready to throw a backhand shot towards the basket. I do a couple of practice throws with the disc in my hand until I finally let loose a shot that stays low to the ground and finally hits the grass near the basket and stops abruptly. Not a bad shot, but still about twenty-five feet from the basket. That's a tough putt.

I put on my bag and walk with the guys to their next shots. Paul and Andy throw their discs well. They both have easy putts to choose from, but Tom and Gary both overthrow their shots as their discs roll down the hill that's right beyond the basket. They start cursing as we all watch Gary's disc continue to roll all the way down to the other basket far below.

"Déjà vu," he jokes as we all laugh.

"Let's just putt out first so we don't have to wait for you to walk a mile to get your disc and come back," Paul says.

I three-putt so I double bogey on this hole. There goes my scintillating run of two holes. I wonder if I'll ever get back to even now that I'm two over— or ever regain the tee for that matter. Oh well, it's about having fun, I remind myself.

We finish the remaining holes of the front nine and go back to the parking lot and throw our bags on Paul's truck as we break open the cooler to get more beers. I shot two more bogeys and the rest pars, giving me four over for the first nine holes. Not too terrible for me, but it would've been nice to pick up a birdie or two. Gary and Tom are two under, and Andy and Paul lead with a four under. I'm way behind.

Paul breaks out a bottle of vodka and passes it around, and I take a nice big shot of it after I make sure it's not the vodka from the billboard.

We stuff our bags full of beer again, and we head over to the back nine and put our bags down at the tenth hole. This one's a rough hole as the basket is far off in the distance, behind a big cluster of trees that only leaves very narrow spaces to get through, on top of that, the basket is situated on a very steep slope. If you overthrow it, you are basically hiking down a small mountain to get your disc. We flip again for teams and I get Andy. Tom and Paul are the other team, and Gary is odd man. We all sip our beers as Andy has the tee.

He starts very high with the disc, reaching over his head in a throwing motion I've never seen before. I'm wondering what the hell he's doing as he moves forward and spikes the side of the disc down on the ground with all of his might. The disc ricochets off the earth, a flash projectile bouncing high off towards the oak trees until it slices back into the rocky surface several times until it finally settles into a barreling role like a runaway train. It's blazing a trail as it screams towards the trees until it slyly maneuvers between them, disappearing for a few moments before reappearing on the other side of the ridge, continuing its scorched earth path up the hill towards the basket.

The guys cheer as the disc starts careening to the right and races up the hill, finally making a broad arc back to the basket, encircling it once, twice, until it finally peters out, falling a mere ten feet to the right of the basket.

Everybody continues their applause as Andy turns and takes a bow. We even hear cheers from the other holes as people all around the course celebrate this magnificent shot.

We approach the man of the hour with our drinks, bringing one over to him, as we all toast this remarkable feat of disc golf. It's moments like this when Andy shows his old championship form from days gone by, when he ruled the disc golf courses with quite literally a disc golf bag of tricks.

"Alright, alright," Andy modestly says as he fends off the adulating hordes. "Back to golf. C'mon, Jeff. We haven't won diddly-squat yet."

I grab my Diamondback disc and meekly step up to the tee. Talk about a hard act to follow. I look dauntingly ahead at the row of trees that block the fairway, and the basket far beyond them. There's nowhere to go but right through those oaks. I move forward and launch my sidearm and the disc flies out of my hand in a nice line drive until it crashes right into one of the oak trees then falls down.

"Boink!" yells Gary.

"That sure was a boink," I lament.

DISC-OVERY

"Let's see if you boink, Gary," Andy pointedly says.

Gary takes a swig of beer as he moves towards his disc golf bag and takes out his Groove disc. He has massive forearms like Popeye. He steps forward and drives the disc forward as he snarls, putting everything he has into his backhand. The disc flies out and smashes right into one of the other pitiless oak trees that guard the basket.

"BOINK!" I hear from all around. Everybody laughs as they keep saying "boink" over and over again. I join in the chorus of "boinks" as Gary goes over to his beer sitting on the bench and pounds it.

"Okay, okay," he says.

The rest of the guys throw their discs right into the trees, too. We grab our bags and make our way down the fairway. I walk along with Andy as if I'm Tiger Woods' caddy. I pick up my disc along the way and put it in my bag. We keep walking towards his shot, sloping down through the oak trees and up the rocky hill moving to our right, periodically looking over our shoulders, making sure we don't get beamed by discs.

We put some distance between us and the guys as they are taking their time trying to figure out how to throw a decent second shot without overshooting the basket and rolling down the massive hill. We're pretty much secluded from the rest of the party as we walk along.

"Hey, Andy. I wanted to let you know that I'm going down into the underground bunker at Oak Grove."

He continues to look out towards his disc, saying nothing for a few moments as he continues to admire his incredible shot. He stops abruptly and brings his brew up slowly, gazing into the bottle as if peering into an oracle about what will happen to me on my impending adventure. He finally takes a swig of the beer and looks back over at his disc, then back at the tenth tee.

"I woulda designed this course so differently," Andy says wistfully.

He turns and walks towards his disc, and I quickly follow. I can see his face is troubled by what I've told him. He brings the bottle up to his lips again as he seems lost in thought.

"There are no known entrances to that base," he dryly states. "I know that area like the back of my hand, and I've looked at every nook and cranny, every possible secret passageway or entrance or tunnel, and I, nor anyone else I've ever known at the park, has ever been able to figure out a way in. It's impossible."

"So you know there's something down there then," I press him.

"Yes. I've heard a lot of stories over the years."

"My brother found a way in. The key is Tibetan mysticism. I can't explain it all right now."

He looks back at the other guys who are flinging the discs up from the oak trees. Andy stares at Paul's shot as it glides high above the basket before it hyzers down far to the left, sailing over the ridge and far down the mountain.

"Shit!" Paul screams from down in the oak trees.

"FORE!" the guys scream from behind us as we both turn around and see a disc wildly sailing straight at us. We both immediately stop as the bright green Parrot disc flies by so close that we can hear the sound it makes as it cuts through the air. We watch it go by us in a flurry as it flies up the hill, hitting the rocks, and skipping to the left another few dozen feet before it skips again and again. Tom's shot finally glides down the mountain following his partner Paul's inauspicious shot.

"Ha! We're gonna take the lead on this hole, maybe even by a couple of strokes. That shot sucked. Paul and Tom bit the dust. Let's see how Gary does," Andy says as he's ignoring the big elephant in the room that I've brought up.

We turn around and watch Gary getting ready to take his second shot from behind a tree. He has to be careful not to slam his arm into its trunk in his follow through. He whips his hand around and grunts loudly as the disc flies too high and starts to angle down to where the other group's disc just went.

"Shit!" he screams.

DISC-OVERY

Andy laughs. "There goes another duck. We're in good shape, Jeff. If you hit this putt, we'll be sitting pretty."

We turn around and continue to walk towards his disc as his face loses his smirk as he grows solemn again, as the gravity of what I've told him outweighs all the disc golf entertainment.

"Why are you going to do this, Jeff?"

"Unfinished business," I reply. "My brother started something, and I got to finish it."

"You're playing with fire, Jeff."

He's looking at me wide-eyed in all seriousness now. I look back at him, then look away. The guys are coming up the hill towards us.

"My life is meaningless, Andy. I've destroyed the lives of people I never even met by orchestrating deals that left them homeless and penniless. And that's just the tip of the iceberg with all the bad shit I did on Wall Street. I've never done anything righteous. I even neglected my own brother who needed me all those years. I was just selfish and self-absorbed, not caring about anyone except for me."

I turn to him and look at him passionately.

"It's high time I do something that puts myself at risk for others. People have a right to know the nefarious shit their own government is up to right underneath a park where they bring their kids to play soccer or go on picnics or go birdwatching. The place they built out of their own tax dollars. I'm tired of sitting on the sidelines, stumbling along in an alcoholic haze until I just fall down dead someday. I can't live like that anymore. I finally have found a mission after all these empty years. And I'm following through with it. Whatever happens, happens."

We finally get to Andy's disc and watch patiently as the guys make their way down the mountain and finally get to their discs. We soak in the silence of the park around us, sipping our brewskis as the wind combs through around us, washing away all the drama as we start to relax again. We watch the rest of the guys throw their way up the hill laboriously towards the basket.

"That's cool you found some kind of quest to be on," Andy says. "Even though it's completely fucked. I kinda have one, too."

"Oh yeah? And what's that?"

"Remember I told you about that course in Switzerland? The one where you can hear the chains ringing throughout the Alps? That's the one thing I really want to do before I die. Otherwise, I got nothing to live for. Except playing disc golf."

I take another long chug of my beer finishing it off. I squeeze the can to bend in the sides before I put it under my foot and stomp it into the size of a disc marker. Andy does the same with his.

Both other teams' discs finally drop near the basket after their long-suffering journeys into putting range. Andy's disc is now the furthest out.

"C'mon let's go putt for birdie," I say as I pick up the smashed beer can.

We walk over to Andy's disc, and I put the crushed can right in front of it as a marker and give him back his disc. The basket sits on that steep slope where a missed putt landing on its side could easily roll all the way down to where the other guys' discs went. I'm wondering if I just throw it conservatively and rest it up against the bottom of the basket to save par, and let Andy really go for the birdie. A fifteen-foot putt is a lot harder than it sounds, particularly with a treacherous slope like this in the backdrop. I'm nervous as hell.

"Go for it, Jeff, make a run at it" Andy says as if he's been reading my mind.

"Really?"

"Yeah. Don't worry about it going down the hill. We need a birdie. Time to separate from the pack. Hit it right in the middle of the fucking chains."

Andy's old killer instinct is rearing its head again. I nod at Andy as I settle into my stance and really focus on the middle of the chains in the basket. I hear the other guys finally walk up to us, and they stop and keep quiet as they see I'm gearing up to putt. I deeply concentrate on hitting the chains. It's very quiet in the park as it seems everything has paused to let me think about this shot. I fling it suddenly to the basket and it starts to veer slightly left and CRASH! It hits the chains and drops down into the basket.

"Yes!" I exclaim.

"Yeah, partner! There you go!" Andy yells.

The other guys come over giving me high fives as everyone celebrates my shot.

"Birdie!" Andy yells.

I feel exuberant. Andy and I are certainly leading the pack now.

We try not to be too gleeful as we all head to hole number eleven, perhaps the signature hole of the course. The tee pad is on a little cliff that overlooks a wide expanse of land, and the basket is far down below at the bottom of the big hill on top of a pyramidal wooden structure. It's a great hole.

"Well, you guys got the tee," Paul laments. "Let's get the show on the road."

I take out my lucky Diamondback and head to the tee pad. The view is incredible from the tee as the cliff overlooks the city of Sylmar. It's really fun to throw discs from this precipice. I emptied my entire bag the last time I was up here.

I take a big wind up and really chuck it with everything I got, praying I don't fall off the cliff. My feet get a little twisted and I let out a big grunt as I fling the disc too high to the right. I immediately know it's a bad shot. I watch it fly up to the sky only to come dramatically down to the left, heading straight for this massive tree that's like a natural castle over this section of the course. I grimace as it starts to head right for the top part of the tree. It hits it dead on as it disappears into the green branches. Then nothing. I wait for it to fall and start making its way down to the ground. It never does.

"Shit!" I yell. "That was my favorite disc! Fuck!"

"Dude, that sucks," Andy says.

The rest of the guys start cursing.

Gary finally gets up off the bench and starts walking down the hill.

"What are you doing, Gary? We gotta throw!" Tom asks.

"Get back here!" Paul chimes in.

"Nah, man. I don't let my friends' plastic get stuck in trees," Gary responds.

I watch in disbelief as Gary walks down to the enormous tree that towers up into the sky. It must be almost eighty feet tall.

"Hey, uh," I stammer, "is he thinking of doing what I think he's gonna do?" I ask in disbelief.

"Yeah, dude," Paul answers. "He climbs trees."

I start walking down to the tree as the rest of the guys follow.

"That's insane. That tree is gigantic," I exclaim.

Gary makes his way to the bottom of the tree and begins to climb up the trunk, wrapping his arms and legs around it as he slowly pushes up the tree. He finally gets up to the first branch which is about ten feet off the ground and does an impressive pull up to get his body around it. The dude is strong. I watch dumbfounded as he then proceeds to climb up branch after branch towards the top of the tree. Before I know it, he's about thirty feet up.

"Dude, Gary is totally crazy," I say. "I can't believe he's doing this for a cheap piece of plastic."

"He doesn't like to see his friends lose their plastic," Andy says matter-of-factly.

"Yeah, but he's risking his life!" I exclaim.

"He doesn't really see it that way," Paul responds as he cracks open another beer.

DISC-OVERY

Now Gary's up to around fifty feet, making his way to the next branch. He disappears as we see the leaves and branches engulf him until he finally reappears another ten feet up. I feel my heart racing as he's almost to where my disc is lodged in the tree.

"I see it!" he yells at us. I can't believe how nuts this guy is. If he falls, he's dead. He goes up another ten feet to the branch that the disc is on, my heart pounding. He then jumps up and down on the branch, trying to dislodge the disc.

"Is he out of his mind!" I yell again. "Jumping up and down on the branch that he's standing on?"

I look around at the guys and they seem only mildly interested in the spectacle far above. I guess they've seen this a million times before.

"He ain't the brightest bulb in the shed," Tom points out.

After what seems like an eternity, and thinking my heart is about to explode, the stupid beat up old disc of mine that probably is worth around five measly bucks, falls from the branch it's resting on that Gary is shaking with his feet. We all watch it hit a few other branches as it falls to the ground far below.

I look back up at Gary who's making his way down the tree now, branch by branch. I walk towards the bottom of the tree to the trunk until I finally see him come into view. After watching him descend the ladder of branches, he finally dangles off the last one, and let's go of the branch and falls to the earth. He gets up and pats himself off. He's covered with all sorts of dirt and tree sap.

"Anyone have any extra beers?" he asks.

"Dude!" I shout, almost in a state of shock. "My beers are your beers, man. Thank you! That was incredible! I can't believe you did that for me!"

"No big deal," he says.

I dig into my disc golf bag and pull out a couple of my beers and give them to him. He gleefully accepts them.

I grab my Diamondback off the ground, and we start to walk

back up the hill towards the tee at the top and I still can't believe what I just witnessed.

"Gary, I don't think anyone has ever risked their life for me like you just did!" I tell him.

"I don't like my friends losing their plastic to no tree," he dispassionately repeats.

I continue to look over at him and the rest of the guys with a big smile on my face as we all walk up the hill. I think about all the people I've known throughout my life. Nobody ever did anything like this for me.

I realize then and there that these guys are my best friends in the world.

11

I spend the next few days on the trails, rising early to see the twilight breaking through the last remnants of the night. As light spreads over the horizon, I'm enraptured as the days comes to life, feeling energized as my courage grows. I'm ready to go down into the underground of Oak Grove, into its mysteries and dangers.

I stay outside most of the time now, sometimes even camping for days on end. As I approach my imminent date with destiny, I am letting nature take me and cleanse me of all the toxic layers of modernity that have long buried away my warrior within. I've quit drinking. I fast. I push myself physically every day. I feel the pounds melt off me, as I'm getting leaner and meaner with each passing day, traveling deeper into the hills around me, going off trail as I test the boundaries of my pain thresholds.

I'm discovering how you can get lost in the pockets of wildlife in the hills and mountains that can happily engulf you, sucking you away from the city. All the machinery of modern life seems so distant, softly echoing from afar.

Occasionally I bump into hikers who look at me oddly. I'm covered with dirt and looking ragged since I've been out here for days. I live off the land, eating berries and catching and cooking little critters over fires that I start from scratch. Before I know it, several months have passed by.

I never planned on doing this at all. I just walked out of my house one day and decided to stay out in nature. It took a life of its own. I go back to the house to change clothes and get supplies, but I immediately head out again into the wilderness. So here I am, months in the bush, surviving like a wild man. Right in the middle of the city. I hear there are others like me in L.A. who do this.

Something has guided me to do this, to find the warrior within me and prepare for the challenges in front of me. I wasn't prepared before. But now I finally feel ready to finish what my brother started. To step into this secrecy going on for decades underneath the park in Altadena, and get the truth out there. I'm ready to risk it all. Ready to die if necessary.

I decide it's time to get ready confront Oak Grove as I've come back from my latest nature excursion that had lasted six days. My neighbor encountered me at my front door, stunned at the sight of me as Ive grown out my hair, grown a thick beard, and lost about forty pounds.

I have to get grounded again, and mentally prepare for my mission. I stick to the house now. No more nature expeditions. It is an adjustment to get back into the swing of regular life again, particularly driving around L.A. and feeling the city lifestyle start to once again make me soft. I must get on with my quest.

One Wednesday in the early dusk of the evening, I finally set off for Oak Grove. A full moon begins to emerge center stage as the darkness of the night settles in, cloaking me in its own furtive mysteries. The night now beckons me to its secrets as the cool air whips through my beard and long hair as I glide in and out of traffic through the intersecting highways seamlessly.

My disc golf bag is beside me in the passenger seat. I might as well play a few holes and blend into the scene as just another disc golfer before I perform the ritual on the course. My Tibetan

DISC-OVERY

singing bowl is in one of the side pockets of the bag, along with my tiny video camera.

I see the mountains of Pasadena in the distance. I've never felt more ready in my entire life as my car speeds along the expressway on my way to Hahamongna Park, that mysterious place where we throw discs.

I get to the park but avoid the entrance since it closes at sunset and they lock the gates. I turn onto a side street into a residential area and park a ways up the hill. I grab my disc golf bag and lock up the car then head down towards the park. Night is rapidly falling upon the city. I gaze up at the full moon staring down at me, wondering what the night will bring.

As I hike down past the entrance, the gate is still open. Cars with their lights on travel past me as I reach the first tee and set my bag down. I zip open the top of the bag and grab my Ogre then step onto the tee. The course looks deserted. Almost everybody has cleared out by now. I look out to where the basket is, and it's in the long position, which is far up and to the left, hidden in between a cluster of trees. I can already feel some of the anxiety of anticipation of the evening alleviate a little bit as I focus on the game. Disc golf always relaxes me.

I take a few deep breaths and glance up at the branch which hangs down from the tree on the left that extends along a large portion of the fairway. I pause as my eyes traverse this gnarly branch who's haunting features I've studied so many times before from this first tee.

As the night blankets the park, the branch starts to transform before my eyes, seemingly shapeshifting into the same ghoulish beings I saw on the billboard that one night with Andy. Eyes of demons start to form out of the dark outline of the branch, followed by mouths, ears, and faces as the monsters come to life with the night's arrival. They group together in a hideous clump of evil, rejoicing in the cover of the evening.

They seem to swarm over the branch as I'm wide-eyed with a new terror. I turn away from this devilish sight, turning back towards the bench where my disc golf bag is. I put my face down into my shaking hands as I tremble from that sight and feel the biting cold wind swirling around me, almost as if the demons' breath is blowing on me from that branch. I'm so cold and start to shake underneath the moonlight. The evil of this place is making its presence known immediately upon my arrival, warning me of its deep malevolent power.

As my face burrows deeper into my trembling hands, I hear the familiar shrill sound of the messenger animal who has greeted me here before. It is the crow, a bird as dark as the night, calling me to keep focused on my mission, to move forward into the ghastly unknowns of the night as bravely as it does. The crow hovers over the vast expanse of this park, nesting and living amongst all dark beings that accompany it during the long, enchanting nights of this haunted place.

I walk along now through the field making my way into the woods as the night now smothers everything. I pass the fourth hole, trudging forward as I finally pass its basket on the right before I crouch down underneath the fallen tree which is the entrance to the fifth hole on the course, otherwise known as the Middle Earth hole.

I pass underneath the fallen tree and make my way up to the clearing above where benches surround the tee on top of the small cliff overlooking the fairway. I walk into the tee area underneath the canopy of trees and sit down on the benches as I look out over the cliff into the black void of the wide open space below.

I close my eyes as I rest from the jaunt over here. The chilly air caresses my face and lulls me deeper into a relaxed state. The crow once again squalls in the distance, seemingly gesturing me lightly to continue. I'll move on in just a moment. It feels so good to relax in the chill of the night.

"Hello, mister."

I almost jump out of my skin as my adrenaline launches into the stratosphere as I bolt out of the bench. I'm completely freaked out and stumble around as my disc golf bag plummets to the ground. Frantically I look around until I find her sitting behind me next to a tree with the red ember of her cigarette sticking out in front of her face. I can feel my heart almost bursting through my chest, it's beating so fast. I collect myself and focus in on her.

"Alisa?" I ask warily.

"Who else, Jeff? You know any other female disc golf regulars around here?"

She laughs as she flicks the cigarette away.

"I haven't seen you in months. You've lost a ton of weight. And I like the new look with the beard," she says as she breaks out her pipe. "You look like you've been living out in the woods these last few months!"

She laughs as she lights up her pipe.

I smirk at her.

"Actually yes. Off and on."

She glances up at me as she spits out smoke and winks.

I pick up my disc golf bag and set it on the wooden bench and look over at her. She's wearing jeans and a padded winter jacket. A few moments go by as she continues to light up her pipe.

"I'll tell you why I'm out here tonight, Alisa."

I look up at her, barely seeing her face in the dark, wondering why I'm going to tell her about the crazy adventure I'm on tonight. She'll probably think I'm insane, but I don't care.

"Well, lay it on me, Jeff. Don't keep me waiting, mister."

"I'm performing a ritual here tonight," I say.

"A ritual?" she asks.

"Yes. Before my brother died, he was going to journey down to the secret base that is supposedly underground at the park here. It houses the secret government, recovered spaceships and even, supposedly, extraterrestrials. All sorts of shit is going on down there. I figure it's high time somebody documents it and gets the truth out."

I take out my tiny video camera and wave it in the air.

"My video is going to unmask this place."

She continues to work that pipe as the smoke escapes from her nostrils. I'm waiting for her response. She takes another long hit and blows the smoke out slowly.

"I don't mean to tell you I told you so but I'm the one who told you all about the UFO's I've seen here at the park. And all the crazy shit that goes on underground here. If I remember correctly, you were the one laughing and poking fun at me when I was telling you all this. Right, mister?"

"Yes, you were right, Alisa. It took me awhile to find out all about the mysteries surrounding Oak Grove, but everything you told me makes sense now. Digging into my brother's life led me oddly to here, and to all the strange secrets of this place. It's a long story but I'm finishing what my brother started. I'm going down tonight."

She smiles as her playful eyes lock on mine. Smoke billows from her lips.

"Sounds like fun," she says. "Can I go?"

Vintage Alisa.

"No. Too dangerous. Too risky. Who knows if I'll even make it out of there."

"I'm not scared, Jeff. I've always wanted to go to this underground base. I just never figured out how to get down there. I'm intrigued that you supposedly have."

Her alluring eyes finally fall upon me, seducing me with her hypnotic gaze as more smoke flows from her mouth, tickling it with her tongue as it leaves her lips and rises into the cool night air.

"Take me there, Jeff."

She moves towards me though the smoke, enticing me with her sultry beauty. Yes, I'll take this enchanting woman with me on this adventure into the magic realms of this ominous place.

"Okay, come with me then," I say to her as I take her hand as we walk down the hill past the cliff. She's seduced me just as

DISC-OVERY

the danger of this mysterious place has. We venture into the area near the cottonwood tree where we had that unforgettable rapturous experience.

I lead my mad princess once again to this site, flirting with a woman as treacherous as the ghoulish night around us. The crow flies over us once again, serenading us with its shrill battle cry as we ready for our ritual that will take us down into the ground.

The bushes surrounding the cottonwood greet us in a wild fury as the wind picks up, the lunacy of the evening crescendos as I walk with this beauty into the crossroads. We both look up at the cottonwood tree behind these dancing bushes as it beckons us once again, shaking to the ecstatic frenzy of this wild evening. Everything's picking up as I turn to Alisa, her eyes are wide with the bewitching fever encircling us.

"I've never seen it like this, Jeff," she says as the wind whips through her dark hair, enrapturing me in her dangerous erotic beauty. We stand at the gateway together, waiting to go to the other side.

Everything continues to cascade around us in the delirium of the evening as the dark realms await our descent. I turn to Alisa and gaze into her lurid eyes as the crow chants fiercely above us under the watchful full moon high above.

"Alisa," I say, "repeat these prayers with me. They were written by Tibetan adepts who helped build the underground tunnels here for the secret government. They lead to the secret base. Their mantras and magical words will bring us into an ecstatic state. Then the teleportation happens. And then we'll find ourselves deep down below in the tunnels. Are you ready?"

"Yes, Jeff," she says as her eyes fiercely meet mine as both of us realize that our paths have crossed now in the same destiny. Everything we've ever been through has prepared us to be together at this very moment.

I recite the prayers methodically and Alisa dutifully chants along with me. Our hands clench together tightly as we start our journey into the portal that will take us to the other side. I start to slowly feel a shift in my consciousness.

I reach down to my bag and unzip the side pocket to get the Tibetan singing bowl with the wooden mallet. I raise it up as I chant the prayers, Alisa wraps her arms around my neck. She patiently repeats them, concentrating intently on reciting them precisely and clearly. I start to feel my soul stir inside of me. The Tibetan words awaken what mystics have known for thousands of years.

My mind erupts into an ecstatic hysteria as I sway back and forth, watching Alisa do the same, a frightening power from a place unseen takes us over. We shiver in communion with the spiritual realms. I begin feverishly rubbing the mallet along the rim of the Tibetan bowl which rings and brings us to an even higher level of consciousness until the sound becomes so loud that we both start shaking uncontrollably. We've reached nirvana. I then throw the bowl into my bag, put the strap over my shoulder and grab her, hold her tightly against me as we convulse violently into a fervor before we are both thrown into a vortex which forms as my vision begins to blur. I clench her as tightly as I can and hold onto her for dear life. The trees around us sway and move, joining us in this mystical dance as this otherworldly tremor beckons us to the other side.

12

All I see is darkness. I don't know if I'm awake or if this is some kind of dream. I am exhausted. I feel dampness against my skin. It's so cold but I just can't get up. I'm at the sandy bottom of something. It's damp, chilly, and I remain lying on the ground, wherever I am. I'm just so tired, I want to keep my eyes closed. Maybe I'm just dreaming all of this anyway, and I'm passed out drunk somewhere in an alley way or outside of a bar on Ventura Blvd. or something. I'm just gonna sleep it off and everything will be okay. Gosh it's so cold and wet.

"Jeff! Jeff!! We are here! Wake up!"

I slowly open my eyes with only darkness greeting me as I squint trying to make out what is going on. The outline of a roof materializes as things come more into focus. Then I see her face peer over mine with those beautiful dark eyes wide with excitement as she starts to shake me.

"Jeff! We actually transported somewhere, those prayers worked! Get up! I need you to get up! Please!"

I struggle to sit up, and I can feel her hands trembling as she holds me as she helps. I guess she had no idea what she was in store for. I reach down to my disc golf bag and zip it open.

"Put this on."

I take out two ski masks from the bag and hand her one. I put the other one on myself.

I reach in again into the bag, grab my revolver and put it in the inside pocket of my denim jacket.

"You brought that?" she asks excitedly.

"Yes, of course."

We both stand and I put the disc golf bag over my shoulder.

I notice that the fright in her eyes has shifted to curiosity, as this girl has walked the tightrope of danger most of her life. The secret dimension to the place that she's always suspected of is now right in front of her eyes.

"Let's go," I say.

We start walking down the dark tunnel. Some light is provided by the lights that are about fifty yards away from each other on the ceiling. It goes on for about a half a mile underground until we finally hear something. We keep walking until the noise becomes more defined, like things you'd hear in a big automotive plant; tools being used, things being welded. Metal work.

As we continue forward, we hear voices echoing throughout a large area. Someone barking orders of where to put things. It sounds like a factory. Finally, the light picks up in the tunnel and we see a ladder in the distance secured to a wall on the right.

I point to it as I glance behind at Alisa and she immediately nods back at me. My heart begins to race as we arrive at the ladder and look up to where it leads. It ascends about thirty feet to an opening where noise from the area is now flooding through. I look over at Alisa and she's wide-eyed with excitement. I lean over to whisper to her.

"My brother's doc had a schematic of this place. We are at the back entrance to the big facility. Follow me."

"Okay," she says eagerly.

I grab the metal steps of the ladder and make my way up. I glance down over my right shoulder after a few moments of

DISC-OVERY

climbing to confirm Alisa is right behind. The noise from up top continues to flow through the little opening at the top of the ladder, and I hear many voices. It's a cacophony of shouting and arguing. All of this in a duet with the loud piercing cries of tools searing metal, and vehicles starting and stopping. There's a lot of activity going on up there.

I finally near the top, and right underneath the opening, I stop and take a few breaths. My heart is fluttering wildly. I wonder if I'll look through the opening above me into the snarling eyes of either an alien or a military sergeant. I finally force myself up the last couple of rings and put my face through the opening.

Holy shit. My mouth drops. I wasn't prepared for such an awe-inspiring sight. I'm looking at an enormous hangar with massive flying saucers. I count four of them. If this were a movie, it would be the perfect moment for that infamous *Spielberg Zoom In*. A phalanx of armed guards and uniformed military people are inspecting the aircraft and talking to dozens of workers in brown suits who are fiddling with the gargantuan spaceships. Sometimes the military personnel would yell and argue with the workers.

I realize Alisa is holding on right below me, so I look around to see if anyone's near the opening, and the only thing near it is a large balcony strewn with brown boxes stacked up against each other right below the view of the hangar. I peer my head in and look all around. Nobody is up here. Just hundreds of boxes.

I slowly pull myself up through the hole and there's a ladder on the other side on the wall that I make my way down. I finally step onto the platform, my heart pounding. I look up at Alisa who's poking her head through the opening at the top of the ladder looking out at the hangar, no doubt having her own *Spielberg Moment* behind her mask.

"C'mon, Alisa. Get down here."

She snaps out of her awe filled gaze and crawls through the small aperture and starts climbing down the steps. I study the barrier of boxes trying to find a little opening to look through. I put down my disc golf bag and grab my video camera out of the main compartment nestled in amongst the discs. Alisa snoops behind me until I find a small opening between all the boxes that has a nice view of the enormous hangar below. I put the camera in the tiny crevice and hit record.

I allow it to record for about ten minutes. The military continues to work on these ships while they continue to argue with the brown uniformed workers. Finally, one of the more authoritative military figures who seems to command a certain respect from everybody, puts two fingers in his mouth and lets forth a high piercing whistle. Everything suddenly comes to a halt and everyone looks over at the decorated general.

"Everybody take a break. Go get some chow in the dining hall. Get on outta here. Go!"

The workers jog out of the area through a door at the far side of the hangar. The military guy who whistled sits down at a table and a few other military people join him there. He appears to be the head honcho down here. I zoom the camera in on him and the military people joining him at the table.

"Private! Whiskey! Now!"

A military person who is near the flying saucers immediately breaks off into a jog in the direction of one of the big offices down in the hangar. When this guy gives orders, people literally run to do them. The head honcho military guy bristles at the rest of the uniformed military personnel who are sitting at the table.

"They want us to figure these things out? By takin' them apart? Are they nuts? We've been tryin' to do that for decades! What makes them think that this time will be any different? We've had the biggest brains in the world down here and it didn't take long for each and every one of them to hit a dang wall. We ain't figurin' nothin' out. The human brain ain't big enough!"

The private returns with a big whiskey bottle on a tray full

DISC-OVERY

of glasses and sets it on the table. The soldier places the glasses in front of all the military brass and leaves.

One of the other military men finally speaks up.

"Regardless, we want all our friends and foes alike to think we figured out how to fly them."

"How you gonna pull that one off, Bob?" The head honcho general shouts. "With your bogus laser light show? Holograms of the ships? You honestly think that'll fool anybody?"

The general laughs as he pours himself a whiskey. As soon as he puts the bottle down, a flurry of hands wrestle for it.

The general downs the bourbon.

"Pass that goddamn bourbon back here," he demands.

The bottle starts to make its way back to him, with some pit stops at empty glasses along the way.

"They're just a bunch of elitist pricks on this committee. I'm surprised they let my country ass on it."

The bottle finally arrives back in front of him. He looks at how much is left and scowls, he then refills his glass to the rim.

"MJ-12, you hear that," the general yells through the hangar. "They're getting a little carried away with themselves and this place. We are not friggin' magicians here. Every time I go see a magic show in Vegas I pay big bucks for, I don't even know how THEM guys do it. So, with a bunch of nerds from MIT or CalTech, I'm supposed to figure out the secrets of space and time of these ungodly flying saucers? Ain't happening! They're getting' a little delusional, thinkin' that we can actually back-engineer friggin' *anything*!"

The general takes a big gulp of the bourbon. He glares at the now empty bottle, shooting daggers with his eyes in the direction of the private patiently standing by. The private dashes away.

"Year after year they throw a new batch of geeks at me, supposedly with some new Einstein rockstar and they always go home with their tails between their legs!"

The soldier comes back with another bottle of whiskey,

opening it up as he rushes to the table, and immediately pours the general another glass. The general motions for him to keep pouring to the rim. The general snatches the new bottle from the private and sets it down next to the empty bottle. The nervous private salutes and heads back to his station near one of the flying saucers. One of the other military men at the table, who has a more dignified look, grabs the new bottle and pours himself another drink then meekly speaks up.

"That laser light show you're referencing...the deputy director from the CIA wants to put a hologram of these ships over Russia and China, showing them we've figured it out and are piloting it."

"That guy from the Agency is a nut job," the general exclaims. "I can't stand that piece of shit!"

He finishes off his bourbon and slams down the glass.

"Bunch of power-crazed pricks!"

"Don't say that too loud," another military man at the table says. "They won't ferry us back home!"

"What are they gonna hear me through tons of earth? Dumbass."

Snatching the bottle of bourbon back, the general pours himself another. Keeping the bottle directly in front of him. "We should get those damn Tibetans to build us another tunnel system that goes from here all the way up to EAD so we don't have to depend on them to hyperdrive our asses back and forth from here. They're friggin' usin' this against us, always makin' us feel we can be left behind down here for good if we don't do their bidding. I'm sick of their shit!"

"Well, general," another one speaks up, "they're coming down here soon so we have to get ready to play the game."

The general grumbles as he drinks his bourbon.

"Now look," another of the top brass says a little nervously, "we don't want what happened at Dulce to happen here. That committee, they play for keeps and so do their little alien buddies. We must placate them or Jesus, who knows what they'll do."

"I don't placate nobody," the general retorts.

The rest of the military personnel nervously drink from their glasses and silence hangs over the meeting. You can feel the tension in the air even where we are. One of the other military guys at the table speaks up.

"Al, you've been very recalcitrant lately. These are not the kind of people you want to piss off."

"I'm a goddamn five star general, they better listen to me. They need me for all this alien bullshit, not to mention all those dirty little wars they fight."

He shoots down the bourbon once again, and he is noticeably getting quite inebriated.

"I'm friggin' indispensable to them. Who the hell else is gonna quarterback all this shit? Can you imagine anyone else in charge!"

The military guys at the table look around at each other sheepishly. They go back to their drinks as they finish off their bourbon.

"Well, someone say something, goddammit" the general blusters.

The other military personnel glance at each other, almost drawing straws in the ether amongst themselves as they wonder who's going to speak up. Finally, a slender general who looks to be in his sixties gathers the courage to say something.

"Al," he says in a very somber tone, "they're getting very impatient with you. I think they're coming down here to set you straight."

There's a long silence as that truth hangs in the air for a while. You can cut the tension with a knife. Even the general looks down into his glass with a newfound sobriety as the effects of all the whiskey he's imbibed can't mask the hole he's dug himself into.

"Well, it don't matter. Y'all got my back, right?

All the other military guys slowly look back at him, expressionless. The silence is deafening until a uniformed military person enters through the doors that the workers had exited out of earlier. He stops and salutes before he addresses the seated military personnel.

"Gentlemen. The ship has arrived."

"All right, here we go," the general says.

What seems like an eternity passes before the doors finally swing open and about a dozen men enter, half of whom are wearing military uniforms brandishing weapons, the others in suits. And behind them is a gray alien. It stands about 4 feet tall. Queue up another *Spielberg Zoom*. Alisa and I glance at each other, exchanging looks of *holy-shit-I-can't-believe-this-is-happening* with our eyes.

This new group make their way to the military men around the table, and the general pours himself yet another drink. The general stares at the bourbon then raises it to his lips as he looks up at the entourage arriving at the table.

"Well, now. What can I do you for?" he asks, setting down his glass and reaching for the bottle of bourbon.

The suited man at the head of the group immediately whips out a gun from his inside pocket and shoots the general in the head. The general, face frozen in his final expression of smug annoyance, slumps out of his chair to the ground. Those standing at the table gasp and freeze. One of them seems to glance at the bourbon bottle, most likely wishing he'd poured himself another drink.

"Nothing, general," the man says coldly. "You really can't do anything for me now."

A bourbon glass crashes to the ground. The uniformed personnel now have their machine guns drawn, waiting to see if anyone makes a move. My hands shake as I'm holding the video camera.

Nobody does anything.

DISC-OVERY

The suited man goes over to the table as he looks over the generals who continue to stare straight ahead, doing a very poor job in masking how terrified they are. He reaches over and grabs the bottle of whiskey out of the dead general's hand. He lifts it up, looking at the label.

"In all the years I've known Al, I could not figure out why he drank this crap."

He picks up one of the glasses from the table and pours himself some of the bourbon. He takes a quick sip and grimaces as he swallows it down.

"Awful!"

He begins laughing menacingly as he walks around the table. The military brass are shitting bricks.

"This was on the government's tab, so he really could've ordered top of the line stuff. But he stuck with this bottom of the barrel garbage."

He looks down at the general sprawled across the ground with his mouth agape. I can't help but wonder what smartass remark the general was about to say.

"That was Al's problem. No taste."

He shakes his head as he looks at the pool of blood now spreading around the General's head.

"Low class. Totally wrong man for the job. I warned every-body! But they were swayed by his—I don't know—what do you call it? Texas hubris? I think some of my colleagues on the committee have watched too many John Wayne movies."

He looks at all the military brass around the table. They are glassy-eyed, looking straight ahead or off to the side, afraid to make any kind of eye contact.

"But the problem is, if you get fired from this job, well, we don't just give you a multi-million-dollar buyout and let you go home like they do when they get rid of the Longhorns' coach. Nah, with this job, if you become a problem, you're done. There's only one way out."

He raises the glass again and studies the bourbon against the light. He finally musters the courage to finish it off and shoots down the rest. He slams the glass down and starts walking around the table, grimacing from the booze as he stares down the military people. They continue to look completely petrified.

"I would hope that all of you will continue to want to work with us. Because, well, you can't just quit. So, are we all good here? Are we all still on the same page, gentlemen?"

They all nod in unison. The man in the suit scans each of their faces for an affirmation. He walks back to his cortege then turns around again to address the generals.

"You know, I'm in the same boat as all of you," he says. "I got people I have to answer to as well. It's a chain of command. Hey, some of those I gotta answer to aren't even people. Right, little fella?"

He looks over at the gray alien standing nearby as the rest of the group all defers to him. He smiles broadly.

"There's only way out for me, too, guys. And that's why I have every intention of staying in. I would advise all of you to do the same. Because, after all, membership does have its privileges. I'm gonna send down a few cases of Maker's Mark on the next shuttle."

He continues to smile as he looks around one last time at all the military generals then starts laughing as he heads out of the hangar towards the exit door as his entourage, including the little gray alien, follows him. He stops when he reaches the doors and turns around.

"Let's keep working on those ships, gentlemen. I'd hate to beam a stupid hologram up over Russia. I'd rather send over the real thing."

He turns and leaves as his entourage follows him out the large doors. The gray alien disappears into the middle of the group as they exit the hangar. The remaining generals let out a collective groan as one reaches for the bourbon.

"Private!" the dignified one calls out to the soldier. "We're gonna need another bottle."

He gestures over to the dead general sprawled out in a pool of blood. "And clean up that goddamn mess!"

"Yes sir," the private replies. "Right away."

The private turns to two of the troops at the entrance of the hangar.

"Go get a body bag from upstairs. They're somewhere in the middle of the hallway with all those boxes. Quickly!"

"Yes sir!" one of them exclaims.

My heart stops as I look back at Alisa who's been looking over my shoulder the whole time. We both look at each other in sheer terror, our Spielbergian awe gone. Shit just got too fucking real.

I can barely move. I look down and see the two military personnel move quickly to the staircase. I grab my disc golf bag and quickly pivot to my left in a panic. My foot catches on to Alisa's leg, and I tumble down. All the discs spill to the ground as I curse myself for not zipping up my bag.

"Shit!" I whisper loudly to Alisa. "Get outta here now! I'll be right behind you. Go!"

"Hey, what was that up there? Did you hear that?" I hear from below.

Panicked adrenaline races through me. I get up and quickly gather the discs around me stuffing them into the bag along with the video camera. My hands are shaking as I zip it up. I throw it around my neck and race up the ladder rungs after Alisa who's already made it through the opening.

I hear the two soldiers making their way up the stairs as I throw my legs through the hole. Glancing down, I see Alisa is almost to the bottom. I put my feet alongside the outer rung of the ladder and hold on with my hands as I slide down the ladder and nearly crash into Alisa who darts out of the way before I slam to the ground.

I grab her.

"Repeat the Tibetan prayer with me, quick!"

As we both recite it, I hear shouts from above as Alisa's terrified eyes start to fade from my view and we escape into another dimension.

13

I spend the next few days hiding out in my house. Talk about going past the point of no return. Well, I'm there. I have evidence of a United States military five star general being murdered along with proof of a secret underground base and our government in cahoots with aliens, working on retrieved flying saucers.

I routinely suffer panic attacks and my place is littered with whiskey and vodka bottles. Occasionally, I pull back my window shades ever so slightly and peer outside of them, into the woods behind my house where just a few days ago I was living wild and free. Now I am a prisoner to the secrets I've discovered.

I'm terrified about Alisa's well-being and I'm kicking myself for inviting her along. I could have gotten her killed down there. This kamikaze mission of mine should have been a solo adventure. Now she's exposed to all sorts of dangerous repercussions. How careless of me.

I've even thought about destroying the memory card in the camera and forgetting this whole thing. But in all good conscience, I can't. I've come this far. I must complete my mission. I just have no idea how to get this out on the internet without leaving some kind of digital footprint. Maybe it's a lot easier than I think it is, but I just don't want to toss it online and have government agents at my door. They have their methods of finding out who uploaded it and where. I need to figure out the right way to do it.

I spiral, obsessing if they could identify us even with the ski masks we were wearing. I seriously doubt it. Even if there were facial recognition video cameras down there, I don't see how they could pinpoint the identity of me or Alisa. Also, I had left my cell phone at home. No way they could have tracked me on that.

I'm still paranoid. Maybe they have cameras all over that area that captured me before putting the ski mask on. Or got a make on my car even though it was far up a hill away from the park. It was dark out but who knows. I'm messing with people who play for keeps.

The next couple of days are spent making sure my offshore bank accounts are squared away. I put anything of value into a couple of boxes and into the trunk of my car. Just in case things get hairy and I have to bolt.

Sometimes the fear and anxiety is so excruciating I want to run screaming out of my house and back into the forest. Instead I pound vodka or whiskey in an attempt to pull myself together.

Then there are other times where I smirk to myself through my tears as I can't believe I actually pulled off what I did. Finally, I did something real with my life, and all for the benefit of the people out there in the dark about the government's lies. I'm redeeming myself for everything I've done in my past.

Every faceless person who went homeless, whose lives I wrecked while profiting from the real estate crash and economic meltdown. Not everyone was a loser in that catastrophe, certainly not my firm and I. But I lost so much from being involved in all of that. I lost my soul. Now, at great risk to my personal safety, I'm getting it back.

DISC-OVERY

After all these lost years, I finally feel at peace, with a forgiveness and a self-respect that have been hard-earned through this journey of self-sacrifice. No matter what happens to me, I have arrived. I'm fulfilling a mission that took far too long to figure out. I'm ready for any and all consequences.

After a few more days, I'm feeling much better and realizing I must get out of the house and do some shopping. The cupboards are basically empty. Funny how buying toilet paper could make you feel so normal again. I appreciate the frenetic activity of the Friday afternoon traffic and the hustle of people finishing their work week and gearing up for the weekend. After my self-imposed isolation it's reinvigorating to be part of the urban scene once again.

I study the people scurrying around and wonder if they appreciate being alive in the moment today, despite the daily pressures or problems they face. Most look hurried and unhappy, with glum looks of stress and hardship. They should be savoring every morsel of fun and freedom they have.

My cell phone beeps with a text alert. I put my grocery bags down on a park bench and take out my phone.

> up for golf tomorrow? We goin to oak grove

I smirk to myself. My disc golf buddies are completely oblivious to my horrifying adventure.

I let out a sigh and shrug. I might as well get on with living. Here I go back to the scene of the crime.

> sure Paul what time?

> 9 am

> confirmed see u then

Playing golf and hanging out with my friends should put

me on a quick road to mental recovery. I need to feel normal again. I have nothing to lose.

Rejuvenated, I smile at the next girl that passes me on the sidewalk. She's oblivious, much like the other lost souls who drearily stare past me into the metropolitan landscape.

I get in my car and drive off, happy to have friends to hang out with tomorrow. Friends to laugh and drink with, and to play the sport that has opened my eyes to so much; not just flying saucers and government conspiracies, but to the joys of friendship and the wonders of nature.

I'm feeling better already.

I chuckle to myself as I drive along Ventura Blvd. recounting their shenanigans, appreciating the friendship they've extended to me. Pulling me out of the dreary depths of this complicated phase of life called adulthood. I spot a liquor store after Laurel Canyon and decide to grab beverages for tomorrow. I can't wait to leave behind this tortuous self-imposed isolation of fear and paranoia and start having fun again. I grab a case of the good stuff, then laugh out loud as I also grab half a dozen of the green apple concoctions.

When I arrive home, I'm whistling to myself and appreciating that I live in such a beautiful area.

As I open the door, I hear the annoying noise of a helicopter which stays around for the next half an hour. I guess they're looking for someone in the park next door, or, god forbid, this neighborhood. I slam the door shut and lock it.

I retreat to a college football game on cable and crack open the first green apple drug-in-a-can I've had in a couple of weeks. Yup. Still strangely wonderfully disgusting. I relish its signature potent buzz as I gleefully toast to myself to the first good day I've had in a while.

* * *

DISC-OVERY

I wake with a splitting headache and a parched mouth. I twist and turn in my bed. There was something I was supposed to do this morning. I lay still in an attempt to will away this hangover. Finally, through the murky depths , it finally dawns on me. I have a disc golf tee time at 9 AM.

I grab my cell phone from my bookshelf next to my bed to check the time. It's 9:30. *Dammit!*

The adrenaline shocks me fully awake. I throw on some clothes, pound some water, then I grab my disc golf bag, slinging it over my shoulder. As I'm about to open the front door, I pause, then rush to the fridge grabbing the case of beer and three remaining green apple concoctions.

The deafening sound of helicopter blades greet me as I head out the door. I ignore the cacophony. One of the drawbacks of living a little too close to Ventura Blvd. and right next to a public park. Shit happens around here all the time. Sirens and choppers are a constant.

I curse myself for oversleeping. Oh well, if I make good time, I'll still be able to play the back nine with them.

I allow my paranoia and fear of the mysterious Experimental Aerolab Dynamics center to slip away. Today isn't about intrigue or my personal mission. Today is about good times, friendship, and disc golf.

14

I make good time arriving at 10:15 AM. I get out of the car stuff as many beers as I can into my disc golf bag. Whatever doesn't fit I stuff into my front sweatshirt pocket. I look like I have an untreated hernia. I walk to hole number nine first. I'll make my way back from there hoping to bump into the guys.

"Yo, Jeff!"

I turn around to the other side of the street at hole number ten, and all the guys are there.

"Yo! What up?" I yell back. I practically run over to them, hobbled by the cans in my sweatshirt.

"Look who's back!" Paul yells. "Barely recognized you with that beard!"

"And that new hairdo!" Gary chimes in.

"You look cut, too, bro. Damn you lost a ton of weight!" says Bill.

"Thanks, Bill! You jailbird!" I reply. "I got your fav beverage!"

"No way!" he says. "Tequila?"

"No, dumbass! That green apple monstrosity you got me hooked on," I laugh.

"That ghetto shit?" he laughs.

"Here, man."

Bill's burly arms reach out to grab one of the green apples. He smiles broadly as we both crack them open.

"Nice to see you again, Bill," I tell him. "I'm glad you're out."

"That makes two of us. No disc golf on the inside."

I hand Paul the last green apple.

"Nice to see you stranger," he tells me.

"Yeah, man, it's been too long. Sorry I'm late. I had a slow start this morning."

"No probs, dude. You made the back nine."

"Where's Andy?"

Paul looks a little dower at the mention of Andy's name.

"Andy's in the hospital, man."

"Are you serious?"

"Yeah, man. Not lookin' too good."

"No way," I say dourly. "I just saw him not too long ago. What happened to him?

"What do you think? Liver finally tanking on him."

I somberly look down at my beer.

"Which hospital is he at? I'll go visit him," I respond.

"He's at County," Paul replies. "Don't put it off. I don't know how much longer he's gonna be with us."

I try to absorb this terrible news as a wave of gloom rushes through me.

"Hey dude," Bill says, "one thing I know, Andy wouldn't want you all sad on a disc golf course."

"Yeah, Bill, you're right," I reply.

"I brought a case of beer for us. Lemme go get it."

"Dude that's awesome but we got plenty. We met these two really cool dudes on the front nine before you came. They've been feeding us beers non-stop! It's like they have an endless supply in their van. Here, lemme introduce you to them."

"Cool."

We start toward the other side of the course to hole number

ten. There's a bench over to the right and the rest of the guys are hanging out there with the two new dudes.

"Look who's here everybody!" Paul yells over to them.

I see some familiar faces. Tom and Hurlie are there along with some other guys we've played with before. Seems like everybody except for Andy showed up for the party today. Or maybe it's just the fact that the new guys brought so much free booze. That has a way of attracting a crowd out on the disc golf course.

The two new guys stand up as they've been laughing with the guys, one of them reaches into the cooler in his van and grabs a beer then walks over to meet me. He's pretty tall, around six foot with cropped dark hair.

"These are two of the coolest dudes we've met in a while," Paul says. "Especially, since they seem to have an endless supply of brewskies!"

The new guy hands me a beer. I take it with one hand and reach to shake his hand with the other.

"I'm Gerald, nice to meet you," he says to me.

"Jeff," I tell him as we shake hands. "Nice to meet you. Thanks for the beer."

He slowly shakes my hand, almost not letting it go. He perks up and becomes more intense. The smile and laughter vanish from his face.

"Jeff," he says looking directly into my eyes. "Awesome meeting you, pal."

I get a strange vibe from him. His grip tightens and his personal space encroaches mine. He has a weird sort of corporate tinge to him. Coming from that world, I pick up on it immediately. He finally releases my hand and continues to give me a penetrating look. His friend comes around his right side and extends his hand.

"Hey there, Jeff. I'm Chuck. Nice to meet you." He also gives me a weird piercing look, like he's trying to read my mind. He's a little shorter than Gerald but cut from the same cloth, like they're right out of a financial house on Wall Street.

"Nice to meet you, too," I lie. I don't like either of these guys. They seem to be sizing me up. I'm reminded of all the yuppies I used to hang around in my other life.

"Yo, man!"

I look over their shoulders at Hurlie who's coming over from the bench.

"Hurlie!"

I gladly pivot around both new guys and walk over to Hurlie. I notice their eyes follow me as I move around them. I slap fives with Hurlie and give him a man hug.

"Glad you made it out today, man. Totally want to catch up with you. It's been a while," I tell him.

"Likewise, partna. Haven't seen you in like, forever. I like the mountain man look."

"Well, c'mon guys! Let's flip for teams. We're gonna have like five or six teams today," Paul says.

We lazily walk over to the tenth tee and set our bags down. Everyone takes out a disc. The tenth basket ahead has a slight curve to the left in its location today. Perfect for my Valkyr. Haven't used that disc in a while, time to break it out. I flip through my discs looking for the yellow disc. I can't find it. I flip through all the discs again. Not there.

"C'mon, dude," Bill says. "We're waitin' for you!"

I look up a little frustrated. The Valkyr is perfect for this hole. *Where the hell could it be?*

"What's wrong, man?" Paul asks.

I look down at my bag and reluctantly grab my Ogre.

"I guess I lost my Valkyr. I loved that disc. And you gave it to me, Paul. That day we all first met. It's not in my bag. Shit."

I get up and join the group . We raise our discs to flip them. Chuck looks over at me with a serious look.

"You lost your Valkyr, huh?"

"Yeah. Sucks. It was perfectly broken in. I'll miss it."

Chuck looks over at Gerald. They both look over at me.

"Yeah," Gerald says. "I hate losing discs. Maybe it will turn up somewhere."

I glance at him and his eyes remain locked on me. These guys are weird. I wish they weren't here and I could just hang out with the guys.

"Yeah, maybe it will turn up," Paul says. "I remember I made you write your name and cell number on it when I gave it to you. Who knows? Maybe there's a good Samaritan golfer out there who'll return it to you. It happens."

"Don't hold your breath," Bill says. There's a chorus of snickering laughter.

We flip for teams and I get Hurlie. Cool. We can hang and talk.

As we begin, everyone throws with varied results. The new guys aren't bad. My shot was awful, almost sailing past the fence far ahead of us where there is a farm. I'm not used to throwing that disc on this hole. Hurlie throws a great shot, though, sailing smoothly until it hyzers beautifully to the left—landing in the dirt, skipping to the left of the basket. A textbook shot.

I haven't played with Hurlie in a while. I'm reminded with this shot how good of a player he is. What he lacks in sheer power he makes up for in being totally smooth with a disc, and superbly accurate. He lights up a cigarette as we wait for the last team to throw. When they finish, we grab our bags and walk toward our discs around the basket. The groups separate and move towards our respective shots.

"How you been, man?" he asks.

"I've been, uh, well, a lot of weird shit has happened. We gotta talk."

"Okay. You want to come over to the house sometime this week?" he asks me.

"Sure."

DISC-OVERY

We take in the serenity of the course as we walk. It sure was a lot different here the other night.

"What do you think of those new guys?" I ask him.

He reaches for another cigarette.

"They been out here non-stop the past week, maybe longer. I don't like them. They too friendly. Tryin' to be best buds with everybody way too quick. I think they might be narcs."

"Yeah, there's something about them I don't like either."

"I hope nobody breaks out they pot here. Because they might bust us on the spot. I know I'm just gonna keep drinkin'. I guess they would've busted us for open container already, but they seem to be interested in somethin' else," Hurlie says. "Maybe the city starting to crack down out here. They might be gettin' complaints from people in the park again. That happens every couple of years out here."

"They remind me of guys I used to work with. I don't trust them at all."

We approach his shot and take off our bags and put them on the ground. I take out my marker and put it on the front edge of his disc and pick it up then hand it to him.

"Thanks," he tells me.

Hurlie's shot was the best of the group, so we stand together and watch the other four teams throw. We are traveling in a big group today.

"You know what they call a group this big?" Hurlie asks me.

"No."

"They call it a sponge. Sponge group."

He laughs as we both sip our beers. Another disc golf term to file away.

We watch everyone throw, and all of the teams get real close to the basket for a decent putt. Everyone's on track to still make par. We have a chance to make birdie, and it would be nice to get ahead of everybody this early in the round. I take out my putter and go to the marker. It's about a 25-foot putt. I concentrate and visualize the trajectory of my putt on a slight hyzer. I raise my disc up to my eyeline and finally let it go. It glides right on the visualized path before hyzering back into the chains.

Everyone erupts in cheers. Hurlie comes over to me and slaps me five. The rest of the teams come up and congratulate me. I almost turn bright red with how much I am blushing.

"Dude," Paul says, "we're gonna start calling you Hollywood Hyzer. You got that shot down, man."

"Aw, thanks, bro. Just lucky," I say.

Bill's team is the only one who misses both their putts. They finish with a bogey as everyone else shoots par. We're the only ones who got a birdie. We move to the eleventh hole which is to the right as we trudge over to the other side of the field.

"We got the tee now, dog," Hurlie says to me as he smirks. "Let's take it to these guys."

We keep the tee for the next six holes before we finally lose it with a bogey on the sixteenth hole to the two new guys. They've been struggling during the round but have managed to keep up with the rest of us, and they finally hit a birdie.

"We got another round of beers for everybody after we're done with this round, fellas," Gerald says as he proudly mounts the tee. "And we got sandwiches for everybody, too!"

Everyone cheers at this announcement except for Hurlie and I. After getting through the next two holes, we sit on the benches at the eighteenth and last hole. Bill breaks out his weed. He tokes up, and then passes it around as Hurlie and I both wait for the two new guys to break out their badges and bust Bill. But they don't. In fact, they both toke up when Bill passes them the pipe. Hurlie and I exchange quizzical looks.

Finishing off the last hole, Hurlie and I win the round with a four under. I pretty much rode Hurlie's coattails but didn't make any huge mistakes I also hit some key putts throughout the round to really contribute to the win.

Back in the parking lot, everyone congregates around the new guys' white van like pigeons at a park waiting for breadcrumbs. They pass out beer and sandwiches, and everyone wolfs them down, also drinking every last beer the guys throw at them.

After about half an hour, Paul has to go. He takes Bill, Gary and Tom with him. We say our goodbyes, and I turn to Hurlie and ask him if he's got another round in him. I haven't had my fill of disc golf yet, playing only nine holes. We also need to talk. He agrees. We nod over to the two new guys at their van as we depart, and thank them for the sandwiches and beer.

They give each other an odd look then Gerald turns to me.

"Hey man. Would you mind if we joined you? We'd really love to play another round before we have to go. We'd bring along a bunch of beers. Whatdya say?"

I exchange a glance with Hurlie, searching for an excuse not to play with them. Hurlie says nothing, and there's an uncomfortable silence as I can't bring myself to turn them down.

"Uh, yeah guys, sure. C'mon, let's go flip for teams," I say.

We head for the first tee, not waiting for the other two to catch up. I'm wonder if it's too late to make up some sudden excuse to suddenly leave the park, but I can't think of anything. I look over at Hurlie who rolls his eyes.

Along the way, we look up to the sounds of another helicopter coming in low, gliding along the tops of the trees. It's one of those weird multi-colored helicopters from EAD. Hurlie lights up a cigarette, narrowing his eyes and studying it suspiciously.

"They never fly this deep into the park," he says. "I never seen nothin' like that."

It noisily swoops through the park traversing far above to the right then moves towards the direction of the highways.

As we arrive to the first tee, be set our disc golf bags down. We sit on the bench, waiting for Gerald and Chuck.

"So you still think they're narcs," I ask Hurlie.

"No," he replies, "but they up to somethin'."

"I went down to the base the other night, man."

Hurlie's eyes widen in disbelief while taking a long drag from his cigarette.

"You actually went through with it. You crazy mofo."

"Hey, have you seen Alisa around lately?" I ask him.

He turns to me and smirks.

"Only in the back pages of the Weekly," Hurlie says, laughing.

Gerald and Chuck approach handing us both beers.

"Flip for teams?" Gerald asks enthusiastically.

Hurlie and I slowly nod as we take the brews. We flip and I get Gerald, unfortunately. I really wanted to have some alone time with Hurlie. But it will have to wait.

We all throw decent shots as my sidearm shot went right under that notorious branch and around into the field.

Both teams split up. Gerald walks along with me as we follow my shot to the left of the fairway while Chuck follows Hurlie off to the far right. We walk along silently towards Gerald's disc and he picks it up.

"You had a real good shot, Jeff. Way better than mine."

"Thanks."

I really don't feel like talking to this guy. When we arrive at my disc he puts his marker above it, then picks up my disc and looks intensely at its underside. I wonder what could be so fascinating about the least interesting part of the disc as, after all, the artwork and the emblem are always on the top.

He's carefully studying my name and cell number written in sharpie on the upper rim of the bottom of the disc. He flashes me a peculiar look before handing me the disc, kind of a mix between a cold-blooded stare and sheer morbid fascination. When I meet his eyes, he turns away and digs into his bag to take out his putter. I take out my putter as well as I watch him get into his weird stance as he concentrates on making the thirty-foot shot. He misses badly.

"Dammit!" he yells. "Sorry."

"No 'sorrys' in disc golf," I tell Gerald as I walk up to the marker. "Didn't anyone ever tell you that out here?" I ask condescendingly like some grizzled old disc golf pro.

I take my time and finally flick a hyzer putt and it sails directly into the chains. I stand looking at it in admiration as it never ceases to amaze me the natural high you get when you hit a shot like that. I'm on a roll with these hyzer putts. I look over at Hurlie and he's smiling broadly. Chuck starts to clap slowly as the sounds of his hands start a methodical beat. I turn around to Gerald's beaming smile.

"Great shot, Jeff."

"Thanks, man."

Gerald picks up my bag and hands it to me then pays me the courtesy of fetching my disc in the basket for me. He grabs the disc and moves off to the side so the other team can shoot. I see he's continuing to gaze at the underside of the disc, once again looking at me with the same bizarre look. Once he notices me watching him, he immediately breaks into a contrived smile and gives me a thumbs up. I look away dismissively to watch the other team shoot their putts. They both miss pretty bad.

Gerald takes out his phone proceeding to text someone as he walks towards the bench on the next tee. He takes a seat while I wait for Hurlie and Chuck to get to Chuck's disc as it's the closest to the basket. It's an easy ten footer which Hurlie hits.

"Nice putt," I say as Hurlie goes to retrieve his putter from the basket.

"Good job, bud" Chuck says.

As we approach Gerald sitting on the bench he quickly puts away his cell phone.

"You're up, champ," he says with that same forced smile.

Setting down my bag, I take out my Ogre. I want something overstable for the sidearm I'm going to throw which will hopefully move uphill to the right where the basket is.

Unfortunately, it slams into a tree which is right over the little corridor that goes through the fairway.

"Shit!" I yell.

Gerald proceeds to throw a nice backhand that ventures to the right. He must've thrown something really understable. It goes over the branch I hit with plenty of juice and sails up towards the basket. A pretty decent shot.

"Nice one," I say.

"Hey, I gotta do something. It's been all you so far," Gerald says as he sits down and opens up his beer. He's very taken with his shot and is all smiles as he downs his beer.

The other team throws pretty good shots as they both sail to the left beyond the tree. They're both out of putting range but still on the way to par. I join Hurlie as we move ahead, Chuck starts tying his shoe while Gerald waits for him.

Hurlie and I walk in silence as we sip our beers. Our tranquil stroll in nature is then disturbed by the roaring sound of that damn helicopter. I look up and see it hover over the enclave of trees above us. We watch as the multi-colored helicopter comes into full view beyond the trees swooping down to our left. It blasts out above the soccer field adjoining the disc golf course.

I pick up my disc that bounced against the tree and glance over at Hurlie who's staring up at the helicopter.

"What the fuck," he says to me.

The helicopter goes to the far end of the soccer field, and then does a long, wide turn as it comes back our way again. It soars back over us as it flies out of the park once again over the highways.

Hurlie and I break off as he goes to the left where his shot landed while I start climbing up to the right to find Gerald's disc. I spot it up the small hill, about thirty feet away from the basket. Gerald lumbers over and joins me as we both look back at Hurlie and Chuck getting ready to shoot.

"Crazy how close that helicopter is flying over us, huh?" I ask him.

He looks straight ahead at Hurlie who's getting ready to putt.

DISC-OVERY

"Uh, yeah," he replies.

I really can't stand this guy. Oh well, maybe I should just concentrate on my game and making this upcoming putt. I'm not here to socialize, after all. I want to improve my game and fucking win.

Hurlie throws a really good shot as Gerald and I watch it sail high then lands right underneath the basket.

"Good one, dude," I say.

Hurlie nods at me as Chuck moves up to take his shot. He lets go of the disc and it sails too high, landing halfway up the hill on its side, and rolls down the hill.

"Oh no!" we hear Chuck yell. The disc is rolling almost on a direct path back to him before he grabs it. The rest of us lightly chuckle. Finally, some fun and levity on this round.

As Gerand and I arrive at his disc, I put my marker above it and hand the disc to him. He takes it and puts it in his bag as I move up to the marker and nestle my foot against it. I throw a pretty good putt but it sails a little to the right of the chains. The disc hits the hill on the other side then rolls back towards the basket, hitting the pole and falling down directly underneath the basket.

"Cool, man," Gerald says. "You just guaranteed us par."

"Yeah," I say, still wanting us to hit a birdie and go up. "Fling it at those chains, Gerald."

He steps up right underneath the marker and concentrates on the putt. He throws it and it sails high, missing the basket. Gerald curses then races up the hill to grab all the discs. My shot and Hurlie's are so close they're gimmes. Gerald snags Chuck's disc as well and runs at his disc, kicking it towards the next tee pad, cursing again. As we begin to walk over to the next tee, he hands us all the discs. Gerald finally picks up his disc and throws it into his bag. Before I make it to the next tee, I look back at the bushes around the basket and realize nobody's behind us.

"Hey guys," I yell, "I'm gonna take a piss, gimme a minute."

"No prob," Gerald yells back as he walks over and joins Chuck and Hurlie on the bench at the next tee. I take out my beer as I walk to find a place in the bushes to take care of my business and simultaneously drink my beverage. When I'm done, I approach the bench where they're all seated. They look up at me solemnly. I immediately sense something's wrong.

"Uh, hey man, I gots to go," Hurlie tells me. "I just got a text about a job in the city. I need the money," Hurlie tells me with a concerned look on his face. It sucks he's going to leave me all alone with these bozos, but work is work.

"Hey, no problem, Hurlie. It was fun hanging out with you today. I'll call you soon and we'll hang out."

He gives me a stern look.

"Yeah. Do that. Later."

He walks off without saying goodbye to the new guys. That was a little weird.

Now it's just me with Gerald and Chuck who are both staring at me intently. Suddenly, I'm uncomfortable being around these guys alone.

"Well, uh, what are we gonna do now, guys? We don't have teams anymore."

They both look at each other, and then back at me.

"I'll be the odd man out," Chuck says. "I like getting the extra shots and work on my game." They continue to stare at me. This is awkward.

"Okay," I say.

We play the next couple of holes barely saying anything to each other. I don't know if it's my imagination but they both have become very serious. Their attempts at sporadic humor have ceased since Hurlie left, giving me odd looks here and there. We finish our putts on the fourth hole and start to make our way into the trees towards the Middle Earth hole. I lead the way and Chuck and Gerald follow from behind.

My cell phone beeps with a text and I pull it up. It's from Hurlie.

DISC-OVERY

> Those dudes flashed a gun at me told me to split dont trip i'm getting my boys together and coming up there to save you hang tight.

My heart flutters as panic races through my body. I almost trip over the roots and rocks I'm stepping over. I tell myself to keep looking forward, moving ahead. Don't look back at them. Play it cool. Buy some time until Hurlie gets here.

I'm doing the best I can to collect myself as I make my way up to the fifth hole. I try to make it to the benches behind it along the rocks, begging myself to just relax.

Once again I hear the helicopter, whipping around the trees and bushes surrounding me. It must be right above us. I don't even look up at it. I just want to make it to the bench and drink my beer. I arrive at the bench and sit down. I sip my beer as the helicopter swirls above and comes into view. It lands in the wide open fairway below.

I take another pull of my beer as I slowly turn to Chuck and Gerald. They are staring at me as both of their legs are slightly apart in what seems like some kind of rehearsed stance.

Gerald shouts over the noise of the helicopter.

"Jeff. I think I got something of yours."

He reaches into his disc golf bag and pulls out my yellow Valkyr disc. He throws it on the dirt in front of me. It lands upside down, and I see one of the 'f's of my name along with my cell number have been smudged out from the endless beating this disc has taken from lakes, creeks, marshes, dirt, dogshit and God knows what else on disc golf courses all over SoCal. I had never noticed until now that only 'Jef' remained from when I first wrote down my contact info when Paul gave me the disc.

The hairs stand up on my neck. *Oh shit.*

"Where did you get that?" I ask.

"Well," Chuck exclaims over the noise of the chopper blades, "that's the million-dollar question now, isn't it?"

I turn and put down my beer, looking straight ahead at them.

"We didn't find it on this course, that's for sure," Gerald pointedly says. "In fact, we found it at a place where no disc golfer would ever be at. Except for us, of course."

They turn to each other and snicker as if Gerald said something incredibly witty. I don't find it too funny at all.

"There are some pretty important people who are not too happy about you playing safari down at their hangar the other night," Gerald continues.

I want to kick myself. I can't believe I left my Valkyr behind when I spilled my discs while bolting to the ladder.

"You got a lot of questions to answer," Chuck chimes in.

I start to panic. I'm cornered up here on the cliff with nowhere to run. They'll easily catch me if I bolt into the woods. That helicopter is waiting for me down below, undoubtedly there to escort me into the bowels of Experimental Aerolab Dynamics as an official guest of MJ-12.

Gerald looks down at my Valkyr with a smirk.

"You know, Jeff. The next time you sneak into a supposedly impenetrable secret government bunker, try not to leave anything with your name and cell phone number on it."

They both laugh as I'm frantically searching for any method of escape. I reach forward slowly to pick up my Valkyr while grabbing my bag with my other hand. I play along and start laughing along with their big joke, then suddenly swing my disc golf bag around, filled with many pounds of plastic and beer, knocking both of them to the ground in a thunderous blow. Both men collapse as I sprint down the steep rocky hill. I somehow reach the bottom without falling.

When I look up, I see the pilot of the helicopter reach for the gun on his vest as he opens up the door of the helicopter. I'm not waiting around to see what happens. I hear Gerald and Chuck both yell at me over the noise of the helicopter as I race forward towards the park below. I look up at the path back towards the sixth hole I've walked down joyously so many times with a beer, only to see a jeep filled with camouflaged soldiers barreling towards me. I veer off to the right and run through the brush. I hear the yelling of the soldiers as they accelerate off the trail following me.

Flailing toward the brush, I hear shots fired. Now I'm officially freaking the fuck out. I slip and pummel to the ground cutting myself on the unforgiving rocks. I squirm my way forward until I'm in the mud. The unpleasant sound—a sound I never thought I'd hear in real life—of a gun being cocked at the side of my temple causes me to freeze. My stomach tightens.

"Don't shoot," I whimper. "Please! Please! Don't shoot."

Three uniformed soldiers hover over me with their guns drawn. The helicopter pilot isn't far behind.

"Put your hands over your head," one of the soldiers says icily. I reach as far as I can above my head.

"Get on your knees and keep those damn hands up or we'll blow your head off!" another one of them yells.

My arms above my head are burning, and I can feel the cuts and bruises all over me come to life. I look up and see Gerald and Chuck sprinting towards us, their guns drawn as well.

"You punk!" Gerald yells at me. "You're gonna pay for that, asshole!"

The helicopter blades continue their monstrous wailing as the wind whips through everything so violently that we can barely maintain our balance. I'm still praying they don't shoot me as I feel blood streaming down from the top of my head onto my nose. MJ-12 may have ordered them to kill me on sight.

"Dumb move, Jeff!" Chuck yells. "Real dumb!"

"Nah, man!" I suddenly hear above the fray. We look towards the helicopter to see about 25 Black men adorned in gray bandanas cock their automatic weapons.

"Y'all the ones that's dumb. Put yo' shit down on the ground now, mothah fuckahs! Now!"

I smile as this voice coming from underneath the masked

bandana is none other than my buddy, Hurlie. I look back at the soldiers, the pilot, and Chuck and Gerald, their guns still pointed at me as they take in the sight of the gang with automatic weapons pointing towards them.

"Do what he say now!" yells another one who looks like he'd be a starting linebacker for any professional football team.

The soldiers look at each other, then at Gerald and Chuck, who both look back at the pilot.

"Do you have any idea of who you're messing with?" Gerald yells at them.

"Y'all know who you messin' with, suckah? You on Hillcrest G Squad turf."

"What?" the pilot exclaims. "We are the United States Government, and this is official—"

"Shut up!" Hurlie yells from his masked bandana. "Drop yo' weapons or you die!"

The moment is tense. Reluctantly, the government people drop their guns. Some of the gang begins to collect them. Blood continues to gush down into my eyes. Hurlie turns to another one of his masked henchmen.

"Tie 'em up. And grab the keys to this thing. We goin' for a ride."

Several of the masked gunmen take out plastic cuffs then kick the government people and soldiers to the ground on their stomachs, tying their wrists behind their backs.

"Give us the damn keys," one of them says to the pilot who's lying prone on the ground.

Another one of the gunmen next to the helicopter laughs.

"Oh shit! Keys in the chopper. C'mon, everybody get in, I flew somethin' like this in Afghanistan. I'll figure it out."

"We just tipped the balance of power on the street with this thing," another masked gunman says. We pile into the large helicopter as Hurlie totes his gun at me from behind his gray bandana.

Before he follows us into the helicopter, he turns to everyone sprawled on the ground squirming and cursing in their plastic cuffs.

"Y'all listen up. This is Hillcrest G Squad territory here. Pasadena. Go back to yo' place behind all them gates and barbed wire down the street. Out here you on our turf. 'Member dat. And if I see that mother fuckin' Rover out here again, we carjackin' that shit and takin' it, too."

We pack into the helicopter and our new pilot takes a few moments before he lifts off jerkily. We bounce around each other as the helicopter finally gets its bearings.

"GPS disabled. We in business," the pilot laughs.

We start to fly off over the park leaving the soldiers, helicopter pilot, Gerald and Chuck on the ground yelling and writhing as they hopelessly try to break out of their cuffs.

"Yo, man," Hurlie motions to me. "Gimme yo' cell phone."

I give the phone to him and he looks it over.

"They had my cell number from the disc I left down at their underground base," I meekly confess to Hurlie.

Hurlie laughs. "Some secret agent you is."

We look outside the helicopter and see the treacherous lake of hole number fourteen below us, the infamous body of water that has gobbled up so many discs over the years from golfers who just couldn't make it over to the other side. Hurlie waves my cell phone in front of my face.

"They been trackin' you on this, dumb ass," he smirks at me. Hurlie throws my cell phone out of the helicopter. It spirals into the water where making a small splash. After being lost in thought for a moment, Hurlie finally looks up at me with that same smirk.

"Bill would find dozens of discs on the bottom of that lake, walkin' barefooted and feelin' the plastic with his toes," he says. "He would get a small collection like that in just one afternoon. Crazy mothah fuckah," he says as he winks at me.

I smile back at my great friend.

"That's why he always has plenty of discs, huh?" I ask.

Hurlie nods as he lights up a cigarette as he takes out two small vodkas from his camo jacket and hands me one.

"I still need to tell you about my adventures from the other night," I tell him.

"We'll have a pow wow when we get to our hideout on the other side of the mountains. We got to stash this in our big warehouse before anyone realizes it's gone."

We both clink our vodkas as the helicopter heads towards the San Gabriel Mountains. I take a moment to admire the big blue sky, sensing Sean out there somewhere rejoicing that his old disc golf buddy Hurlie has saved the day.

15

I coast through the San Gabriel Mountains on my brand-new motorcycle, given to me courtesy of the Hillcrest G Squad gang. They figured it was the least they could do since I led them to such an easy heist of one of the latest and greatest helicopter models of the United States Military. They assured me the bike had legit plates.

I'm on my way out of the country but I have to be careful. I must find Alisa and tell her everything that's happened. She's clueless about the events of the day, and they might be looking for someone who fits the description of the 'plus one' I took down to the little whiskey party those Generals threw the other night. I need to warn her; I owe her that much. And, of course, before I leave, I have to say goodbye to Andy.

I zoom along feeling free as the wind whips through me, looking up at the city panorama that comes into view sporadically as I dip up and down between the San Gabriel mountains. I glance up at the endless concrete jungle that this beautiful rocky terrain leads into, knowing that somewhere down there, Alisa is surviving the way she only knows how to.

It's too risky to go back to my house. The helicopter that was circling around my neighborhood last night was more than likely looking for me, trying to pinpoint my location from my cell phone. I've always gotten spotty reception in there anyway, so the chopper was probably getting something muddled. But now they have my cell number. Hell, they probably know all about me now: my full name, my address, my social security number, everything. I have to lay low. I'll go back to my car in a day or two. It's still parked outside the park.

I figured this day would possibly arrive if I actually went through with going down into the secret underground base. Even if it went without a hitch, getting the footage onto the internet would leave some kind of digital footprint, and might necessitate me leaving the country. I've prepared for such an eventuality. Now that it is happening, I'm ready. There's nothing in this country for me anyway. It almost feels like a natural progression to leave and go somewhere else after completing my mission.

I have plenty of cash on me, and I'd transferred my life's savings to offshore accounts weeks ago, so all I have to do is make it south of the border. In the meantime, I need to stay in the shadows, living off the grid as I did when prepping in the woods weeks before.

I pull into a convenience store and buy one of those prepaid cell phones you don't have to register your name on, then head out to the hospital to say goodbye to Andy. I'll figure out my next moves after that. Under the hot sun, I'm feeling good. I finally feel like I'm living the adventure I've always yearned for. All those years in oppressive, stuffy offices in my soulless grind in New York seem like a million years ago. I'm confident I can get out of this last part of the maze of intrigue I've found myself in.

The expressway finally takes me from the glistening rocky expanse of the mountains into the grim edges of the city, whose angry urban sprawl rudely greets me coming in from the San Gabriels with traffic and hurried people impatiently moving over a paved mother earth. Strip malls and stop signs, red lights and crosswalks crowd and impede me, forcing me into the slow grind of the city.

I pivot and move my bike around traffic as I travel towards the county hospital. I wonder how my old friend is doing, and I'm hoping he's okay. I speed down the highway in a sea of cars, looking up at the green exit signs as I finally near downtown.

I arrive at the hospital and park my bike, then find the entrance and approach the nurse at the front office. I inquire about Andy but only know his first name, but as I describe him, they finally know who I'm talking about. They keep asking me how I know him., I just tell the nurses that I'm a buddy. They tell me Andy has no family, that the only people who have come to see him occasionally over the last few months are a handful of his friends.

It's sad to me how somebody can be so alone in the world like that. I wonder for a moment, when I'm at death's door, if anybody will come see me. It's a pretty humbling thought. I push those thoughts away and focus back on Andy. I pry a little bit, and they tell me that he has cirrhosis of the liver. He doesn't have long to live. They finally let me in to see him.

I make my way to his hospital room with the nurse and she opens the door. We enter and she proceeds to check his IV and tinkers with some of the other machines that he's hooked up to before she leaves me alone with him. Andy looks very ill laying on his hospital bed as his age seems to have caught up with him in here. His wrinkled skin from years of homelessness underneath the L.A. sun, along with his chronic drinking and drug abuse, combine to make him look way past his fifty-something years. I approach the bed and sit down on a chair next to it. I look into his face and wait.

"Andy," I whisper.

"Andy," I say a little louder this time. I let that linger in the air a bit.

His eyes start to pry open. He looks over towards the direction of the voice in the room, and squints as his eyes rest on me.

"Hey dude. Sucks in here. I can't play golf," he says.

"Yeah, I bet. I caught up with the guys on the course. They told me you were in here."

He looks up at the ceiling with a glassy despondency in his eyes. It appears he's resigned to his impending bleak fate. We say nothing for a long while. I decide that now is the time to open up.

"You know, Andy, when I worked on Wall Street, I did a lot of things that I really regret now. Things that were wicked; that impacted so many people. But at the time, I didn't know. It was like I was just putting a puzzle together. And when I figured out how to put all the pieces together, it would create money.

"I would do this day in and day out, month after month, year after year, never realizing the human cost of what I was doing. People like you who lost their houses and their jobs from all of the stock manipulations we were doing, all of you seemed so far away, miles and miles beyond those fancy offices with pricey leather chairs where us executives in expensive suits orchestrated all of that. Then we'd all meander over to our posh bars and restaurants, slapping each other on the back celebrating with yet another drunken evening, riding high with the euphoric adrenaline of getting richer that day and thinking we were all winning again. And the faceless multitudes of people we were affecting, well, they just weren't around to be seen."

I look down as I start to tear up, wallowing in the lost years I spent in New York, and the toll they've taken on my soul.

"But with you, Andy, I finally caught up to one of those faces. To one of those people who were affected by the meltdown that I was a party to. And, well, I just want to say I'm sorry. Sorry for you being on the receiving end of all of that."

I wipe my tears away with my shirt sleeve. I've wanted to say something like this to somebody for a long time. It just happens to be Andy. He keeps his eyes closed. I'm wondering if he's awake, if he even heard anything I said. I sit there, slouched, looking over at him. A heavy silence descends upon the room. He finally speaks in a heightened whisper.

"I was a goner before I ever lost that house, Jeff. Things happened to me when I was younger. Things I could never understand. That no one really had any explanations for. And all I could is stumble through my life with the weight of them as they slowly wore me down. Finally broke me down, into what you see in front you now."

Through my teary-eyed gaze, I see a tear travel down the left side of his face. He slowly opens his eyes and I'm reminded of his haunted gaze from the day out in front of the liquor store, when I realized why he slept under the bridge.

I feel tears travel down my cheeks as I look up at my dying friend.

"Andy, you and the guys gave me a gift I never had before. Friendship. I've learned a lot out there on the disc golf course," I say. "Things about my brother, about what our government's doing there, and what they're all about. About friendship. About evil. About my brother. About nature. About real people. It's been a real discovery."

A smile slowly creeps onto his face.

"You mean, a *disc*-overy," he laughs as he's taken with his play on words.

"Yeah, man," I chuckle along with him. "A *disc*-overy."

I wipe the tears away from my face. I'm feeling very cathartic but relaxed as the talk and tears seem to cleanse away something I've been holding inside for a long time.

"Jeff, will you do me a favor?" Andy asks.

"Of course."

He raises his right hand and points over to the corner of the hospital room where his backpack hangs on the doorknob of a closet.

"Some of my discs are in that backpack. Can you look through there and grab my red Valkyr?"

"Sure," I say, walking over to it and zipping it open. I flip through the discs until I find the lone red disc. Funny he should bring up a Valkyr considering what I've just been through with my own. I turn around with it and start back to Andy.

"Don't give it to me," he says. I stop, waiting for him to tell me what to do with it.

"Remember I told you about that course they opened in Switzerland?"

"Yes," I say.

"I've met a few disc golfers on the courses who've been to it. They tell me how wonderful it is, high up in the Alps, where the air is so crisp, and you're so high up that the clouds start to blanket you and take you into their white haze. They say it's like you're walking along in a dream as you play golf, the discs flying out of your hand, hovering in and out of the clouds as they spin through the sky."

He turns and looks at me misty-eyed, temporarily lost in a dreamworld far away from this sterile, dreary hospital room.

"They say it's like playing disc golf in heaven."

Andy's eyes fall back on the Valkyr that I'm holding, and he looks at it longingly.

"Like I've told you, I've always wanted to go there. It was the only thing really keeping me going these last few years, the chance to play on this course in Switzerland."

He continues to stare at the disc, remaining quiet for a few long moments as the missed chance of going to play on this course weighs on his soul.

"The people I met who have been there, they kept talking about this one amazing hole. The basket is situated in just such a place in the mountains that when the disc hits the chains, you can hear the ringing for miles. The sound just reverberates through the Alps, traveling all the way up to the tee pad and throughout the entire mountain range. They tell me it's like hearing the bells of heaven."

He pauses as if trying to picture the scene in his mind's eye.

"I want you to take that disc, Jeff, and do what I really wanted to do with it but won't be able to. Throw it on that hole at that course in Switzerland. Hear the ethereal ringing of those chains when the Valkyr finally hits them. And listen to those celestial sounds cascade throughout the mountains and on up into the heavens. I'm sure when you do this, I'll hear it up there, too."

His teary eyes look up into mine again.

"Will you do that for me, Jeff?"

I can feel my own tears travel down my face as I look into Andy's pained eyes.

"Of course, Andy. I would be honored to do that for you."

He looks away and closes his eyes. I can hear his delicate breathing. This deeply emotional conversation has left him exhausted.

"Thank you, brother. Let me rest now, Jeff."

I take one last look at my friend before I leave the room with his Valkyr.

* * *

Exiting the hospital, the early afternoon heat hits me like a punch in the stomach. I hop on my bike. My emotions thrash around inside of me as the realization of the finality of saying a last goodbye to a dear friend festers. His red Valkyr is in my zipped-up jacket, nestled against the left side of my chest right up against my palpitating heart. I try my hardest not to start bawling like a baby as I rev up the engine and speed off into the flurry of cars. I grip the handle bars tight in my hands, weaving the motorcycle in and out of traffic. This well of emotions inside me want to burst through. The visor of my helmet hides the tears that continue to stream down my face as I just speed off to nowhere.

I find myself riding into Hollywood. I see the throngs of people bustling around the famous theaters on the boulevard.

Tourists scour the stars on the walk of fame, addicts hustle for a score, and the homeless badger everybody for spare change.

As much as there is desperation and despair in the air, there is also the energy of hope. All seem to come here to fulfill their dreams. Kinda like how I came here trying to find a purpose and found a mission. Actors from all over the world come here, wide-eyed and ambitious, looking for Hollywood immortality. And then there are those who have failed and dropped out of life who come here to die, like this place offers some kind of safe passage to the afterlife.

I start laughing at it all as my sadness dissipates and I speed along with the Hollywood sign looking down on us from its mountainside perch, tantalizing all of us who are far below on the boulevard. I pass by the people dressed up as superheroes bullying tourists for money after they pose for pictures with them, and pass by the loud racket of street performers who bang on plastic bucket drums, annoying everybody around them.

Even with all its faults, Hollywood always seems to put me in a good mood. I continue down the boulevard as it gets seedier and sketchier passing Vine Street. It's fun to ride so I just keep going, but the task of finding Alisa sooner rather than later starts to gnaw at me. As I finally reach the outskirts of Hollywood, I stop and chart my next moves at a cafe in Los Feliz, Sean's old stomping grounds.

I park in front of one of the trendy cafes with hipsters shuffling in and out with their beards, trendy clothes and expensive sunglasses. I get off the bike and feed the meter and head in. A cute blonde greets me at the counter, and I order a latte. I look back around at the café. It's populated mostly by twenty-somethings who quietly talk or sit alone, brooding over their laptops, coffee drinks and cell phones. The place is adorned with fancy colored tapestry and pretentious paintings on the walls, strewn pillows on the couches. I plop down in the middle of all of them and clutch them close around me for several minutes as I let my body catch up to itself.

My latte is finally ready and the cute blonde girl smiles at me as I take it then sit back down. I take a few sips. The foam nestles on my lip and I wait a few moments to lick it off while I settle into the dark, cool interior of the cafe. There's a tiny stage in the corner with a microphone stand where I guess they have open mics.

I take the Valkyr out of my jacket, bending it back and forth as I inspect all the cuts and scrapes on the edges of Andy's disc. I put it down and lift the latte up to my lips again as I look up at a bookcase that's in the middle of the store. I peruse the titles and come to a book on mythology. I glance down at the disc. I know the Valkyr is some kind of mythical figure, but not much more than that so I get up to grab the book. It's a thick book that has sections on mythologies from around the world. I flip through and find the Valkyr entry under the Norse mythology section.

> Valkyr: a female figure, a maiden of Odin, who chooses those heroes to be slain in battle, and leads them to Valhalla.

I smirk as I think of the female figure I'm looking for now. Alisa. What a woman. She's managed to survive strips clubs, escorting and porn shoots...and God knows what else. I bet she is dealing just fine with the experience we had together the other night.

I don't need to warn her about anything. If anyone from EAD bothered her about knowing me on the course, she wouldn't flinch at all. She can take care of herself. And who am I kidding anyway about finding her; it would be like finding a needle in a haystack. I don't even know where to start. She has no website advertising her services or porn career, no contact info anywhere on the internet. Weird how someone in her line of work can be so off the grid. I wish I had gotten her number.

I sip from my latte again as I look up around the cafe. I like this place. The vibe is real mellow. There's some cool music on in the background, and everybody is just chilling out. I take the mythology book back to the bookcase and look at the other titles. Finally, my eyes rest on the table to the right scattered with various pamphlets for yoga classes, postcards of theater productions, business cards of photographers, and the Weekly.

I look at it and smile, remembering the snide comment that Hurlie made about Alisa being in the back pages of this very publication. Was he joking or just being insulting? Or could it be this easy? There's only one way to find out. I grab a copy and go back to my table.

I turn to the back pages to all the medical marijuana ads and keep turning the pages until I hit the 'Adult Massage' and 'Escort' sections. I'm looking at all pages of the girls and out of the corner of my eye spy a middle-aged lady sitting at the table next to me looking at me funny. I continue turning page after page of seedy ads and then...I don't believe it. There she is in a scantily clad outfit holding a whip by her side.

> For a deliciously painful time, call Bella Biotch.

My heart almost stops as I see her in this outfit. Hurlie was not joking. I can't believe I'm looking at her in this ridiculous ad. I blurt out a laugh and the woman next to me gives me another condescending, judgmental look.

I read a couple of articles while I finish the rest of my latte then smile at the lady next to me before I get up to leave the cafe, taking the Weekly with me. I exit and step into the alleyway right next to the cafe. The city noise from the Los Feliz streets abates as I walk to the end of the alleyway where I see a rat scurry underneath a large pile of garbage.

I dial the number in her ad and it rings for a while. Finally, she picks up.

"Incall or outcall?"

I bite my lip and try not to laugh.

"Um, Alisa. It's me, Jeff."

There's a long silence on the other end of the phone.

"How did you get my number, Jeff?"

"Well, you're not a hard woman to find if you look in the right places," I reply.

There's another long silence. I wonder if she might just hang up.

"What is it, Jeff? Are you okay?"

"I'm leaving town. We need to talk before I go."

"I'm shooting something now. But I'll be done soon. Meet me downtown at Broadway and fourth in two hours. Gotta go." *Click.*

* * *

Arriving downtown, I pull my bike into a parking garage. The sun is setting as shop owners are hurriedly closing up, pulling their sliding metal doors down and locking them up frantically before the light fades, almost like they are preparing for a hurricane.

Making my way towards Broadway, the street people begin to claim their turf as the night descends upon these mean streets. It's starting to get cold as everyone hunkers down and burrows away, disappearing into lofts, apartments, alleyways or underneath cardboard boxes or tents on sidewalks.

Alisa is in the distance, standing confidently on the corner. She is a powerful creature of these city nights. Like a she-wolf. She's as much in her element in the L.A. urban underbelly as she is on the disc golf course.

I wave at her from about a block away catching her eye. She walks towards me. She is in a very stylish leather coat with knee-high boots and a tight leather miniskirt. Men give her hungry glances as she walks by them. She smiles at me as I approach and approaches me like one of those comic book bad ass superhero chicks. She owns the night.

"Well, hello there, partner in crime," she says with a wink.

"Hi, Alisa."

"Walk me to my night club. On the way, you can tell me all your earth-shattering news."

She puts her arm through mine as I turn to walk with her. She guides me to her lair, almost like how the Valkyr took their fallen warriors to the Otherworld. I feel like a million bucks with this gorgeous girl by my side.

"It's been an eventful few days, Alisa. I guess I dropped one of my discs, that yellow Valkyr I always throw, when we were getting out of that underground base."

"I don't like Valkyrs," she says. "Way to understable. They always flip on me. No big loss, replace it with something more stable."

I smile.

"That's not really the point. They found the disc at the base, and it had my name on it. They put a couple of agents on the course at Oak Grove. To make a long story short, they found me there."

She looks up at me in wide-eyed excitement without a hint of fear. I feel like I'm in some film noir movie with this scintillating woman on my arm, walking the downtown shady streets of downtown L.A. on the run from government agents. The thing is, I'm living this. It ain't no movie.

"You silly man, leaving behind your name for them."

She laughs out loud, like this is some big game. I bet if we turned the corner and the face of death greeted us, she would laugh the same exact way.

"You might want to rethink your career as a secret agent man," she quips, squeezing my arm. We laugh together as I move a little closer, continuing to walk along.

"I was able to get away from them with Hurlie's help. I don't know if you know him or not."

"Hurlie from Oak Grove?"

"Yes."

"Of course I know him. He has a grudge against me because I've hustled him. More than once."

I smirk. Hurlie left this part out while explaining his dislike of her.

I stop and turn towards Alisa.

"But they obviously know who I am now and I have to leave the country. I just came here to warn you. I don't think they could identify you but I just wanted to let you know what's happened, so you could be mindful out there on the course."

She looks up at me, defiant and self-assured.

"They've got nothing on me. I'm not worried. Even if they did, I would never stop playing there. If they killed me at hole five, well, let them bury me there."

She begins walking and I turn with her as she slips her arm through mine once again.

"Plus, I'm no runner. And I can't go home."

"Why not, Alisa?"

I wonder if I'm being too intrusive.

"My family has banished me for what I am."

We walk along silently, the city streetlamps illuminating a path for us, sirens wailing throughout the streets. She grips my arm tighter and lays her head against my shoulder affectionately. We finally reach a nondescript night club off the main street with a couple huge bouncers stationed in front. She turns and puts her arms around me.

"We had quite an adventure together, didn't we, Jeff?"

"We certainly did."

"I always knew something was going on underneath the park from all the crazy things I'd seen there over the years. I finally saw it all up close. I was right in the middle of it. Thank you for that, Jeff."

"It wouldn't have been the same without you."

Alisa's tone becomes serious and her eyes meet mine.

"What are you going to do with the footage?"

"I'll upload it when I get down into Mexico."

"I can't wait to see it."

Her beautiful eyes have a special alluring power, I could easily get lost in them. I hug her again and she pulls me close to her, pressing up against me. I hold her tightly.

"I want to see you again someday, Alisa. I don't want this to be goodbye."

She steps away as she holds my hands, rubbing them softly. She reluctantly lets me go.

"Well, you can always find me at Oak Grove."

She turns and one of the burly bouncers opens the door to the entrance of the club for her. Alisa vanishes into the nightlife.

EPILOGUE

I'm lightheaded and short of breath being this high up in the Alps. But it's invigorating. There's barely anyone up here. The worst part is retrieving the discs from the snow. If I didn't have gloves, my hands would be frostbitten by now. But I'm not complaining as it's so beautiful out here. The sun is shining and blue skies abound as the snow crunches under my feet. I'm playing disc golf in God's country, otherwise known as Switzerland.

I've played eleven holes so far, and I'm four over. Not a great showing but I could care less because I'm living out Andy's dream. It might as well be mine, because there's nothing I'd rather be doing and no other place I'd rather be. I'm playing disc golf on top of the world. Right next to heaven.

I take out a little flask filled with some vodka and take a swig. It doesn't matter where you are, you can't play disc golf without a drink. And this vodka is as crisp as the air I'm breathing. I'm so far up I feel I can reach out and touch the blue of the sky.

I'm almost at Andy's dream shot. The fifteenth hole. I really want to make a great throw off it. It's not every day that you're throwing a dead man's disc on a hole to fulfill a dying man's wish. I know he's watching up there somewhere. I take another drink from the flask.

During my time in Mexico, there weren't many disc golf courses. I had to make up my own courses. *Playing natural* as they say in disc golf parlance. It was fun. Plenty of tequila to drink and senoritas to hang with. But at some point I had to make it over to the Alps to fulfill Andy's deathbed request. Funny, Switzerland is where most of my overseas accounts were anyway.

My old life in America seems like lifetime ago. The only thing I miss is being around the guys (and one scintillating lady) playing disc golf. The only real friends I've ever had. Andy I'm sure has crossed over by now. But maybe one day I'll cross paths with my old buddies again on a course somewhere. If I get my disc stuck in a tree again somewhere in Europe, maybe Gary will miraculously appear high up on a branch again, snagging it for me. Or perhaps Alisa will suddenly emerge from a hollowed-out tree after I hit my next ace, demanding some cash. I could only hope.

I live day to day on the very fringes of society, traveling to and fro across Europe with a backpack and a big bundle of cash on me.

Sometimes I just camp out and sleep in my tent stowed on my motorcycle. I blend into the periphery of every town I visit in, trying not to attract any attention as I lurk in the shadows. Kinda like how Andy lived. I have no fixed address and I'm off-the-grid, sometimes living in the woods like I did in L.A.

I have my occasional bad days. I get paranoid that MJ-12 agents might be on my trail. Sometimes I just want to crash my bike and end it all, but I always get through the tough moments, and live to see another day.

The video I took has gone viral for quite a while now and has made some waves. It disappears off sites, then reappears on others. It's been doing that for about sixteen months now, and I know Sean must be pleased with what the video has been doing, looking down from the heavens.

I've even met people on my travels who have brought up the infamous video from the underground base at Oak Grove. It's achieved a certain cult status among conspiracy circles. There have been official denials from the government, and it's fun to watch the disinfo agents spinning wild stories about the video. Their puppet corporate media has poked fun at it, too, when they're not totally blacking out the story. But the truth is out there. I'll let the public decide.

I take out the flask again as I think about my approach shot for the eleventh basket which is nestled against the edge of a small cliff. If I miss this, I might as well forget ever making par for the course. I take my Ogre disc out as I sidearm a shot that thankfully plants into the snow about nine feet from the basket. I hit the putt solidly and move to the next tee pad.

I bogey the next three holes as this course continues to be treacherous and tough. I'm way over par now. I finally make my way up to the course's signature fifteenth hole. There's a small hike to the tee pad which is at the summit of one of the peaks. As I finally climb my way up there, I'm greeted by several guys smoking a joint at the top.

"Hey guys," I say.

They all nod as they pass me the joint.

I take a big toke and give it back to a tall, spindly blonde dude who looks to be in his mid-20s. I step up to the view. It is magnificent.

"This is the famous hole, right?"

He nods as he takes a hit off the joint.

"Where is the basket?" I ask.

He points off at a massive mountain in the distance.

"It's far off to the left behind that mountain," he says. His buddy makes his way over and he hands him the joint.

"You can't see it from here. But you can hear it," his buddy says. He's a pretty scruffy burly guy also in his twenties who kind of reminds me of Bill.

"The last group just went through about a half an hour ago," the tall spindly guy continues. "We heard the chains ringing from all the way up here."

"Has anyone ever hit an ace from here?" I ask.

All three of them laugh at this. The one that's still sitting on a bench further back speaks up as he starts rolling another joint.

"Not even close, my friend," he says.

I step out from the benches under the enclosure where we've been talking and go out on to the cliff where the tee pad is. I'm buzzing hard from the vodka and the pot as I walk out to the tee pad which is right at the edge of a cliff overlooking the vast mountain range. I set my disc golf bag down and take out Andy's disc.

The crisp coolness of the air hits me again and I breathe it in, trying to focus on how I want the Valkyr to fly. It can be an unpredictable disc to throw, though I certainly loved my old yellow one. Ideally, it will hold its line and venture far to the right before it settles into a long fade to the left around the mountain where the basket is hiding. I want to honor Andy with a good showing on this particular hole. It would be awful if I threw a triple bogey here at the site of Andy's dying wish.

I notice the stoner guys have walked up behind me to get a view of my shot. They've brought their disc golf bags with them. Maybe they'll throw after me and join me for the rest of the course.

"You mind if we join up?" another one of the guys asks, practically reading my mind. "We already threw. Just been putting off walking down. It's hard to leave the view up here."

"I'd love it," I say as I look around at the Alps, feeling like I'm throwing this disc from on top of the world. "Been playing all alone this whole time."

I step up to the tee as I bring the disc up, concentrating as I slowly bring it back as I step forward. I feel my legs moving and

DISC-OVERY

my feet feeling spry as they start dancing on the tee pad as my body feels nice and nimble. My right arm goes way back with the disc as my hips start to turn around. My entire body twists forward, I feel the disc stay very level as I'm moving it along an imaginary table just like Andy trained me to do.

I twirl around as I finally spring forward and my wrist makes a loud snap as the red disc erupts out of my hand and I spin around on my follow through, whipping my legs in a circle as the disc launches out into the Alps like a bat out of hell.

I know immediately it's a good one. I watch the disc fly to the right, spinning wildly over the mountain range. As it descends into the valley below, it follows the course I envisioned it, thankfully not flipping over to the right, but instead keeping the trajectory I had planned for it as it starts to make its way behind the mountain in front of us.

"Good shot, dude," I hear one of the stoners say behind me.

"You got all of that one, man," another one says. They take a few steps forward to join me as we're all transfixed on Andy's red Valkyr blazing its trail through the snow-covered Alps.

"That is the best shot we've seen up here today," the spindly blonde one says as he takes another toke from the joint before passing it to me. I take it and pull on it as I see the disc finally disappear behind the large mountain far ahead of us that blocks the view of the basket far off in the distance.

I take another nice big toke on the joint before I hand it back. There's nothing to see now as the disc is blocked from our view by the mountain. We all wait for a couple of long moments.

As I feel the marijuana hit me with its sedative effects, I look off into the spectacular array of mountains I see before me before I hear the shrill crackle of a plastic collision into metal that starts to spill out of the deep valley below, gushing up towards us like a tidal wave of music as the chains of the basket sing with the symphony of victory reverberating throughout the range.

As the ringing reaches up to where we are, a gust of wind

whips through us. The heavens so close above seem to join in rejoicing my shot. I feel the chills go through me like an electric shock as I know Andy and Sean are with me on this mountain top, sending this flurry of wind my way applauding my unthinkable ace.

I look at all the other guys standing next to me, and their formerly subdued, stoned countenance has changed to astonishment. We stand for several long moments in a state of shock.

"Dude, that was just a religious experience," one of them says.

"Did I do what I think I just did?" I ask.

"Yeah, man. You just hit the ace of all aces."

We stand spellbound by what we all just witnessed.

I grab my wallet and pass out Swiss francs to everyone. They slowly take the bills. We stand still in a semi-state of rapture. After another moment, I collect myself and take out the flask of vodka from my disc golf bag, noticing the sharpie lodged in there. I take that out, too, and hold it in my hand, clenching it tightly. I take a sip of the vodka and pass the flask to one of the dudes.

"Let's go, guys. I want you to sign that disc for an old friend of mine."

My new friends and I grab our disc bags and start making our way down the mountain.

AFTERWORD

Thank you for teeing up and reading DISC-OVERY.

More than ten years ago, I was tormenting myself with the fact that I hadn't written my novel yet. Suddenly, almost out of nowhere the story of DISC-OVERY presented itself to me—well, really *blindsided me*—as the novel I was supposed to write. This started a multi-year effort of getting it done (99% of that time was spent procrastinating). After lots of drafts, and tons of great feedback and luckily meeting Sean Duregger online, my novel is finally coming out. To my knowledge (and everybody at Encyclopocalypse), DISC-OVERY is the world's first disc golf novel.

If you see me on a disc golf course around L.A. feel free to say hello and you can let me know what you think of the book. Oh, and don't forget the drinks.

Jed Rowen
Los Angeles, 2024

ABOUT THE AUTHOR

Jed Rowen is an actor living in Los Angeles. You might have seen him in *The Ghastly Love of Johnny X* as Sluggo, or in *Space Wars* as the Mighty Manx. Or maybe as the title character in *Pretty Boy*, *Axegrinder* or *The Electric Man*. If none of those ring a bell, maybe you saw him in Full Moon's notorious *Giantess Attack vs. Mecha Fembot* as the hapless General Kilgore, or Gordon in the post-apocalyptic *Impact Event*, or the goofy photographer in *That's A Wrap*.

Still nothing, huh? Maybe you caught a glimpse of Jed in *Piranhaconda* on Syfy? In *Camel Spiders* you might have heard his voice, and in *Eruption L.A.* he was leading the charge in all camo with a machine gun.

Enough of the the third person.

If none of these strike a chord, well, yes I was Det. Ray Garton in the notorious worldwide phenomenon *The Amazing Bulk*. Now you probably know me.

Regardless if you've seen my movies on late night cable or the $5 bin at Walmart or excoriated on any number of social media sites, I have finally achieved something that has eluded me for decades, and has always been on my mind. Thanks to

Encyclopocalypse Publications, I'm officially a published novelist.

www.ingramcontent.com/pod-product-compliance
Lightning Source LLC
LaVergne TN
LVHW032005070526
838202LV00058B/6296